"He is a talented and very promis[illegible]
no mistakes, he deserves the promotic[illegible]

But when gay Detective Sergeant Dave Lyon is assigned to Detective Inspector Claire Summerskill's team as part of the Service's 'positive discrimination policy', no-one at Foregate Street Station is happy. And that includes Summerskill and Lyon.

Mutual suspicion and mistrust must be shelved however, when a young man's beaten body is found on a canal tow path, and a dead-end case of 'happy slapping' unexpectedly turns into a murder investigation.

Why would someone want to kill middle class arts student Jonathan Williams? And how is his death linked to that of rent boy and would be 'adult' film star Sean?

As Summerskill and Lyon's investigations proceed, the newly-promoted detectives begin to untangle a web of connections, false assumptions and sheer prejudices that force them both to question closely not just their relationship with each other but with the rest of their colleagues at Foregate Street Station and with the Police Service as a whole.

"It's A Sin" is the first in the "Summerskill and Lyon" police procedural novels.

This is a work of fiction. All characters, places and events are from the author's imagination and should not be confused with fact. Any resemblance to persons, living or dead, events or places is purely coincidental.

Published by
NineStar Press
PO Box 91792
Albuquerque, New Mexico, 87199
www.ninestarpress.com

Warning: This book contains sexually explicit content which is only suitable for mature readers.

Print ISBN #978-1-911153-77-1
Original Cover Art by Aria Tan
Print Cover by Natasha Snow
Edited by Elizabeth Coldwell

IT'S A SIN

Summerskill and Lyon

Steve Burford

Dedication

For Neil

Chapter One

Three people walked past him on the canal path that cold November morning before anyone realised something was wrong.

The first, a professional man, out early for the morning paper, saw him sitting under the small footbridge that crossed the narrow strip of dark water. He took in the face-concealing hoodie, the flashy and doubtless ridiculously expensive trainers, and kept as far away from him as he possibly could without actually walking on the water itself. The skin on the back of his neck prickled nervously as he walked past the youth, and the *Guardian* was rolled tight in his fist ready to beat the lad off if he leapt on him from behind. But the slouched figure remained immobile, his back to the bridge's crumbling brickwork, and the man passed by unscathed, relieved and curiously exhilarated.

A young mother pushing her pram had been next. She hesitated when she came upon the sitting figure, glanced nervously at the precious bundle in front of her, then steeled herself and marched straight past him, arms stiff, pram a small juggernaut. She passed safely, and laughed a little to herself at the frantic hammering of her heart and her breathlessness. She cooed nonsense to her child about 'silly mummys', and inwardly vowed never to go that way again at that time of the morning.

It was the elderly man walking his dog, diligently employing his pooper scooper, who wondered what a young lad would be doing sitting on the damp grass, propped against a dripping stone wall so early in the day, and who asked himself if, maybe, something might be wrong. He moved a little closer, pulling slightly at the dog suddenly grown restive on its lead. Perhaps the boy was drunk. Well, he'd had a couple of mornings like that himself when he'd been that age. Or maybe he was stoned or high or whatever the hell they called it nowadays. And what were you supposed to do then? He hesitated. His dog whined.

And then it hit the old man: what if the boy in front of him was dead?

Chapter Two

Foregate Street Police Station. He'd liked the sound of the name. It had a vaguely medieval ring to it. And Worcester—that was an historical city, right? Something big in the Civil War, if he remembered his history lessons. He had, however, reckoned without the city planners, specifically the ones who had been in charge during the Sixties who had fallen out of love with history and deeply in love with that new wonder material of modern architecture, concrete. Worcester Foregate Police Station was an ugly, functional block of a building with all the medieval charm of a giant brick. With a sigh and an involuntary check of his tie, Dave Lyon entered the building, presented his ID to the desk sergeant and was pointed in the direction of the canteen where he was told to wait until he was called. All very cold and efficient. At least it wasn't hostile. That'd probably come later.

"You new to the station, then?"

Dave dragged his attention away from a menu in its uncertain black marker pen to the smiling face asking the question. "Yeah. Starting today."

The woman in canteen whites restocking the sandwich shelf poked him playfully with a baguette. "Uniform?"

Dave gave a look of mock wounded pride. “Sergeant me. Starting that today, too.”

“Good for you.” She sighed, taking in the height, the lean build, the short, dark hair and surprisingly blue eyes. “So, suppose we shan't see that much of you around here, then? You'll be off having your pub lunches and meals on expenses.”

Dave laughed and nodded at the greasy whiteboard. “Depends what your egg and bacon sandwich is like. Reckon you could tempt me here on a regular basis?”

The woman laughed, too, just a little more breathlessly. “I'll see what I can do. My name's Eileen,” she added. “By the way.”

“Hello, Eileen. Pleased to meet you. I'm Dave.”

“Hello, Dave.” And she was gone back behind the counter, taking with her a blush that was quite surprising for someone used to the heat of a kitchen.

Dave scanned the canteen, still empty that early in the morning. Spotting a paper abandoned on one of the tables, he went over to it and sat down. It was the *Mail*. He sighed, opened it and began to read.

Chapter Three

The question, Claire thought as she took her seat, was did she now flirt more with Madden or less? Promotion had brought her one step closer to him in rank, but did it also take her one step further away from that sort of behaviour? She smoothed her hand along her skirt, a reflex action and not really intended to draw attention to her legs. She ran her hand through her short blonde hair, another reflex but this one intended to draw attention to her new cut. If she did flirt, she decided, it would be because they both expected it, and because they both knew it meant absolutely nothing. The bottom line was she was there because of a ton of bloody hard work, not because of her appearance or how she could make an older man's heart race just a little bit faster, even first thing in the morning before his cup of wake-up coffee. Besides, a girl should never turn her back on her mam's lessons, even if that girl was, as of 0800 hours this morning, a fully fledged Detective Inspector.

"Good morning, sir," she said with a commendably straight face.

"Good morning, Detective Inspector Summerskill," replied Chief Superintendent Madden, equally po-faced. His emphasis on her rank gave her all the pleasure she'd known it would. "I trust I find you ready and eager for your first day in your new position?"

"Most definitely, sir," she said. *Bring it on.*

Madden nodded, toyed for a while with the manila folder he was holding, then finally held it out over his desk. Claire took it and opened it immediately. Madden leaned back in his more comfortably upholstered chair and watched, his faint smile unnoticed by her as she skimmed the papers, any traces of amusement well concealed. It took less than a minute.

"Happy slapping!"

"Assault."

Sod flirting. Claire glared at Madden.

Chief Superintendent Madden returned the expression with the impassivity of a stone Buddha. "Your point, *inspector*?"

My point, as you well know, you patronising old goat, is that there is a major arson case going down, and what is almost certainly a gang-related pair of killings right here, right now on our turf, and you've given me for my first case as a DI... "Kids. It's kids larking about."

"That's 'youths', inspector," Madden corrected her, "and it is technically assault." He paused. "And possibly hate crime. You had noticed that, I trust?"

"Of course. It's just..." Claire transferred her glare to the folder in her lap as if hoping the intensity of that expression might get rid of the damn thing by causing it to spontaneously burst into flames. Damn it. Maybe this was how you got to rise further up the ranks, not by flirting but by the speed with which you could pull carpets out from under people without apparent effort. She'd noticed what the report referred to as the 'unifying feature' even before the single sentence final paragraph. And it was just another off-pissing factor that she'd given Madden an opportunity to make it appear as if she hadn't seen it or didn't care.

"We're here for all sections of the community now, Inspector Summerskill," Madden went on, steepling his fingers. He leaned forward. "And we have to be *seen* to be here for all sections of the community."

"Yes, sir." She gritted her teeth and prayed that giving in now would cut short any sermon. The stinging irony was they both knew she actually believed what he'd just said more than he did.

"Imagine what a field day the local press would have if they thought we were behind in our civic duties."

"Yes, sir," said Claire, determined to ride it out. There was one good thing about this poxy first case as DI. It could almost certainly be tied up quickly. With kids there were bound to be some mates, or mates of mates, who'd grass each other up pretty sharpish with just the right application of pressure. It might not even be too bad a start to her new job, to have something quick and clean on the record. *Yeah. Right. DI Summerskill bursts on the scene with a major collar*. She could actually feel her jaw beginning to ache under the pressure of the expressionless face she was maintaining.

"Even when the rest of the time they're doing the bashing

themselves," Madden concluded.

"Yes, sir." Was he testing her mettle in her new post, or just rattling her cage because he liked to? It didn't really matter either way. *All right, you smug sod. If that's the way you want to play it.* She looked him straight in the eye. "Do I get Trent?"

Madden slid a second folder across his desk. "WPC Trent?" he said, pausing to give Claire a moment to take in the rank he'd used. "No. I'm afraid not."

"Jenny worked damn hard on the Robinson case."

"I know."

"She deserves the promotion."

"I know."

Claire frowned, unbalanced by the lack of resistance. "So, why...?"

Madden leaned forward again. "She'll get her stripes, don't you worry. Just not now. For now there are...other matters that have to take precedence. It happens. Consider it your first lesson in life at your new exalted rank, inspector." He passed the second folder across to her. "Sergeant David Lyon," he said, "from the Redditch station. It's still a new promotion so you can break him in to your way of working. I think you'll get on like a house on fire."

Claire was too busy scanning the information on her new sergeant to give that comment the ironic response it almost certainly merited. She had the strong sense of something—not a trap exactly, but a *situation*—being set up around her. It took her less than thirty seconds of scanning the papers she had been given to find it. "What's this?" she demanded, holding up a sheet and rapping it with one finger at a particular point.

There was no way Madden could see which line she was jabbing at but he wouldn't have needed to. He'd have known very well beforehand which one would light her fuse. "New policy," he said. "You don't have to fill that part in but you can if you want to. Sergeant Lyon wanted to. You know how keen our superiors are to be modern, fair and *all-inclusive.*" To his credit, he managed to say the last words with only the slightest hint of a grimace.

"So I get this guy because of that?"

"You have to admit, Sergeant Lyon could bring a useful perspective to this case."

"It's a routine line them up and shake them down procedure."

"And in any case," Madden continued, as if she hadn't interjected, "he is a talented and very promising young policeman. Make no mistakes, he deserves the promotion."

Claire glanced again at the opening lines of Sergeant Lyon's CV. "So why's it taken this long to get to sergeant? With his background, and if he's as good as you say, he could have been made up years ago."

Madden regarded her with one eyebrow skilfully raised. "You tell me," he said softly.

Claire studied the passport-sized photo staring up at her from the CV. She thought she'd been ready for everything when she'd got this job. She'd been wrong, and it had taken less than ten minutes for Madden to show her. *Damn it, he's good!* "Cortez and

Rudge will have a fit."

"Cortez is a sergeant. You're a DI. He'll do and think what you tell him. And Rudge." Madden shrugged. "Rudge is Rudge. Deal with it. That's also part of the job."

Madden pushed his chair back from his desk, and Claire recognised it as the sign that their interview was over. But she couldn't hold back one last important question. "Why me?" she said as she stood up. "Why this case and why this sergeant on my team?"

Madden pursed his lips. It might have been because he was thinking. It might have been because he was trying to suppress a laugh. "It was thought," he said finally, "that you might be sympathetic. To the situation of...minorities."

Claire regarded him incredulously. "Because I'm a woman?"

"No," said Chief Inspector Madden, with benign reasonableness, "because you're Welsh."

Chapter Four

Madden's office was only two floors up from the basement canteen. By the time she had walked the stairs, Claire had gone through over half a dozen scenarios for this first meeting with her new sergeant. With Jenny it would have been easy: a handshake, maybe a girly hug, maybe not, and it would have all been done and dusted. And then they could have gone and had a good girls' night out later and really celebrated when no one was around to see. Instead she had a brand new officer to induct, and less than five minutes to get the ground rules for their working relationship sorted out in her head before she began to lay them down. And lack of time wasn't the main problem. The main problem was she was mad as hell. Mad at not getting her choice; mad at the Super's manipulation; mad at the bloody political correctness that had shoved it onto both of them, and mad at being mad at a policy she'd have applauded under every other possible circumstance. Not that that was this sergeant's fault, she reminded herself on the stairs between first and ground floor. Shoving her way through the canteen double doors, she had no trouble identifying the only man to be seen. Drawing herself up to her full five seven, Detective Summerskill strode over to him.

"Sergeant Lyon?"

Dave lay the paper down and got smartly to his feet. "Ma'am?"

"Inspector Summerskill."

"Inspector."

For a moment they stood regarding each other. Sizing me up, Claire thought. Typically male. Well, actually perhaps not. "Please." She nodded to his chair and pulled out another for herself as he sat back down. That at least dealt with the extra six inches or so he had on her. She noticed him quickly shuffle the paper he'd been reading out of sight under the table as if embarrassed by having been caught reading it. Odd, she thought. It was only the *Mail*.

"Welcome to Worcester Foregate Station," she began. "And congratulations on your promotion."

"And on yours, ma'am."

"What? Oh, yes, thank you." It hadn't struck her till then that obviously someone had briefed him on her just as she'd been briefed on him. "I've just been reviewing your details with Chief Superintendent Madden, and..."

"Hope you like it." From somewhere between them a plate materialised, hovered at eye level before descending to land neatly in front of Dave. Above it was the still flushed but beaming face of Eileen.

"Great!" said Dave. Claire could see he was trying subtly but unsuccessfully to indicate to the girl through rapid eye movement alone that this was not the best moment to deliver breakfast.

"I've popped on an extra rasher," said Eileen, blind to Dave's signalling. "As it's your first day like."

"Thanks, Eileen." Dave smiled and waited for the station cook to return to her hot lamps. Eileen stood, smiling back and obviously waiting for him to sample her temptation. "I'll have it in a minute," he said, inclining his head not so subtly towards his boss.

This time Eileen got the message. "Oh. Right. Morning, Claire."

"Morning, Eileen," Claire muttered.

"Or should I say *Inspector* Claire now?"

"No. No, you really shouldn't," Claire said.

Eileen nodded towards Dave's plate. "Don't suppose you'll be wanting one of those, will you? Not even as a bit of a celebration, like? Not with that new diet you're on. How's it going?"

"Just fine, thank you, Eileen."

Finally, something of the frost in Claire's words seeped through even Eileen's warm cheeriness. "Ah, right, then. Well, I'd best be off, let you two get on with getting acquainted."

"Thank you," said Claire crisply.

"Hope you enjoy the sandwich, Dave," she couldn't resist adding.

"I'm sure I will."

Claire watched her go then looked back down at the sandwich. "Extra rasher," she said. Dave smiled, clearly not quite sure what you said about something like that to a new boss who was on a diet. "Garnish, too," she added, with reference to the rather limp lettuce leaf Eileen had thoughtfully balanced on the edge of the plate. "D'you know, I don't think I've ever got garnish here. I don't think *anyone's* ever got garnish here."

"Well," Dave assayed carefully, "my dad always said there are two people in any new station you have to get on with: the desk sergeant and the canteen cook."

"You certainly seem to have made a good start with Eileen."

"She seems a nice girl."

"And you'll notice how she packs them in." Claire waved a hand at the empty room.

"I'm not fussy when it comes to food," said Dave with a smile.

"Neither's Eileen. You should get on like a house on fire. You're from a police family?"

"My dad. Retired now."

"Division?" What she wanted to ask was *rank*?

Dave gave a deprecatory shrug. "Just a plod. Twenty years."

The suspicious thought forming in Claire's mind evaporated. Nepotism would hardly have accounted for Lyon's less than meteoric career anyway.

"You?"

"Me?" She somehow hadn't expected to be answering questions herself about her background. "No," she said. "Definitely no police in my family." Deliberately she brought the conversation back round to the direction she had mapped out for it. "People had good things to say about you in Redditch. I'm sure you'll be an asset to the team here, too. We're a smaller force. You may not find the premises and facilities as cutting edge as you've been used to." She paused to allow Lyon to interject some kind of token protest. "But there are good people here," she said, when he did not. "They work hard. I work hard. And I hope that you'll—" she paused again, uncomfortably aware that her rhetoric had somewhere lost the sparkle she'd hoped for "—work hard, too."

"Yes, ma'am."

She waited, but he said no more, his expression one of entirely appropriate enthusiasm. She was impressed that he was able to keep his eyes off the egg and bacon sandwich on the table between them, which she had to admit smelled bloody good. "So, what I suggest is you finish your breakfast, unload your stuff at your desk upstairs—" she indicated the holdall at his feet "—and then we'll get down to our first case."

"Sounds good! What is it?"

She saw it in his eyes, that same anticipation that must have been in hers as she waited for Madden to reveal her first tough new challenge. "I'll tell you on the way there," she said. "Meet me out front in ten minutes. Okay?"

"Okay. Thank you, ma'am."

She stood, turned to go, then, "I think you should know," she said suddenly, without planning to, but unable—right or wrong—to hold it back, "that I don't believe in quotas. I don't think they're a good idea at all. I think we should all get where we want to be on our merits." She automatically went to flick her hair out of her eyes, still surprised by the fact her new cut left none there for her to flick. “I just wanted that to be understood.”

Dave had risen and now stood, obviously processing what his new boss had just said. “Me, too, ma’am.”

Claire nodded, “Good. Good. All right, then. Second floor, third door on the left. You get the desk by the water cooler. Handy for water and station scuttlebutt but a pain in the arse on hot days. Ten minutes, remember. Okay?”

“Okay.”

Claire turned on her heel and walked smartly out of the canteen. That, she reflected, as she stepped through the double doors, had gone all right. Firm, professional, but honest. She wasn’t sure about ’ma’am‘, though. Right form, but Christ it made her feel about a hundred. Based at Worcester Foregate as she had been for five years, everyone knew her well enough to use her first name, and as she’d just found with Eileen, that was a situation that could turn round and bite her on her newly elevated bum. It certainly wouldn’t be right to let this newbie be so familiar. Especially not until she’d got to see how he’d work out. Fair start on his part, though, she conceded. He could have taken the hump at her forthright expression of views but hadn’t. And in today’s political climate, people who thought their feathers had been ruffled could make life quite awkward. She might even have had to... Abruptly she stopped, an echo of Madden’s earlier words suddenly coming back to her. *Hang on a minute!* He had understood, hadn’t he, that when she’d been talking about quotas she'd been referring to *him*?

Back in the canteen, Dave wolfed down the lovingly prepared egg and bacon sandwich, which was actually quite good apart from the lettuce leaf which he rolled into a small ball and took like a pill. Having wiped his mouth on the piece of kitchen roll Eileen had thoughtfully also provided, he grabbed his holdall and strode from the canteen, winking at the cook who sighed expansively and unhealthily over a tray of cooling sausage rolls and waved goodbye. He dropped the copy of the *Mail* in the bin on the way out.

That went all right. Dave bounded up the stairs. That statement about quotas had been a bit unexpected, but he'd dealt with worse. A lot worse. He'd vaguely wondered whether having a woman for an immediate boss would make things easier. No reason why it should he supposed, but somehow...

Shelving the question for a later time, Dave strode along the corridor on the second floor until he came to the office DI Summerskill had indicated. Through the glass he could see it was empty. And small. He went in. He took in the four desks that practically filled the space, the currently blank incident boards, and the water cooler. So that desk by it, conspicuous by its empty top and noticeable smallness compared to the others, had to be his. Dave grinned. Just what he'd expected. *Can't put the new boy straight in the lap of luxury, can they?* He dumped his holdall on his chair, which, he noticed, had a shaky leg, and began to unpack its contents.

The scrap of paper was waiting for him in the top drawer. The message was short and nasty, the writing almost convincingly illiterate. *Well, it just wouldn't have had the same kick if it had been copperplate, would it?* Dave screwed the paper up, holding it there in his fist for a moment. *Okay, so news travels fast. Really fast.* He went to throw it in the bin down by the side of his desk but held back at the last minute and instead pushed it deep in his pocket.

He turned back to the holdall. It was practically emptied now, just that one last thing. He hesitated. He could feel that scrap of paper still in his pocket, its spiteful little 'welcome' message holding him back. *All the more reason...* Deliberately, he thrust his hand into the holdall and pulled out that remaining item. He tried it in various positions on his desktop, first to one side of his computer screen, then to the other, stepping back to examine it critically before deciding the first place was better after all. More people could see it clearly there. With a grim smile, he folded the holdall up and shoved it into the desk's capacious lower drawer. "There you go," he muttered, touching the top of the framed photograph once briefly. The face of a handsome young man grinned maniacally back out at him, the words *For my darling Dave. All my love!!! X* written in bold felt pen underneath. "You're out of the bag. And I'm out of the closet. Again."

Dave turned and left the office, heading back downstairs for his meeting with his boss. As he re-entered the stairwell, Inspector Summerskill's parting words came back to him and, perhaps inspired by the small gesture he himself had just made, their meaning suddenly appeared in a completely different light. "Shit! I hope she's not a dyke!"

* ~ * ~ *

Jenny bumped into Claire in the ladies'. "Congratul..." she began.

"Don't!"

"Why not? You deserve it. I'm pleased for you, really I am."

Claire regarded her friend closely, and not for the first time wished that women were as easy to read as men were. "I'm sorry Jen. I tried."

Jenny shoved her hands under the washer/drier machine and rubbed them briskly in the stream of tepid water and cool air that followed. "I know you did. Thanks. Maybe next time, eh?"

"Definitely, if I have anything to do with it."

"Still up for that drink?"

"Still want to?"

Jenny's laugh was a little forced, but it was there. "Of course I do. It is still a cause for celebration, you know."

"Thanks, Jen." Claire felt the relief. Women might be harder to read than men, but at least they didn't let their egos get in the way of their friendships. She wondered briefly whether she could have been as generous if her position and Jenny's had been reversed. She shook her head and quickly decided it was best not to go there.

"So what's he like then, the new wonderkid?"

It was on the tip of her tongue to ask how the hell Jenny knew about Dave Lyon already when she herself had only found out less than half an hour ago, but she held back. Always best not to snoop after a colleague's narks, even if they were in the station itself. "Hardly a kid. I'll let you know. Good record."

"Yeah. I know about his record."

News does travel fast. Claire found herself wanting to ask Jenny exactly what she had heard, and perhaps even more importantly what she thought about it, like she would have done when she was just a sergeant. But that was then. And now, she was an inspector, and Dave Lyon was her sergeant. She wouldn't spend the first hour of her new post in gossip about one of her team. No matter how much she wanted to. Gloomily, she wondered just how much more of the anticipated pleasure of her new rank was going to fade away in the cold light of its first day. "And I'll let you know when we can have that drink, okay?"

Jenny frowned. "Thought we'd said Friday?"

"Yeah—well, hopefully. It just depends how this first case goes, all right? Shouldn't be a problem."

"Right. Yeah, of course."

* ~ * ~ *

Lyon was waiting for her at the front desk, chatting with the desk sergeant. Chatting *with* or chatting *up* she wondered, before she could stop herself. She took in Sergeant Dennison's nose, hairy ears and bald patch. *No way*, she reproved herself. *Surely*. She signed out the car keys and threw them to Lyon. "You can drive." They went to leave.

"Inspector Summerskill!"

Chief Superintendent Madden was walking towards them. Was Madden already checking up on her? Making sure she was playing nice with her first recruit? "Sir?"

"You're off to the canal?"

"Yes, sir. Can't have those happy slappers running amok while we're dragging our heels here." She was sure she could feel Lyon beside her react to her words, was certain she felt his enthusiasm for their first case begin to drain away, just as hers had, as he began to suspect its true nature.

"Yes—well. You might like to know that the situation has suddenly become that bit more challenging."

"Sir?" Claire waited unenthusiastically for whatever fresh twist the old bastard was about to add to her first day as an inspector.

"They've just found a body down there."

Chapter Five

"Oh, great." Claire swore under her breath as she and Lyon approached the knot of uniforms and civilians gathered under the small bridge.

"Ma'am?"

"Aldridge." She jerked her head in the direction of a man in SOCO overalls kneeling down by something on the ground.

"Difficult?"

"Only on working days."

Dave grimaced. "Had 'em like that at Redditch, too. Reckon it's something to do with the chemicals."

"Only the ones in his hormones."

At their approach, Aldridge rose. "Sergeant!" he exclaimed, his face breaking into a toothy smile. Dave started, racking his brain for a memory of this man who sounded so pleased to see him before realising the nature of his mistake. "Sorry," Aldridge apologised theatrically to Summerskill, "I mean *inspector*." He nodded cheerily to Dave. "And sergeant, too." Dave nodded back. The guy didn't seem too bad. He wondered why his boss had such a downer on him. Not ugly, either. But then he noticed that, after having given him the nod, Aldridge's attention was all for

Inspector Summerskill, and that as far as he was concerned Dave could have been in the canal, not merely standing by it.

*

"Aldridge." Claire nodded coolly. She stepped closer to the focus of activity. The boy's body was still sitting against the wall. At first glance he could indeed be taken for someone sleeping. It was only as she knelt down and peered up under the hoodie that she saw the open, unblinking eyes, the pallor of the face, the thick line of now crusted blood stretching down over the cheek. "What do you know?"

"More than can readily be explained over a series of late night meals. But if you mean with reference to this case..." Aldridge paused, drew breath and then chanted, "Male. Caucasian. Age probably late teens, I don't think he's twenty. Cause of death severe trauma to the head. And now, if you're here and will allow me to do the honours?" Claire nodded, only just hiding her irritation at Aldridge's faux gallantry. The doctor knelt and, with professional gentleness, pushed back the hood that covered the boy's head. "Yes. Well, there wasn't really any doubt about that was there?" Claire steeled herself and leaned in closer. "It's rather unpleasant."

"I'd guessed that." It wasn't the most extensive injury she had seen, but it was still enough. It had killed a human being. It was that appalling fact that sickened her, not some childish squeamishness over blood. She'd got over that a long time ago. She stood up. “Who found him?” A PC indicated an old man with a dog. Claire nodded towards him and Dave walked over, pulling out his notepad as he went.

Aldridge was standing again and removing the thin white gloves he wore.

“May I?” She indicated the box on the ground and snatched from it a pair for herself before he could pick it up and offer it to her as a gift. She removed the one ring on her right hand and pulled the gloves on. She hoped Aldridge wouldn’t say what he always said. She really, really hoped he wouldn’t say it.

“Ah, always so keen to snap on the latex, inspector.”

He’d said it.

Claire rolled her eyes, took a calming breath and focused again on the body, blocking the SOCO man out completely as she tried to take in everything about the way it was positioned, the ground beneath it, the stones behind it. Slowly she reached in, ran her fingers over the jeans pockets, then across the chest. She found what she was searching for in a shirt pocket: a thick card wallet, expensive black leather, unmarked. Flipping it open revealed a number of cards neatly held in transparent plastic pockets. At least three of them had photographs, all of the same person, the dead boy before her. She stood and signalled to the two men standing by with stretchers who came over and carefully set about removing the corpse.

Aldridge was closing up his bag of tricks. “I’ll know more when I’ve had a chance to get up close and personal, of course,” he said, "but from prelim scene analysis I'd say he's been dead between six to ten hours."

"When can you let me have the details?"

"For you, I'll do the autopsy as soon as I get back. Should have it all sewn up, so to speak, in under two hours. Then, if you're there by my side, I can pass on the fruits of my labours immediately."

"Call me," Claire said flatly.

"You'll give me your number?"

"You'll find me at the station."

"I prefer the personal touch."

You'll get such a personal touch in a moment, mate. She was unable to suppress a sigh of relief when Aldridge left the scene, passing under the black and yellow cordon tape a uniformed officer lifted for him. She'd had a vague hope that her higher rank might have cooled Aldridge's annoying ardour. Her fear now was that it actually acted as an aphrodisiac. As if the man needed that.

"I see you have a close working relationship there, ma'am."

She turned to her sergeant who was back at her side. "If he gets any closer I'll have him up in court. Anything?"

Dave shook his head and flipped his notepad closed. "Mr Roberts there was trying to be your basic Good Samaritan. Time of discovery, that's all."

Claire scanned their surroundings. Fewer than a hundred yards away and you were on the streets. Mostly shops which would have been closed at the time of night Aldridge was suggesting the murder had been committed, but there were flats and some houses, too, so that was as good a place as any to start making inquiries.

"Already on it," Dave said. "I've put a couple of uniforms to knocking up the nearest."

"Right." *Initiative. Which is good. Not jumping the gun at all. Initiative.* She opened the card wallet in her hand, flipping again through its pockets.

"We've got a name?"

Rail card. Student card. Library card. One after the other. "Yes," she said. "We've got a name. Jonathan Wilson." She flipped the wallet closed and dropped it into a plastic evidence bag. "And he's local." She took a deep breath. "Ready for the shitty part?"

Dave grimaced. "The family?"

"The family."

Chapter Six

Dave gave a low whistle. “Impressive,” he said.

“Thought it might be.”

“How’s that?”

“The wallet. The clothes. Hoodie, jeans and trainers—all labels. None of it cheap stuff.”

“So do you think the lad was killed for his money?”

Claire shook her head. “And the card wallet left behind? Shouldn’t think so.”

Dave killed the engine and took a closer look at the house they had just pulled up before. “*Very* impressive,” he amended.

“Most of the houses in this area are.” Claire leaned back momentarily in her seat, gathering herself. “God, I hate this bit,” she said, more to herself than to him, then, “Come on.” She threw the door open, stepped out, and strode purposefully to the large front door.

The address on Jonathan Wilson’s cards, confirmed by a call back to the station, was ten miles from Worcester in Malvern, one of the outlying towns. Sprawled across its famous hills, Malvern was actually a collection of picturesque small towns rather than one single place: Malvern Link, Great Malvern, Little Malvern,

North Malvern, West Malvern, all places with their own personalities, reflecting the different periods they had been established, the different nature of their inhabitants. The sizable late Victorian house they now stood before was in Malvern Wells. Where the rich people lived.

There was an ornate brass knocker and a doorbell on the sturdy wooden double door facing them. Claire used the bell. The door was opened almost immediately by a young man—early twenties, Claire estimated—and the speed of the response made her wonder for a moment if he was some kind of butler, before deciding that the decidedly casual jeans and T-shirt ruled that idea out. There was also something familiar about his face that... With an unexpected twist of the stomach, Claire recognised the line of the nose, of the jaw, last seen streaked with blood and leached of life against a dank stone wall, and knew she should have prepared herself for something like this. Jonathan Wilson had a brother. "Good morning. I'm Police Inspector Summerskill and this is Sergeant Lyon. May we come in?"

The young man's eyes flicked over the proffered cards. "Of course," he said, though with understandable uncertainty. He stood back and opened the door wide to let the police officers enter. They stepped into a spacious hallway, and stood in an awkward group. "I'm Simon Wilson. Is it me you want to talk to or my parents?"

"I think it would be best if we spoke to you and your parents."

Simon Wilson nodded, almost as if that was what he'd

expected her to say, and indicated for them to follow him down the hallway. They walked along an intricately patterned, thick carpet, past a sweeping staircase and sideboards heavy with ornaments and framed photographs. Pictures lined the walls, mostly of vintage cars from what Claire could see. They stopped in front of a door and Simon turned to face them. "It's bad news, isn't it?"

"What makes you say that, sir?" She mentally kicked herself for that automatic reaction. Of course it was bad news. Inspectors didn't turn up on your doorstep to tell you you'd got a parking ticket. *Great first impression to make on this young man. Not such a good one to make on Lyon, either.* "I'm afraid it is. I... I'd rather not say anything until I see your parents." At least that way she wouldn't have to break the news twice. Simon nodded once and took a second as if to brace himself before he opened the door and showed the police officers in. *Handsome lad. Quite a heartbreaker, actually.* She wondered if Jonathan had been in life, and she felt again that sick anger at the violence that had cut such a young life short.

The room was what she guessed you'd call a morning room. Larger than her living room and dining room combined, lit by the midday sun streaming through floor to ceiling windows, and heavy with the same gilt ornamentation and decoration she'd noted in the passageway outside. Across the room she made out a woman seated on a long leather sofa. Her attention was on the officers as they entered but she did not get up. Standing by a small bar nearer to them, a glass in his hand, was, Claire presumed, the woman's husband and Jonathan's father. The boys' looks, she couldn't help feeling, had to have come from the mother's side of the family. "Mr Wilson? Mrs Wilson?" She braced herself to shatter their world.

"This is Inspector Summerskill," Simon said. "And Sergeant...?"

"Lyon."

Simon gave Dave a small smile of mingled gratitude and apology. It was obvious that he was apprehensive about what they had to say, had almost certainly guessed the essence of it if not the full facts, and Dave gave a small smile back, clearly wishing he could do more to lighten the blow that was about to fall.

"Inspector?" Mr Wilson said evenly. "What can I do for you?" A stocky man, he stood at his bar, his free hand lying proprietarily on its marble top, and addressed his question to Dave. Claire cleared her throat. "You are the parents of Jonathan Alan Wilson?" The man redirected his attention to her with obvious reluctance, and nodded once. Claire took a steadying breath, aware of Mrs Wilson across the room raising herself up, a small woman dwarfed by the sofa, by the size of the room. Conscious, too, of Mr Wilson's unfriendly regard, his hand clenched on the glass he was holding, like a fist held out in front of him. Already, the words she'd been going over again and again in her head on the way there sounded completely inadequate to her. "I'm afraid I have some bad news for you about Jonathan." She paused, uncertain which of them she should be facing when she actually broke the news, settling finally on the father. "I'm so sorry."

Mrs Wilson leaped up from the sofa, then just stood there, her fingers skittering to her throat, fluttering uselessly down the front of her dress. "Jonathan?" Her voice was cracked, as if unused to sudden expression. Mr Wilson stood rock steady, face unreadable.

"Yes. It's my duty to... I'm afraid I have to tell you...that Jonathan is dead. I am so very sorry." And now she felt sick.

Mrs Wilson gave a choked gasp and Claire instinctively moved towards her then stopped. She'd had to do this horrendous duty three times before in her career. Mercifully, she hadn't been the one in charge on those occasions, and each time she had been the one who had gone to support the woman; a mother, a wife twice, but now...? Dave moved awkwardly towards Mrs Wilson but it was Simon Wilson, whom they'd both momentarily overlooked, who swiftly stepped across the room to put his arms around his mother and hold her as he stared back at them, his face pale and stunned.

"How...?" began Mr. Wilson. Then, "An accident?"

Claire shook her head. "No. I'm afraid not."

"Killed. You're telling me he's been killed? He's been... Jonathan's been murdered."

The path lab report wasn't in yet. Aldridge was probably only just scrubbing up as this ghastly interview unfolded. She knew the official line was circumspection. And she knew that wasn't what families wanted at times like this. "Yes, we think so." Out of the corner of her eye she thought she saw Lyon flinch very, very slightly at this break from correct procedure. Well, he was damn well going to have to get that rod out from up his arse if he was going to work with her. Even if he liked it there.

Mr Wilson stood still, eyes turned to her but focused elsewhere, most likely on some unimaginable scene playing out in his mind. “Do you know...?” He stopped, looked briefly at the glass in his hand as if surprised to find it still there. “Who?” he spat out finally.

“I'm afraid we don't know that yet. The... Your son was only found this morning. But rest assured...”

Wilson turned his back on her, head down, shoulders hunched as he leaned on his bar. She heard the hard rap of the glass tumbler as it hit the marble, found herself wondering if it had cracked. “We'll leave you for the moment,” she said, guiltily aware of just how badly she wanted to get out of that house. “You'll want some time alone. I'm afraid we'll have to come back later. There'll be some questions. We'll need to know as much about Jonathan as you can tell us. And you will have to...” She glanced across at the mother, her face buried in her son's shoulder. “I'm afraid you will have to identify your son. Is there anyone you would like us to call for you?” There was no reaction from either Mr or Mrs Wilson and she wasn't even sure they had heard her, but Simon Wilson shook his head. “Right. Then we'll go. Sergeant? We'll see ourselves out.”

She and Dave made for the door. Simon Wilson gently forced his mother back down onto the sofa, disentangled her clinging arms with a few murmured words, softly stroked her mutely agonised face, then walked towards the two officers. "I'll be back in a minute," he said as he passed in front of his father. "Please, just a minute." He followed Claire and Dave out. Claire got one last sight of the room before Simon closed the door behind him. Mr Wilson remained standing at the bar. Mrs Wilson remained silent and stricken on the sofa. They did not move towards each other.

"Thank you," Claire said out in the passageway again. "I think your parents are going to need you, Simon. You have a very difficult time ahead of you. I..." She knew she was about to repeat herself and wished there was something else, anything, she could say, but if there was it was well beyond her. "I really am so very sorry."

Simon nodded dumbly.

"Were you and your brother very close, Simon?"

And now it was Claire's turn to flinch at her sergeant's question. *Time enough for questions like that later. Right now, let the family grieve. Let us get the hell out of here. And what sort of question is that to ask a bereaved brother anyway?*

Simon, though, didn't react badly, seeming instead grateful for something that wasn't just another platitude. "I suppose you'd say so. You know how it is with brothers." Claire did. She had no idea yet whether Lyon did. "I suppose we had been closer, but then I went away to university and that meant we couldn't talk as much as we had, and... I suppose we started to drift apart."

"Right. Which university?"

And here Simon did blink as if in surprise that on a day like this people could still ask the routine day to day questions they always did. “Bristol. I read history.”

Dave nodded in a way that might have suggested admiration for Bristol, history or both.

“It’s good that you’re at home at the moment,” Claire said, masking the irritation she felt at her sergeant’s apparent penchant for pointless, ill-timed questioning. “You’ll be a comfort to them.”

“Mum perhaps.” Simon glanced back at the morning room. “It’s so unfair, y’know? I mean, I know Jonathan hadn’t been happy for a while. Things getting him down. But I really thought he was starting to work them out. And now...”

“Things?” said Claire, unprepared for this flash of earnestness.

From behind the door came a woman’s thin voice, pleading, “Simon? Simon!”

The young man ran his hand over his face. “I’ve got to go,” he said unsteadily.

“Could I just have a quick look at your brother’s room, Simon?” Dave asked. “I promise I won’t touch anything.”

Claire shot him an irritated glance. This was not something they had discussed.

“He hardly uses it,” Simon said doubtfully. “He’s got a bedsit in town, you know.”

“No, we didn’t,” said Claire. She assumed that would be a part of the information the desk staff back at the station would have waiting for her when she got back. *It had better be.*

"Just a quick look. Through the door?"

Simon glanced between them and the morning room door, obviously torn between his desire to help them and to return to his mother. "All right. I suppose that's okay. It's up there." He pointed up the sweep of stairs. "Second door on the left."

"Thanks. We'll only be a minute and then we'll see ourselves out. You go and be with your mum and dad. They need you right now."

Nodding uncertainly, Simon turned back to the morning room. Claire heard only one more querulous, "Simon?" before the door closed behind him.

Dave waited a couple of seconds then spoke to his boss. "Shall we?"

"No, no, sergeant. You go ahead with your own investigations. I wouldn't want to get in your way."

"Right. Shan't be a tick." Unaware of, or deliberately refusing to acknowledge his superior's sarcasm, Dave bounded up the wide stairs while Claire made her way back to the car, where she waited in the passenger seat. And quietly seethed. Lyon's unanticipated striking out in his own directions had irritated the hell out of her, his apparent imperviousness to her sarcastic putdown only increasing her annoyance. She wasn't handling him properly, she was sure of it. It had all got off to a bad start and she was having trouble getting it back on track. He was smart. He was confident. These were good things. Yes. But you could be *too* confident. Cocky. Or was this just her showing her own lack of confidence?

Shit, this would have been so much easier with Jenny. Then she could just have concentrated on the case.

She took a deep breath, held it for five and let it out again slowly. She wasn't sure why. She wasn't even sure it made her feel any better. It was just something she thought she'd heard about on telly once. She made herself think about the family they'd just met, the people they would almost certainly have several dealings with over the course of the forthcoming investigation. *Keep it simple,* Jeff Conlon had told her years ago, back when they were both on the beat, she just starting out and he nearing retirement age. *One word should do it.* Advice she'd smiled at, nodded in agreement with, and laughed at in private. Until the years had proven to her what sound sense it made, though by then Jeff had been long gone in Devon and she'd never been able to thank him. So, one word to sum up the Wilsons. What would it be?

Contradictions.

That was the one that came immediately to mind. Right from the start: contradictions. A boy in hoodie and trainers, with a wallet stuffed with credit cards. Okay, so perhaps that wasn't so odd, and explained easily enough by the demands of street fashion. An elegant home in the country, then, stuffed with garish ornamentation and furniture. A fine-featured son and a father flushed with drink by midday. She pictured again the hand grasping that glass, the thick gold rings he'd been wearing. Had Jonathan been wearing any rings, or jewellery at all? She couldn't remember. She didn't think so, but could they have been stolen from him? She'd check with Aldridge. Most rings would have left an impression on the flesh if they'd been taken off recently. All this and a murder, in a place where before there had been only minor assaults.

Contradictions.

~~*

Back in the house, Dave stood outside Jonathan Wilson's room. Ignoring the automatic impulse to knock, he opened the door. The room was large, at least three times the size of the one he'd had to share with his brother when he'd been living at home, and considerably tidier. Dave went to walk in then held back, mindful of what he had said to Simon. He could see enough from the doorway, for the moment. No clothes on the floor, no magazines strewn about the place, not much like his and Andy's room at all. But then Simon had said that Jonathan had been living away from home. Where, Dave wondered, and why when you had a place like this to call your own? He took in the posters on the walls, old film posters mostly; a few for Japanese anime, some for bands, a couple he recognised, one he really liked himself. He took in the books over the desk. The shelves of CDs and DVDs, even some videos by the looks of it. *Which is a bit surprising, isn't it, for a lad of Jonathan's age?*

And he took in the things that weren't there as well. Not so completely different from his own old room, after all.

He nodded to himself, closed the door softly behind him and

went back down the stairs to join his new boss.

* ~ * ~ *

"You realise we'll have to do that again later?" she said, as he climbed into the car. "Thoroughly."

"I know. But I wanted to do it now, wanted to get a sense of the boy."

Okay. Claire had to admit she approved of that, at least. "So?"

"Just impressions at the moment. Nothing definite."

Great! "You done many of these family visits?"

"Five. And that's five too many."

It was also two more than she had. "Come on, get us back to the station. I want to get the routine stuff sorted before Aldridge sends his summons."

"Thought you were keeping him at arm's length?"

"If I could I'd keep a lot more than the length of an arm between us. But there's no getting away from some things. I need to see that boy again. I need to be there when Aldridge tells me what happened."

Dave nodded and started the car up. "Understood."

Was it, she wondered. Not really. What she'd said about Aldridge had been true enough, but that wasn't the only reason she wanted to be back at the station now. It was the other item on her agenda she wanted to get out of the way as soon as possible so she could properly focus on the job at hand. The working day had well and truly kicked in. It was past time to introduce Sergeant

Dave Lyon to the rest of his new colleagues.

She found she was not looking forward to that at all.

Chapter Seven

When they got back to their office at the station, the two desks other than their own were occupied. Claire made the introductions and as she did so, Dave sensed the change in her manner, almost as if she were bracing herself for something. "Chief Inspector Rudge. Sergeant Cortez. Meet Sergeant Lyon. Transferred from Redditch today."

"Hi," said Dave.

Cortez nodded. Rudge merely leaned back in his chair. "Murder already then, eh? Aren't we the lucky one?" He spoke as if Claire had entered the office alone. Quickly Claire brought them up to speed on the case while Dave took a moment to size up the guys he'd be working with. Rudge was definitely older than all of them, but his shaved head made it hard to actually pin numbers to his age. The indeterminate colour of his moustache made it hard to imagine what colour his hair had been originally. He had what, in gay personals at least, was charitably called a 'rugby player's build'. Cortez was young, younger than all of them in fact, and Dave noted the sharp jacket and good build underneath it. He approved. All that pounding the beat kept uniforms pretty trim as a rule, but give a man more time at a desk than on a pavement and a beer belly was never that far behind.

"So, *inspector,*" Rudge was saying, "how are you going to handle it?"

Claire smiled at him with mock sweetness. "Didn't work under you for five years, Jim, without picking up a tip or two. I thought I'd hang around here for most of the day, drink coffee, let some keen sergeant do all the work, then step in when all the hard graft has been done and claim all the credit."

Cortez clicked his fingers. "That's got to be why you made inspector before me," he said with a grin that wasn't entirely without an edge. "You've studied at the feet of a master."

"Your turn now, Terry. And the first time he asks you to make that coffee you know where to tell him to stuff it."

"You're working the nearby houses?" Rudge continued, without any sign of reaction to Claire's words.

"Mostly shops, but we're already on it." It was Dave who answered.

Rudge finally turned to face the station's newest sergeant. "And you'll want to be checking out the local gay clubs and pubs, I suppose?" he said. "If you haven't already."

Claire bristled visibly, though Dave knew she must have been expecting this. Maybe just not so soon. "What's your point, Jim?" she asked levelly.

"I've read the briefing. There's been a series of assaults on that path over the past few weeks, all on a Sunday evening. Sunday night is gay night at the Pharos nightclub. Clubbers leaving the

Pharos walk along that path to get to the main road. You see the connection, inspector?" He leaned back still further in his chair and put his hands behind his head. "Some of them have admitted it anyway."

"Putting aside for a minute the idea of *admitting* to something that doesn't require a confession," Claire said carefully, "the assaults you referred to were minor at best. People..."

"Men," Rudge cut in.

"Boys mostly, were ruffled, little more than that. No one was struck with anything other than a hand, far less did they have the backs of their heads cracked open. So we don't know if there is any link between those attacks and this murder. And we definitely don't know yet if Jonathan Wilson was even gay."

"Actually," said Dave, "I think he was."

Claire whirled round. "What? What makes you say that?"

Rudge was smirking. "Haven't you heard? It's what they call 'gay radar'."

A policewoman walked into the office without knocking and came to a halt, no doubt sensing the building atmosphere. "Jenny, come in." Cortez beckoned her to him, and she walked over with the message she was carrying though her attention was wholly on Lyon and Rudge.

"That's gaydar," said Dave, nodding at the passing Jenny as if this was a perfectly calm, everyday conversation. "But that tends to work best when the guy is giving you the eye or smiling at you, buying you a drink or grabbing your bum, something like that, y'know? Not when he's lying there dead with his head cracked open." He turned to Claire. "It's just the impression I got from his room. Nothing definite. Just a feeling."

"So you said."

"Woman's intuition." Rudge snorted.

"You'd have to ask Inspector Summerskill," Dave said evenly.

"Boss," Cortez said, waving the piece of paper he'd been handed. "Fielding case. Think we've got it."

"About time." Rudge heaved himself from his chair. "Come on, Terry. Let's leave the ladies to their work." He tipped an imaginary hat to Claire and Jenny. "Ladies." He smirked and left. Terry Cortez followed, exchanging a brief glance and a very small shake of the head with Claire.

Claire took stock of the suddenly much less crowded room. "Sergeant Lyon, this is WPC Jenny Trent. Hardest worker still in uniform." As soon as the words were out of her mouth she grimaced, as if she'd somehow spoken out of turn.

"Hi," said Jenny and then she, too, swept out of the room.

Claire turned to Dave, who was rummaging in his waste paper basket. As she watched he pulled out a framed picture, gave it a quick wipe on his sleeve and set it up on his desk next to his computer screen. He knew she had to be curious about it but there were other things that needed settling before that. "Okay, sergeant. Care to tell me why you think Jonathan Wilson was gay? Any little insights you'd care to pass my way? Before broadcasting them to all and sundry."

As before at the Wilsons' house, if he spotted any irony in her words or tone, Dave gave no indication, though he was not completely comfortable being drawn out on what he had said. "It was just...well, memories I suppose. Jonathan's room reminded me a bit of mine when I was his age."

"You're going to have to help me here. I didn't realise bobbies on the beat could run to houses and rooms like that for their kids."

Dave snorted. "Shit no! Jonathan's room was way bigger than mine was. It had more TV, video and hi-fi equipment in it than the whole of my family house put together, and more books and DVDs on the shelves than our local library."

"But otherwise identical?"

"It was what *wasn't* there." Dave gave a thin smile of not entirely happy reminiscence. "I shared my room with my older brother, Alan. One of our biggest arguments was over what we put up on the walls. When we were little it was fine. We worked our way through fluffy animals to superheroes without too many problems. We almost made it through rock groups together but then the hormones kicked in and he wanted pictures of topless women and I wanted pictures of, well, topless men."

"I see," Claire said slowly, then, perhaps because she couldn't think of anything else at that moment, "Tricky."

"Yeah."

"So, in the end...?"

"In the end we compromised. We put up pictures of footballers. Alan could tell any visiting friends they were the team he supported, and I got to go to sleep every night surrounded by loads of fantastic legs. Footballers do have great legs."

"They do, don't they?" She shook her head. "And this has precisely what to do with Jonathan Wilson's room?"

"There were no pictures of girls on Jonathan's walls."

"Ah. I see." She nodded. "Hardly conclusive evidence, sergeant."

"No, ma'am."

"Pretty much a guess, really."

"Yes, ma'am."

"So your reason for coming out with it at that time was...?"

"Basically to get up DCI Rudge's nose, ma'am."

"I see." He waited for her to make some point about superior officers and first days at new stations. It didn't come. "So which team did you support?"

"Man U," Dave said immediately. "Great thighs."

Claire nodded. "That's what I've always thought."

Chapter Eight

"So how was your first day, *inspector*?"

Claire sighed. That had just got to be the last time that day anyone would place an excessive emphasis on her new title. "Long."

Ian, her husband, grimaced sympathetically as he joined her at the kitchen table with the beers he'd poured them. Claire accepted one gratefully. "Thought so," he said.

"Sam in bed?"

"For the past hour at least. I put my head round the door a minute ago but he was sound."

"I'm sorry, love. I meant to be here tonight to read that new book with him."

"No worries." Ian chinked his glass with hers. "Even he knows mummy's starting a new job. He was very understanding about it all. 'She'll be even busier now, won't she, Daddy? We'll have to help her.'"

"And they said my brainwashing wouldn't work. I'll go up in a minute to tuck him in." She took another long pull at her drink. "And Tony?"

Ian grunted. "Not yet back from his 'football practice'. Must have eyes like a bat the amount of football he plays in the dark."

"They hear, don't they? Bats." She leaned back and closed her eyes, resting the cool glass against her forehead. "I don't think they can actually see very well at all."

"Well, Tony certainly isn't able to hear me. Or his teachers for that matter. You know what his last report said?"

"Of course."

"Well, I'm already getting the hints that his next one's going to be even worse. Old Mason could barely keep the smile from his face when he was telling me what Tony's maths report is going to be like."

"You know we probably wouldn't get so worried if you weren't both at the same school. All the other kids only get bad reports once a term. Poor old Tony can get one every day just through people bumping into you in the staffroom."

"Then poor old Tony should pull his socks up," Ian remarked astringently. "You shouldn't always try to find excuses for him, Claire. We need to have a united front on this, for his own good."

"Yes, sir," she said, with mock obedience. Hell, she could fake it for Madden, she could certainly fake it for Ian. She tipped up and emptied her glass.

"What are you smiling at?"

"Nothing."

Ian would be quite right to suspect that Claire wasn't taking him seriously, but any further comments were cut off by an insistent pinging from the cooker, and he rose to adjust a simmering pan and to check on the chicken. "So," he said when he came back to the table, without, Claire was mildly disappointed to note, another beer, "apart from the length of it, how was the rest of the day? Jim and Terry okay with your new power?"

She considered. "I think so. Jim'll treat me like a little woman whatever, but I gather that behind the scenes he actually put in a good word for me." She thought about that for a moment, feeling slightly guilty now about her irritation at Rudge's obvious displeasure with her new sergeant. "Terry could have been awkward about it I suppose but he's being cool. He's good at cool. He knows it's his own fault he didn't get on this time. Needs to spend a bit less time in the gym and in front of mirrors, and a bit more behind his desk and his books. God, you know I really am starting to sound like a teacher."

"Not such a very bad thing," Ian remonstrated mildly.

Claire stretched in her chair. "Terry'll make inspector next time as like as not."

"And did you get Jenny? Are you two set to be the Cagney and Lacey of the Midlands?"

Claire swirled the remaining froth of her beer around in her now empty glass, hoping maybe Ian would get the hint. "No. No, I didn't. Jenny didn't get the promotion."

"No? That'll put her nose out of joint."

"It's not like that, Ian. It happens sometimes. She'll get made up, too, when the time's right."

"Now you're sounding less like a teacher and more like a chief superintendent." Claire glared at him. "So, do you get a new sergeant of your own or are you and Jim going to have to share Terry?"

There were times when she regretted telling Ian quite so much about office politics. She'd just assumed he wouldn't be that interested. She never wanted to talk about his staffroom. "No, I've got one of my very own, thank you very much."

"Anyone I know?"

"No. A new lad." She thought about that. She'd have to stop saying 'lad'. He wasn't that fresh off the assembly line. And it made her sound old. "Dave Lyon."

"Where's he from?"

"Redditch station."

Ian tutted with slight exasperation. "I didn't mean that. I meant, where was he born?" He affected a mock, plummy tone. "Who are his people?"

"I don't know," Claire had to admit. "I think he's fairly local."

"Not another emigrant from God's own country then?"

"The English police force should be so lucky."

"Well, I hope Madden's fixed you up with someone congenial."

"What d'you mean?"

The cooker pinged one last time and Ian rose to set about dishing up their tea. "Someone you can get on with. Do you think you're going to like him?"

"I guess so. Too soon to tell, really. Don't suppose I'd thought of it that way." And, rather to her surprise, Clare realised she hadn't. She'd been thinking of Dave Lyon more as a problem to be solved than as a person she was going to have to work closely with for at least the next month or so.

"Do you think he likes you?"

"Everyone likes me. What's to dislike?"

Ian began dishing up. "Married? Kids?"

She smiled to herself, trying to work out just how offhand those questions were. "No." Now would be the moment of course to tell him that her new partner was gay.

She didn't.

Well, why should I?

"He might have a partner," she said doubtfully before adding with much more conviction, "but he's definitely not married."

"You're slipping," said Ian, laying two steaming plates on to the table. "Time was you'd have had his life history by now."

She thought about that one for a minute. Annoyingly, Ian had a point. She probably would have taken the time to find out more about him if...if things had been different. As it was, well, it felt like prying. Except now she realised it must have looked as if she simply didn't care. Or didn't want to know.

"So, when are you going to invite him and any significant other over for a meal?"

"What?"

"Bit of a getting-to-know-you session. You are the boss now, you know. Have to be the gracious hostess now and again."

"It's not like at school, Ian."

"Jenny was always coming over."

"That was different. And she wasn't *always* coming over."

Ian wisely passed over the last part of the statement. "She was less of your partner than this guy is."

"He's not my 'partner', Ian. We're policing the semi-urban streets of Worcester, not the downtown ghettos of New York."

"Well, I'd still like to meet him," Ian insisted as he ladled out the veg.

I'll bet you would, and I know why, too. One word would have been enough dispel her husband's mingled curiosity and jealousy. One very small word. "All right," she said. "In between keeping the world safe for decent people I'll invite him over for sherry and nibbles. Okay?"

"Good. Can't wait."

"Me neither. It should be interesting." Claire reached for her knife and fork. "I do know one thing about him," she added.

"Oh yeah, what's that?"

"He supports Man U."

"Really." Ian appeared to be more surprised by his wife knowing that fact than by Dave's choice of team. "Didn't you tell him we were more of a rugby family?" He laughed. "At least we can be sure he and I will have one thing in common if he does watch the rugby. He'll be bound to support England over Wales any day, won't he?"

Depends on which team's got the better legs.

* ~ * ~ *

"So how was your first day?"

Dave lay back in the bed, staring unseeing up at the ceiling, and let Richard trace patterns on his chest with his index finger. "Interesting," he said.

"Solve any juicy murders?"

Dave sighed. Sometimes Richard's treatment of his job as being like something from a television cop show was a bit of a laugh. Sometimes it just got on his tits. And not in the rather pleasant way Richard's finger was at that moment. "Not on the first day, no. I thought I'd leave it till maybe the end of the week before I showed them all how it should be done."

"Put you on traffic duty, eh?"

"No. In fact, there was a murder if you must know. I expect it'll be on the news tomorrow."

Richard left off his tracery and propped himself up on one arm. "Sorry," he said simply. "That was crass, wasn't it? Must be hard not to bring something like that home with you. And then me asking for all the gory details probably doesn't help."

"'S'okay," said Dave. In point of fact he didn't find it hard at all. He just didn't like talking about his work with Richard. Which bothered him a bit. He did like Richard dragging his fingers over his chest, though, and wished he'd just shut up and get back to that.

"So what's your new boss like?"

Dave sighed inwardly and considered. "Okay, I think," he said eventually. "Early days. Be different working for a woman."

"No handsome boss to take you under his wing? Make you his protégé?"

"You can rest assured that DI Summerskill and I will enjoy a purely professional relationship."

Richard sank back down and laid his head on Dave's chest. "And what about the rest of your colleagues, hmm? Any pretty policemen likely to try to entrap you?"

Dave pretended to think about it. "Couple of the uniforms are quite tasty," he admitted, "but as an officer I shall have to show some restraint."

"Mm, restraint! And what about your fellow officers?"

Dave cast his mind back over the day. "Sergeant Cortez is a bit of a looker," he admitted. "Got the feeling he knows it as well. And then there's Inspector Rudge..." He trailed off as he thought about Rudge. Truth be told he probably found the chief inspector the more attractive of the two. He'd always had a bit of a weakness for shaven-headed, burly guys, more than for the classic model type, which was what Cortez definitely was. But there was also Rudge's undeniable...coldness. He thought back to that bit of paper in his desk, now tucked away in the pocket of his trousers hanging over a chair. And then there was his framed photograph, rescued from the bin. "Not your type at all," he said finally. "And not mine, either." He turned into Richard and nuzzled briefly at his neck. He knew him well enough by now to know that, given half a chance, he'd natter away all night, and what Dave really needed at that moment was some sleep. "Night, darlin'." He kissed Richard, reached over him to turn out the bedside light, then wrapped his arms tightly around him in the dark.

"Night. *Sergeant.*"

"And don't start that again!"

Chapter Nine

"If you're going to be sick..."

"I'm not going to be sick," Claire snapped.

"Really, it'd be okay. I'd understand," Aldridge insisted, with palpably mock concern.

"I am not going to be sick. Sergeant Lyon is not going to be sick. Are you, sergeant?"

"No, ma'am, I am not going to be sick."

"We are neither of us going to be sick. Now, will you please tell us what we need to know, doctor, so that we can go away and get on with our jobs?"

With an expression of mild disappointment and what looked uncomfortably like a flourish, Dr Aldridge pulled back the pale green sheet covering the body on the table between them. The two police officers stepped forward. Claire could feel Aldridge's eyes on them, especially on her she suspected. She forced herself to concentrate on the sad sight in front of her. In point of fact, she did feel sick, but not in the way Aldridge had hoped for.

"Young Caucasian male, age nineteen..." Aldridge had come closer now, reading his preliminary notes from a clipboard in that annoying routine sing song. "Cause of death, blow to the head."

"Just the one?"

"Hard to tell. The substantial bruising to the face and upper body shows that he'd been in a fight. Or, to be rather more accurate, that he'd been on the receiving end of a couple of pretty heavy punches before the fatal blow."

"No bruising or abrasion on his own knuckles?" Dave said.

"That's right." Aldridge acknowledged Lyon's presence briefly, appearing to weigh him up before dismissing him as a possible rival for Summerskill's attentions.

"And the weapon?"

"Something large and heavy, of course, and, judging from the nature of the impact fractures and stress lines, something with a degree of curvature to it. I'd suggest some kind of bat."

"Or a hammer?" Dave said.

Aldridge turned to him again, with obvious reluctance. "Given the size of the depressed area of the skull and the aforementioned degree of curvature, I would say that was unlikely."

"A lump hammer, maybe," Dave persisted. "You know, one of those really large ones."

"I know the type of hammer you mean, but if someone had swung one of those into the head, I would have expected the weight of the thing to have created a much deeper depression. If not to have completely burst the head like an overripe melon."

"Ah, right."

"If I might continue?"

"Of course," said Claire.

"A cricket bat?" Dave suggested.

"Perhaps," Aldridge snapped. "If it had been swung edge on. More likely, though, is something along the lines of one of those American baseball bats. Possibly metal. A wooden bat, particularly an old one, would almost certainly have left material in the wound or in the clothing that we could have found, but there was nothing there."

"Nothing?"

"Beyond the fibres of the hoodie that he was wearing, no."

"So I suppose really he could have been hit with anything and the hoodie would have masked the nature of the blow."

"Not to the extent that I wouldn't have been able to determine the rough shape of the object used, sergeant, no," Aldridge said, with just enough irritation to please Claire.

"Of course. Of course. Thanks. Please—" Dave gestured to the body "—go on."

Aldridge glared at him suspiciously. Claire suspected that Lyon was winding the doctor up deliberately. She liked that.

Aldridge flipped more quickly through his notes. "Time of death was somewhere between midnight and three in the morning. The soft ground, overnight rainfall and the fact that half the world and his dog, literally, walked past the poor sod before anyone thought to ask if anything was wrong means that it's been impossible to lift any tracks or footprints worth a damn."

Claire nodded. That much she had at least been able to guess for herself as soon as she'd arrived on the scene of the crime.

"Thanks. Okay, well if there's nothing else then...?"

"I didn't say that."

Summerskill and Lyon turned back reluctantly to the table and waited while Aldridge took his own sweet time to reread his recently made notes before finally delivering his last piece of information. "There was evidence of recent sexual intercourse."

"You mean...?" What *did* he mean? "You can tell that he'd had sex before...?" She saw Aldridge's raised eyebrow. "Ah. I see."

"Our boy had been banged up the canal path in more ways than one, inspector."

Claire felt her hackles rise at the man's callousness even as she studiously avoided catching her sergeant's expression where he stood beside her.

"You mean he'd been the passive partner in a gay sex act," said Dave.

"Yes, sergeant, I do." Aldridge shared a wry inclination of the head with Claire, inviting her to laugh with him at the newbie's naivety. Claire fixed her attention on the body.

"Had he been raped?"

"Possibly."

"Possibly," Dave repeated, and Claire glanced at him, alerted by the deceptive softness of his tone. "Forgive us, doctor. We don't have the benefit of your...experience. Was there any evidence of the use of unnatural force?"

"The boy had been buggered, sergeant," Aldridge said with a barked laugh. "There's precious little natural about that."

"I think—" began Claire.

"Was there any evidence it had been done against the boy's...against the young man's wishes?" Dave persisted with icy calmness. "Bruising and bleeding beyond that caused by the blows to body and head. Evidence of restraint?"

"No. But less than an hour or maybe two after the sexual act this boy was dead with a dent in his head you could rest a small grapefruit in. Draw your own conclusions, sergeant."

"Thank you," said Dave. "We will. Now, if you'll excuse me. Ma'am." He turned to leave the cold white room. "I find I am starting to feel a little sick after all."

"I'm sure I can rely on you to forward all the correct paperwork to my office as soon as is possible," Claire said formally as the doors swung shut behind her sergeant.

"For you, inspector, I'll get on to it straight away."

"And I'm also assuming the DNA samples you've recovered have been forwarded for analysis?"

"Of course."

"Then that, I think," she said, "is our cue to leave and proceed with the investigation."

"What's his problem?" Aldridge nodded at the doors that were still swinging in the wake of Lyon's exit. "Something he ate?" He winked at her. "Or is it that he can't stand a little healthy competition?"

She smiled at Aldridge, even as she was visualising how satisfying it would be to plant a fist in his face. "I think," she said, "he has a bit of a dicky tummy when it comes to greasy things." She left, happy enough that if she couldn't have the imagined image of Aldridge's battered face she had at least the memory of the puzzled and uncertain expression her comment had caused.

* ~ * ~ *

"All right?" she asked when she was back in the car.

"Yes thank you, ma'am," he said stiffly.

She inspected her sergeant more closely. He was good looking, and she was surprised to realise she hadn't noticed that before.

"Actually," he went on slowly, "I am quite angry."

"Yeah?" Claire braced herself. A brief assertion of sympathy for his grievance was, she thought, probably what was going to be called for.

"I should have spotted Jonathan's hands myself."

Yes. A definitely handsome face: strong jaw, good teeth. And a decided poker face when he chose to use it.

"Well, we can't all be Aldridges, can we?"

Dave started the car. "No, thank God."

* ~ * ~ *

Jonathan Wilson's bedsit turned out to be an attic room in a converted Edwardian house off one of the leafier roads in the city. A glance at the doorbells outside told them the house had been divided into six flats. Even so, as a whole, it was still smaller than the Wilson family house just ten miles away.

"Cosy," Claire commented laconically, taking in the extremely compact room, the shelves with their books and still more CDs, videos and DVDs.

"Still nicer than anything I had when I was at college."

Claire ran her eyes along the rows of discs and tapes, taking in the precise numbering on the spines. "And a damn sight neater than any room I had when I was his age. Anything with the desk?"

Dave shook his head. "Notes? Letters? No." He picked up the laptop on the desk's working surface. "In here, I'd guess, or on a memory stick or some such."

"Which you haven't found in any of the drawers?" Dave shook his head again. "No, that would just be too easy, wouldn't it?" She stood in the centre of the room, which wasn't hard to find in a space so small, trying to get a sense of the place as a whole, of the young man who had lived in it until so very recently. "This doesn't feel right."

"Woman's intuition?"

"Say that again and you'll be back on the beat quicker than you can say—" she searched for a cutting word "—demotion." Okay, she could work on that later. She hurried on. "I may not have been to college, but I've got a teenage boy. *Just* teenage," she added quickly, "and this doesn't feel like a young lad's home from home to me." She was half amused and half irritated by Dave's involuntary but obvious surprise about the age of her son, but she'd seen it before. Gratifying, really, and she supposed she'd get used to it. Maybe by the time Tony was in his twenties. "Anyway, you're the one with a feel for rooms. What do you feel about this one?"

Dave teased out a couple of DVD cases. All were numbered, starting at 151, while the two he was holding now were numbered 212 and 213. "I presume discs 1 to 150 are back at the family home. While these..." He opened the cases and checked the dates written in precise black pen on the discs inside. "Both of these are from over a month ago. So where were the discs he'd recorded since then? Malvern wasn't home. And I don't think this place was home, either. Maybe just somewhere to leave his things."

"So the question is, where is home?"

There were two main Further Education colleges in the city, Claire told Dave. The City Sixth Form College had been an old grammar school, and its focus still tended to be on the 'traditional', more academic subjects, a large portion of its students going onto universities and the professions. The Severn Valley Technical College, on the other hand, had a more practical bias, offering a range of vocational subjects at a variety of levels. Both establishments still clearly reflected the eras in which the majority of their buildings had been put up: the sixth form college a Fifties monument to public school aspirations which even then must have felt slightly outmoded and on the verge of extinction; the Tech a Sixties example of naively optimistic futurism set in concrete, which now, after several decades of city pollution and student wear and tear, presented a considerably more depressing face to the world.

"Funny. I would have thought the Wilsons would have preferred their son and heir to have gone to the sixth form college," said Dave. "I mean, they're obviously not short of a bob or two."

"The sixth form isn't fee paying."

"I know, but I bet that's the one the families with money send their kids to. You know how it goes." As she, Lyon and their small team of uniforms made their way up the cracked grey steps into the main entrance foyer Claire had to admit that she did. "In fact," he went on, "you'd think they might have paid to send him somewhere private and altogether more upmarket."

Claire thought back to their first meeting with the Wilsons. "Maybe," she said, "although I have a feeling Mr Wilson may be one of the 'School of Hard Knocks' types. You know: 'I made my way in the world without a fancy education, etc etc'."

"Prejudice, inspector?"

"Experience, sergeant." *Cheeky so and so!*

Their first meeting was with the principal of the college, someone Claire was amused to note she had already had professional contact with. Five years previously, when she'd still been in uniform, she'd had to book him for a minor speeding offence. She doubted he'd recognise her now. A nervous man with a grey complexion that suggested he'd been breathing in too much of his college's concrete dust for too long, he had little to tell them about Jonathan Wilson, having had no personal contact with him at all. There were a few vague, faintly complimentary comments, obviously culled from hasty discussions with staff who actually had taught him, and that was all. The officers asked for class lists and a couple of rooms they could use for the interviews, possibly for the next two days. They were granted the use of a pair of demountables located a considerable distance from the main body of the college.

The day stretched out before them, a long series of interviews with students and staff, a succession of faces young and not so young, the order largely dictated by whether they were free or in classes. Gradually, from what was said, and sometimes from what was not said, Summerskill and Lyon built up a picture of the young man whose life had been cut short by the side of the canal.

The opinions of his fellow classmates were fairly well represented by the girl from one of his graphic design classes. “He was all right, I suppose. Pretty standoffish and not so fit as you'd make an effort, you know? Not that that really matters. Shit, does that sound bad now he's dead?” Claire assured her that it didn't, and wondered glumly how long it would be before Tony started bringing home girls like this. “And always filming or taking pictures. Bit weird, really. Shit, there I go again.”

The high hopes they had of the form tutor, Miss Humphries, the woman supposedly responsible for Jonathan's pastoral welfare, were soon dashed. “Pastoral welfare,” she had exclaimed bitterly. “Do you know how much time they give me to be responsible for the pastoral welfare of thirty-two hyperactive adolescents?" Claire and Dave had to admit they didn't. "None," she had said triumphantly. "None at all. I'm supposed to teach twenty lessons of politics a week, write up all the bloody paperwork the government wants, mark and grade essays and turn up for the sodding end of term Fayre, and then with the other hand monitor the whereabouts and welfare of every kid in my form whom I don't actually see from one end of the bloody day to the other."

"So I take it you didn't really know Jonathan Wilson then?" Claire asked mildly.

"If you showed me a picture now I doubt if I could recognise him," she concluded. And then she leaned forward. "I suppose that sounds bad now he's dead, doesn't it?" Claire assured her that it didn't.

Miss Humphries consulted the ring folder she had brought with her. "Three A levels in Graphic Design, Media Studies and English, though the English was probably just a makeweight for him judging by how little work he did in it, and the only area of the Graphic Design syllabus he seems to have put any work into was the Moving Image modules."

Dave thought back to Jonathan's room: the movie posters, the shelves of videos and DVDs.

"And I suppose you know," Miss Humphries said, bringing the folder up more closely to her face, almost as if to conceal it, "that he was a member of Woggles."

Both officers regarded her blankly. “Woggles?”

“Worcester Gay and Lesbian Society. WGLS.”

“Ah.”

Miss Humphries drew herself up to as full a height as she could manage in her chair. “I hope you’re not going to let that influence your approach to this case,” she said with new primness.

“I can promise you I won’t,” said Dave.

“Oh. Good.” Miss Humphries deflated slightly. “It’s just that, well, Woggles wasn’t established in the college without some...resistance from some senior members of staff.”

“The principal?” Dave hazarded.

“Some members,” Miss Humphries went on with dogged and not very convincing loyalty, “thought it wouldn’t be right to agree to a group that didn’t represent the ideals of the college.”

“I can well imagine,” said Dave.

Just before the end of the first day, the college tracked down the president of Woggles for them and he was asked to go to Demountable One for an interview. Tom Adams came across as by far the most uncomfortable of the people Summerskill and Lyon had interviewed that day. He settled warily into the chair before their desk and then deliberately drew himself up as if displaying for their benefit the various badges on his denim jacket: the pink triangle, the rainbow flag, the Rufus Wainwright T-shirt.

“I expect you’ll know by now why we’re here,” Claire began.

“This is to do with Jonathan Wilson, isn’t it?” Tom had a nasal tone to his voice, the sort, you’d get very tired of hearing very quickly.

"Yes it is. I understand he was a member of your group."

"Society. The Worcester Gay and Lesbian Society," Adams repeated with unnecessary emphasis on the last word. "Yes, he was. It's not illegal."

"Of course it's not," said Claire.

"Though there ought to be a law about bad acronyms," Dave suggested. Adams glared at him as if suspecting the comment to contain hidden hostility. "Sorry," Dave murmured, frowning at his paperwork to conceal a smile.

"Was he a popular member?"

Tom gave a sound that was somewhere between a snort and a laugh. "We're not about being popular, inspector."

"Was he liked within your...society?"

"Yes. He was *liked*."

Claire glanced at Dave. They could both tell something was being said or understood here that had passed them by. Tom didn't keep them in the dark for long. He turned his attention more obviously to Dave. "He was good looking, wasn't he? That's all your average queer is after in a boyfriend these days."

"And did he have a boyfriend?"

Tom kept his eyes on Dave. "Not that I was aware of."

Blanked by the boy, Claire watched Dave meet his gaze steadily. Tom Adams was young, presumably bright and not especially attractive physically. How quickly the kids were getting bitter these days. "Did Jonathan bring a camera along to any of your, what would they be, meetings or functions?"

The boy snorted. "Jonathan brought cameras along to everything. Probably another one of the reasons we didn't see very much of him in the end. He was *asked* not to. Your young queen is a very shy animal. She doesn't like being filmed. Especially if she isn't out to mummy and daddy." He shifted a little in his chair as if preparing himself for something. "You're very cute," he said.

"Thank you," Dave said matter-of-factly.

"You'd be very popular at our functions. Fancy coming along one day to talk to us about police relations with the gay community?" It wasn't an invitation, it was a challenge.

"I think that would be a very good idea," Dave replied evenly. "Who knows, we might even make a few new recruits. The police service is an equal opportunities employer, you know, in every sense of the phrase."

"Yeah, right. Oh, I'm sure you'd make several new recruits."

Claire cleared her throat. "If Jonathan didn't have a boyfriend was there someone in the group that he was especially close to?"

"You mean someone he fancied? Oh no, not him."

"You say that as if there was some reason why he shouldn't have."

With an elaborate sigh and an exaggerated display of reluctance that made Claire want to lean over the desk and slap him, Tom Adams dragged his eyes from Dave back to her. "Jonathan was a member in name only. We hardly saw him after his first few appearances." *Here it comes again. The same story we've been hearing all day.*

"Why was that?" asked Dave. "There aren't that many places where young gay men can meet and socialise in these parts. Okay, so you didn't want him bringing his cameras along with him, and we're beginning to see they were very important to him, but were there any other reasons he didn't want to mix with your group?"

"No, there aren't many places for gayboys, sergeant," Tom said, with a scorn that might almost have suggested that had something to do with the police themselves. "But we weren't *real* enough for Jonathan. Too 'gay' rather than 'queer', if you understand what that means?"

"Yes, I do, actually," Dave said quietly, and Claire was pleased he did, because she damn well didn't. She was also pleased to note Tom Adams's surprise.

"You ask me," the boy pressed on, in a dogged attempt to shock the inspector and, especially, her sergeant, "I think Jonathan was into rough trade, and there just isn't enough of that in a small city college like this one." He sat back and narrowed his eyes in a deliberate close inspection of Dave to see how he had taken that statement.

"Maybe, maybe not. But you don't exactly have to search very far in any city for a bit of rough if that's your thing, do you? Did Jonathan go cruising?"

Tom's incipient grin faltered, unbalanced by Dave's easy acceptance and apparent understanding of things intended to unsettle and dismay. "I've no idea. Wouldn't surprise me, though.

I mean, that is his background, isn't it? The apple never falls far from the tree and all that."

"Now there you've lost me."

Tom gave a mirthless small smile. "Jonathan may have been born into money, but only by the skin of his teeth. Daddy's a used car salesman made good. I think Jonathan was the first one in the family to get GCSEs let alone go on to further ed."

"Actually, Jonathan had an older brother who's a university graduate," said Claire. "Bristol," and she couldn't help enjoying proving this insufferable little prat wrong about something, even if it was about such a comparatively unimportant fact. This interview, she decided, was going nowhere. It was time to end it. "Well, thank you very much, Mr Adams. If you remember or hear of anything else that might help us with our enquiries, I hope you'll us know straight away, please?"

Tom sat for a moment, appearing slightly surprised that was all there had been to his interview. He went to stand, but then sat back down and faced Dave again. There was a smile on his face, but his body noticeably tensed. "Maybe you'd like to leave me your number, sergeant?" he said through his brittle smile. "So I could get back to you straight away. If anything comes up."

"That wouldn't really be appropriate, Mr Adams," Claire said crisply.

"And maybe we could have a drink sometime, see if that jogs my memory about anything?" Tom continued as if she hadn't said anything at all.

Dave met the request with complete equanimity. “That’s very kind of you, Tom, but as Inspector Summerskill has said, it really wouldn’t be a good idea for a police officer to mix socially with members of the public involved in an ongoing investigation, would it?” Tom smirked at Claire as if to confirm that he had in some way scored a point. And then Dave continued, “Besides, I don’t think my boyfriend would approve, do you? Good day to you.”

“Do you think that was a good idea?” Claire asked when the boy had left the room.

“Maybe not,” Dave said with a chuckle, “but it wiped the smile off his face, did you see?”

“So, tell me that was gaydar in operation? I mean, was that why he was coming on to you, because he knew you were gay?”

Dave laughed again. “He was hitting on me because he thought I was straight!”

“What would be the point of that?”

“He’s young. He’s here, he’s queer and he bloody well wants the world to know. Making straights feel uncomfortable is a bit of payback for all the times he’s probably been made to feel bad about himself. He’ll get over it. Probably when he gets his first real boyfriend, poor sod.”

“Do you think he fancied Jonathan?”

“Probably. Like he said, the Wilson brothers are good looking. Tom might even have come on to Jonathan and been given the brush-off, who knows? It’d explain the backbiting we saw there, wouldn’t it? But unless Tom Adams is some kind of festering psychopath and managing to hide it very well, I don't think there was anything more to it than that." He leaned back. "It's like the bedsit, isn't it? Jonathan Wilson was here but didn't leave much of an impression."

"He made enough of an impression somewhere for someone to want to kill him."

"You don't think it was a random thing? Maybe even mistaken identity?"

"Mistaken identity, maybe, and if it was, then we're really stuffed because who the hell was he mistaken for. Random?" Claire ran her fingers through her hair. "I can't accept that."

She was uncomfortably aware of Dave regarding her, presumably wanting to ask her why she couldn't accept the randomness of such evil. He hadn't been in the service for much less time than her but he obviously did.

By the end of the day, Summerskill and Lyon had seen everyone they thought might have anything relevant to say with the exception of Jonathan's visual media tutor, John Elijah, whom the secretary rather sniffily said was ill that day. The detectives got the impression that maybe Elijah was ill more often than she would like. At the very least, the woman seemed not to like him for some reason. They decided he could be left for the next day when a couple of uniforms would be handling the mopping up of less promising interviewees.

"Were you ever anything like young Adams there, then?" Claire asked, as they were gathering their papers together before leaving the college for that day. “All badges and T-shirts? Rainbow-coloured trousers, that sort of thing?”

Dave smiled slightly to himself. “Something like that,” he admitted.

Claire was intrigued in spite of herself. Questions for a later day. And there was, she realised, something else, too, something fluttering about at the back of her mind, since... *Got it!* Something Dave had just said. *The Wilson brothers are good looking.* He’d been quoting Tom, except Tom hadn’t said that, had he? Tom hadn’t even known about Simon. She shook her head. What was she worried about? Simon resembled Jonathan, and Jonathan had been good looking. So why did she–? Her thoughts were interrupted by her mobile’s ringtone.

“Celine Dion?” Dave grimaced.

“My husband put it on. Been meaning to change it.” She unlocked the keypad. “But I don’t know how to. Jenny? Hi.” As Dave drove, Claire listened. After less than a minute and a, “Thanks Jenny,” Claire shoved the phone back into her jacket. “Okay, change of plan. Take us back to the canal road.”

Dave swung the car round. “Another lead?”

“Not exactly,” Claire said grimly. “Another body.”

Chapter Ten

Inspector Summerskill looked down into the face of the second dead boy she had seen in as many days. Once again she forced herself to lean in closely, to make her eyes move down past the swollen features, the protruding tongue, to the ugly puckering of the skin around the throat. The grim inspection completed, she turned away and walked around the room they found themselves in, taking in the peeling wallpaper, the cracked and dirty windows with the tattered curtain hanging in front of them. A different kind of killing from the one she and Sergeant Lyon had begun to investigate and, judging from surroundings, a different kind of boy. Probably no connection. And yet the view from those dirty windows was of the canal path where Jonathan Wilson had been murdered. And it was in the air, wasn't it? The smell of shit, that no one tells you about though it's almost always there. But that other smell, too. The sickly sweet smell her conscious mind was trying to deny. Decay. Rot. The smell of a body two or three days gone. Which would put the murder at just about the time Jonathan was killed.

Cortez forced his way into the small room, elbowing his way past the police photographer who protested automatically but without much expectation of being heeded. He stopped in surprise at the sight of Summerskill and Lyon, acknowledged her with a brief nod and then addressed himself to his boss. “Okay. The lad’s name is Sean, last name probably Flanagan or Flatterly, the little old dear down the corridor was none too sure about that. Quiet lad. Didn’t drink. Didn’t smoke. Always polite.” He closed his notepad. “And he was almost certainly on the game. String of men here at all hours. Mrs Kidd said she thought he had ‘a lot of friends’.”

“Rent,” said Rudge, in a tone that steered clear of contempt while falling well short of neutrality.

“Yeah.”

“So someone’s out for rent boys?”

“Jonathan Wilson wasn’t rent.”

“He was gay.”

“It’s not the same, Jim,” Claire said with forced calmness.

“I don’t remember sending for backup, inspector.”

“We were in the area.”

“And someone thought you’d like to call in, eh?”

“Just as well someone did, eh? Weren’t you going to call me, Jim? A second murder within a stone’s throw of the one I’m investigating?”

Rudge gave a slow smile. “You’ve got a lot on your plate, Claire. First big case.” He gave the merest flicker of a glance in Dave’s direction, the only acknowledgement he’d made of his presence. “New recruit.”

A uniformed WPC poked her head round the door, interrupting the sharp retort that was so obviously on Claire's lips. "Wagon's here, sir," she said. "Can I tell them they can take the body?"

Rudge nodded, and the officers stood back while the SOCO people cleared away their gear and made way for the removal of the corpse. "Bodies piling up, Claire. Madden's not going to be happy."

"This one was killed about the same time as Wilson."

"Pathologist as well as inspector now? You've been spending too much time with Aldridge."

"Knock it off, Jim. I think we both reckon this death is connected with the Wilson boy's."

"Do we? Convince me, inspector." The body removed, Rudge left the room and Claire was forced to follow after him, leaving Cortez and Dave alone in the cold bedsit.

*

Cortez let out a long whistle. "Fun and games," he said dryly.

"She has a point. Were you...was he going to let the body be carted off before we got to see the scene?"

"Foregate's a small station. Rudge knew who was up to speed. I reckon he knew the news would get back to Summerskill without his having to whistle for her. It's how he likes to work. Keeps people on their toes."

"We tended to work a bit more closely at Redditch."

"Yeah, well, things are different here."

Dave stopped on the point of leaving the room and turned to Cortez. "Yeah. How so?"

Cortez picked at an invisible thread on his jacket. "Claire's an inspector now."

"Ah, right." The two men left the room and headed out after their respective bosses who were already a way ahead of them. Dave strained to catch their words but they were too far away for him to catch anything more than the tone of their discussion. It sounded heated. "Always this busy in Worcester?" he asked Cortez.

"Nah, you've come on a good day."

By now they were out of the drab block of flats and back on the street. Up ahead, Dave could see Claire animatedly sharing her opinion about something. Rudge reached his car and stood stolidly by it, a broad grin on his face. *Patronising git.* "Listen, up for a drink tonight?" he asked Cortez. "Fill me in on all the local detail? Bring me up to speed on who's who, and who's with who at the station? Clue me in on the different way you do things here."

Cortez hesitated. "Can't tonight, mate," he said finally.

Dave nodded. "Okay. Some other time, then."

"Yeah. Right." Cortez walked over to his boss, and Dave went to wait for his by their car. When she finally joined him she was red in the face.

*

Claire threw herself into the passenger side of the car. Dave got in and sat there but did not start up the engine. “That looked like an...animated discussion with Chief Inspector Rudge, ma’am,” he said blandly.

“Chief Inspector Rudge is determining whether or not we should treat this case as linked with ours. Like there is any bloody doubt about it whatsoever!” With a visible effort she reined her temper in, sitting stony-faced and glaring unseeing ahead of her through the windscreen. “In the meantime he suggests we proceed with our own investigation which, he has helpfully pointed out, is going nowhere.”

“And was that all he was saying, ma’am?”

Claire opened her mouth to reply before fast-developing professional instincts kicked in and she bit back her original words. “You’ve got to admit there’s a gay angle here.”

“Do two deaths constitute an angle?”

“They’re practically within sight of each other.”

“And if the two boys had been heterosexual would we be talking about a ‘straight angle’?”

“So you’re saying it’s just a coincidence?”

“I’m saying...” Dave ground to a halt, gathered his thoughts and started again. “What I’m saying, what I’m *asking*, is why was I offered this post here?”

Claire blinked, caught out by the apparent change of direction. “You didn’t...? I mean...it’s promotion. The post became available.”

"And I'm gay and you had a case of happy slapping, apparently directed at the gay community, so enter Sergeant Pink in a nice bit of low profile, community-friendly work. Except a significant section of your station isn't quite ready to 'embrace the rainbow', is it, and to make matters worse things have all suddenly got a lot heavier, and sexuality's being shoved down everyone's throat. And not in a fun way."

Lyon's sudden display of bitterness took Claire by surprise. Madden hadn't been upfront with her, she'd accepted that. She hadn't thought that he might not have been upfront with Lyon either. "Realities of the job, sergeant," she said, not sure how far she was ready to accept that herself. "I've been picked to fill a woman's role in the past. Does it bother you?"

"No. Yes. I suppose not. Did it bother you?"

Claire considered. The official line? The truth? "Yes," she said. "And I got over it. And now I'm an inspector."

Dave gave a small laugh of grudging acceptance. "You've read my record. You know how many times I've been passed over for promotion?"

Claire didn't, not exactly. But she knew how surprised she'd been at his length of service and comparative lack of progress. "Sometimes that happens. I'm not saying it's fair but... It happens." She thought about mentioning Jenny Trent but held back. "Wrong place, wrong time."

"Wrong sexuality?" He held up his hands. "Don't worry. I'm not some kind of radical fairy ready to go to the unions at the flap of a wrist. I don't even think that's what slowed me down. Much. You just reach for something when you see guys you know are complete tossers getting on ahead of you." He shook his head, a trace of his more familiar smile on his lips. "I had one friend who swore he'd hit a glass ceiling because he was ginger." He gave a mock shudder. "That is unnatural, though, right?" The smile faded again. "The irony is when I got the posting here I thought I'd finally cracked it, on merit alone. But it wasn't, was it? You just wanted a gay boy to talk to the queens."

"Your appointment wasn't anything to do with me," Claire said quickly. "I mean, not that I'm saying I'm displeased with what you've done so far. Not that you have done much so far. I mean..." She endeavoured to choose her next words carefully. "Do you want to be taken off the case?"

Dave considered, for slightly longer than she would have expected. "No," he said finally. "No. I want to know who killed Jonathan. And this new lad, too. That's what it's all about. I just didn't want...other things getting in the way."

"Right," she said, wondering in fact how she felt about that. "Good. So let's talk about the case rather than our careers, yes?"

"Okay." He nodded, and she wondered just how strong the resentment that she had just caught a glimpse of was. Had she dealt with it in the way a good superior officer should? Had she just side-stepped it? Yes, she really wanted to talk about the case. It was a lot simpler by comparison.

Dave began. "This all started as a series of minor assaults, right?"

"If those cases of happy slapping are in fact linked to this, then yes. Several men were jumped on their way home from the clubs. Or, more specifically, from the Pharos nightclub. The assailant was always alone, did little more than shove his individual victims around a bit, laugh a lot and run off. There was no attempt at theft."

"But whoever attacks Jonathan does a great deal more than just slap his face. Maybe the killer knew in advance he was going to kill Jonathan and the previous assaults were a smokescreen."

"That's a hell of a lot of predetermination."

"Which implies one hell of a motivation."

"And will have to be linked in some way with the death of this Sean lad."

"And at the moment we have no link with that." They both let that one hang in the air and fell back into silent thought. "They were all gay, weren't they? The men who were slapped around before the attack on Jonathan?" Dave asked.

"The assaults on the canal path were all on a Thursday night. Thursday night is gay night at Pharos, about fifty yards from the canal path. The men weren't specifically asked about their sexualities, but a couple were quite open and the inferences overall were pretty clear, yes."

"And they were all interviewed about their assaults?"

"The ones who came forward. Yes."

"Which we know means that several will not have come

forward either because of some suspicion of the police, heaven knows why, or because they're closet cases and don't want the world to know the dreadful things they get up to in a city nightclub once a week." Dave kept his tone carefully neutral. "And the uniforms who interviewed them...?"

Claire kept her tone as carefully neutral as his. "Trained in diversity awareness and community policing."

"Great." Dave started the car's engine, signalled and pulled out. "Fancy a drink?"

"What?"

"Pharos is gay once a week between seven and one, yes? My extensive research has shown me there is only one other 'official' gay venue in the city, The Old Navigator pub on Angel Street; just opposite Pharos, in fact."

Claire arched an eyebrow. "Extensive research?"

"The listings in *Gay Times*."

"Impressive initiative, sergeant."

"Yes, well, I wanted to make sure my new patch had somewhere I could get a drink and unwind a bit."

"With...friends?" she said, mindful of that lack of information she'd had for Ian.

"Yeah," he said unhelpfully. "Good idea to make some personal contact with the people on the ground don't you think? Put our own diversity awareness to the test?"

Pushy. Damn pushy. And right. She sat back and folded her arms. "Well, as we appear to be on our way there anyway, why not?"

"I hear The Old Navigator serves a mean piña colada."

"Anything with an umbrella and I'll tell them where to stick it."

"Show me a gay man who hasn't tried that at some point in his life."

* ~ * ~ *

"So," Claire said, as she and her sergeant stood outside The Old Navigator, "how can you tell if a pub's a gay pub?"

"If you wake up in the morning after a few pints and it's gone and hasn't left its number, chances are it's gay."

"So young, so cynical."

"Half right."

"I'm serious."

"Word of mouth. Listings in gay magazines. Telephone helplines will usually give you the lowdown on the local scene, or the internet. It's not that hard these days if you're really looking. And, of course, you'll often see something like that." Dave pointed to a peeling sticker of a rainbow flag on the inside of a smoke-stained window.

"My son's got one of those in his bedroom," Claire said. "I thought it was some kind of eco warrior thing."

"Yes, well, it can be that, too," Dave admitted, "which can cause the odd bit of confusion. The number of gay men who've ended up saving the humpbacked whale when they'd walked into a building expecting to end up humping…"

"Thank you, sergeant." Claire ran her hand through her hair. She didn't like this new cut, she really didn't. "Won't I stand out just a bit?"

Dave regarded his boss critically. "Well, with those shoes and that jacket you might raise a few eyebrows but I think you'll get away with it in a dim light."

"I meant being a woman in a gay bar." *He's joking, right?*

Dave lowered his voice conspiratorially. "There are gay women, you know."

"Great, so I'll get taken for a dyke."

"What? In the police force? How unlikely would that be?" Dave pushed open the doors to the pub. "In we go."

Claire followed. She didn't want to, but she *had* to ask. "And what's wrong with these shoes and this jacket?"

The Old Navigator was typical of many of the pubs in Worcester's city centre: an unconvincing fake Tudor exterior, built about the Sixties and allowed to go to seed ever since. The evening had only just begun so it was quiet. Fewer than half a dozen punters all told, all of them men. The two police officers walked up to the bar. "What'll you have?"

Claire went to say that she would pay, but decided against it. Her sergeant appeared to have momentarily taken the lead so why not let him carry on the same way financially? His turf, after all. She asked for a tonic and Dave ordered a pint.

"Pretty quiet," Dave said to the young barman who brought

them their drinks. The lad nodded his head non-committally. “Get busy?”

“Depends.” The boy glanced at Claire by Dave’s side.

Dave affected not to notice. “Was thinking of dropping by some time with my boyfriend.”

“Oh. Right.” The lad brightened noticeably. “Yeah, varies a bit but can get quite crowded. Thursdays are good. Gay night at Pharos over the way there and people pull in here on their way over.”

“Good range of guys?”

“Not bad. Well, it’s about the only place to go round here at the moment. There’s a couple of things go on in Cheltenham and Gloucester but they’re only once a month. Apart from that you have to go into Brum.”

“Right.” Dave drank deep from his pint. “Nice.”

“You just moved into the area?” Dave nodded. “What do you do?”

Dave took another deep draught of his pint. It stopped him sighing. He’d found The Old Navigator in *Gay Times* soon after he’d moved in with Richard, and had hoped he’d be able to keep the city’s only gay pub and his work separate for at least a short while. His frequent answer when out socially to the inevitable question about what he did was ‘quantity surveyor’, mainly because no one ever knew what that meant, and there wasn’t the inevitable freezing of the atmosphere when he told the truth, especially in gay pubs, which left the conversations free to move into other more interesting topics. But now… "I'm with the police, stationed at Foregate Street." He pulled out his ID. "Sergeant Lyon. And this is Inspector Summerskill." Claire already had her card out and was smiling at the lad.

"Oh. Right." The barman went to move away, not hastily, but very deliberately.

"Just a moment, if you please." Claire called him back, still smiling. "We'd like to ask you a few questions."

"It's about the assaults on gay men that have taken place recently," Dave added, seeing the boy's worried expression.

"I haven't been assaulted."

"No, I didn't think so. But these assaults all took place on Thursdays on men making their way home after a night out."

"Right. So that's why you were asking about the disco."

"Yeah," said Dave. "Plus, I really do want to bring my boyfriend along sometime."

The boy looked sceptical, obviously suspicious of some clumsy attempt at undercover work or, at the least, a piss-take. "This is about that lad that got killed the other night, isn't it? I saw it in the paper."

Dave reached into his jacket pocket and pulled out a picture of Jonathan, taken from his student records and enlarged. "Do you know this lad? Did he ever come in here?"

The boy took the photo and studied it closely for a few seconds, but in the end he shook his head and handed it back. "I'm new here," he said. "Only started a month ago and only work during the days."

Dave nodded and pocketed the photo again. "All right if we just have a word with people here? See if they know anything. About the assaults, I mean?"

The boy was doubtful and unhappy. "Not sure the boss'd be too keen on the police asking questions. Not really good for business, is it?"

Claire swirled the tonic in her glass. "Not half as bad as a couple of uniformed coppers doing the same thing. Every day. For the next two weeks." She smiled at him again, sweetly.

"Is your boss in?"

"He's not here right now." The boy glanced over at the small group of men in the corner who were now watching them. "Hang on a sec." He moved from behind the counter and over to the other side of the bar and the men.

"So, you much of a pub and club man?" Claire asked as they waited and watched.

"The term is 'disco bunny', and no, not especially. Not at the moment, certainly."

"That would be because of your...boyfriend?" She hesitated slightly over the word that Dave had so conspicuously avoided earlier but had seemed happy enough to use in front of this barman.

"More to do with starting a new job, ma'am. You're working me very hard, you know."

"Right." Claire thought back to the photo on Lyon's desk. If she had that waiting for her at home every night she wouldn't be out at the pubs much either. She wondered how hard he worked Dave. *Lucky sod.* "You have got a boyfriend, though?" *God, I've known murder suspects who were easier to crack!*

Before Dave could answer, one of the men from the far group detached himself from his fellows and walked over to them. "Pete says you're asking questions about the muggings by the canal?" He was a big man, a good beer belly on him, the short sleeves of his black T-shirt showing both the impressive size of his upper arms and their liberal tattoos. Old school designs, Claire noticed, number one haircut, probably to disguise as much as possible the greying and thinning effects of age, though you had to wonder why men went to that kind of trouble and then wore T-shirts with faded Iron Maiden pictures on them. His regard slid quickly over Claire before settling on Dave where it took a much more detailed inventory, top to toe, which, Claire noticed, Dave took in his stride. Professional sang-froid or familiarity with being cruised in gay bars? *Take a picture, why don't you*, she thought with irritation. Or was that jealousy?

"That's right. I'm Sergeant Lyon and this is Inspector Summerskill."

The big man glanced again at Claire at this mention of her rank, but his attention quickly reverted to Dave. "I've already been down to the station. Gave my statement. They weren't that bothered by it then."

"You were one of the men assaulted?" Claire asked.

"Yes, I suppose so."

"You *suppose* so?"

"Hardly what you'd call assault. Some kid jumped out at me then ran off. If he'd actually laid a hand on me I'd have knocked his head off his shoulders."

Claire took in the beefy upper arms. She didn't doubt that the man could have been as good as his word. "And when was this?""'Bout three weeks ago."

"And you reported it, even though you hadn't felt in any particular danger?"

"I reported it when I heard that some of the other guys had the same thing happen to them. I can take care of myself. Some of the others—" his glance flicked over to the group he had left "—aren't so handy. And the policeman is our friend now, right?"

"Who took the statement?" Dave asked, ignoring the sarcasm.

"Can't remember. Ugly little guy. I don't remember ugly little guys."

"You'd have to narrow the field down a bit," Claire said, and that at least got a small twitch at the corners of the big man's lips.

"Suppose it's all a bit more serious now someone got killed. Straight lad, was he?"

"No," said Dave, "we think he was gay. This is him. Name was Jonathan Wilson. Know him, Mr...?"

"Evans. Phil." He took the photo, held it for a moment then handed it back. "No. I don't think so."

*

Dave returned the photo to his pocket. “What about a lad called Sean? Flannigan or Flaherty? Do you know him?”

“Sean?” Another man had come up to them, one of the group Phil had been with. Phil put his arm around the man’s shoulders in a gesture that was either protective or defiant, Dave wasn’t sure which. He’d seen it before when police confronted gay men: a muted version of that defiance they’d seen earlier from Tom. *You don’t need to do this with me, guys.*

“This is Mikey,” Phil said.

Shorter, fatter and balder than Phil, though what hair he had left had been allowed to grow longer than his friend’s, Mikey might actually have been a couple of years younger. He was wearing the kind of polo shirt that a young gay skinhead might have thought quite hot twenty years and three stone previously. When he spoke his voice was softer and more hesitant. “What about Sean?”

“Do you know him, sir?”

Mikey looked up at Phil who spoke for him. “Yeah, we know Sean. What about him. You’re not saying you think he had anything to do with that lad’s death, are you?”

“May I ask how you knew Sean?”

Dave saw something like panic flare in Mikey’s eyes and watched as Phil pulled him in that bit closer. “It’s all right. There’s nothing wrong in that.” He directed his words to Claire. “Why should we have to tell you how we know people? I thought you were supposed to be trying to find out..." His words petered out. "He's dead, too, isn't he?"

Dave watched as his boss hesitated. They both knew what the official line should be. "There hasn't been a formal identification yet, but yes, we think he is." *Rudge is going to have your head for that!* He was quietly impressed.

"Was he a friend of yours?" Dave directed the question at Phil though his attention was on Mikey.

"We...we knew the lad, yes."

"I liked him," Mikey said quickly, before drawing himself even closer into the shelter of his large friend's encircling arm.

"I'm sorry. I have to ask, how did you know him?"

"Not like that, if that's what you mean."

Dave seized the nettle. "You knew that he was rent, then?"

"I knew he'd do it for money," Phil agreed. "It's not quite the same, is it?"

"No, it's not."

"According to the law—" Claire began.

"When he did...meet men," Dave interrupted, "did he do it here? Was he here recently, with anyone?"

"Not recently, no, I don't think so." Phil looked down at Mikey who, wide-eyed, shook his head.

"He was all right was Sean," said Mikey softly. "I liked him."

"He was a bit wild but there was no harm in him," agreed Phil. "He'd have settled down eventually, if he'd found the right guy."

"So there wasn't anyone regular?" Phil shook his head. "And

you never saw him with this lad?” Dave showed him the picture of Jonathan again.

Phil took the picture. “No.”

“Mikey?”

Dave gestured for Phil to pass the picture to his companion, and Mikey took it, holding it for a second as if not sure what to do with it, before being gently urged by Phil to inspect it. He furrowed his forehead and shook his head then quickly gave it back to Phil who returned it to Dave.

One of the other men from Phil’s group had wandered up to the bar, ostensibly to buy another round, though fairly obviously to have a nose at what was going on, and Dave passed the picture to him without much hope of a reaction. He was surprised when the man began to frown at it, crooking a finger to cover parts of it up. “It could be, you know,” he said, quietly, almost to himself, and then with growing vehemence. “It bloody well is, you know.”

“What?”

He jabbed a finger at the picture. “I’m bloody positive this is the poxy little toe rag who jumped me.”

“Jonathan!” Claire exclaimed incredulously.

“You were assaulted?” asked Dave.

“Aye. Well, assaulted is putting it a bit strong like,” the man said. “About a week ago, it was. And this is the cheeky bastard who did it.”

“What’s your name please, sir?”

“Andy Robins.” Andy’s mood of gleeful recognition abruptly

changed. “Eh, you’re not trying to say I was involved in any murder, are you? I didn’t lay a finger on the kid. I wouldn’t have done anything like...”

“It’s all right, Andy,” Dave said, holding his hands out in a calming way. “Nobody’s saying that at all. You made a statement at the time?”

“Well, no. I mean it was only a wee slap. And Phil had told me it had happened to him, and so had one or two of the others and they’d gone to the police and nothing had happened so I thought...”

*

Just how long had these reports been trickling into Foregate Street, Claire wondered bitterly, before someone had decided to do something about it? *Before someone decided to dump them on me?* “Could you tell us about it please, Andy?”

Unhappy now he had let his enthusiastic identification of the picture get the better of him, Andy pressed on. “Well, I was heading back home from here. Bit pissed, really.” There was a snort from somewhere behind him. “Drunk I mean,” he said sheepishly, with deference to Claire, who bit her lip to keep from laughing. She had a feeling Dave was doing the same. “And all of a sudden this lad jumps out in front of me and he, like, hits me, twice across the face.”

“*Across* the face?”

Andy ducked his head embarrassedly. “Yeah. Well, like this.”

And he mimed the attack.

Claire nodded, a carefully composed expression of seriousness on her face. “You mean he slapped you?”

“Yeah, well. Like I said, I was pissed, right?”

“And this was where?

“Down on the canal path. By the bridge.”

“And did he say anything?”

Andy shifted uncomfortably. “He said... I think he said...” He took a deep breath. “He said, ‘Your money or your life’.”

There was a silence in the pub, broken only by the faint sounds of a distant fruit machine going through its electronic routines in a bid to attract custom. It was clear that all of the punters there had heard the story before and now they were waiting for the police reaction. Claire cleared her throat. “Was that all he said?”

“Yes.”

“And then he ran away?” Andy nodded. “So he didn’t make any real effort to take your money?”

“No. Yeah, I know what it sounds like but I was on my own and for all I knew the guy had a dozen of his mates round the corner just waiting to bash me and throw me in the fucking canal.”

There was a murmur of agreement among the gathered men and Claire noticed the very slight nod from her sergeant as if he, too, was agreeing with or at least understanding the general feeling.

“Thank you,” she said. “Andy, I know it’s a nuisance but it really would help us in our investigations if you’d go down to the station and give a full and proper statement. We can take you there now if you like."

"No, no that's fine," Andy said, backing off slightly. "I mean, I'll do it, all right? Just, in my own time, if that's okay? Today, but not taken in by the polis."

"Understood." Claire addressed the rest of the men who were by now all gathered around her and Dave. "And the same goes for the rest of you. If you've had a—" she chose her words carefully "—less than satisfactory reception before, then I'm sorry. But this isn't just some kids' prank now. There's been a murder." She tried to put the image of Jim Rudge's face out of her mind. "Possibly two. And for all we know they were targeted on your community."

From somewhere behind her there was a snort. She didn't turn round to see the source, but she noted Dave did. She noted, too, the flash of anger across his face. "If you go, *when* you go, please use my name. That's Detective Summerskill. Or my colleague's, Sergeant Lyon. I promise you you'll be taken seriously and anything you say will be treated in confidence."

"Will you be taking the statements, Sergeant Lyon?"

Dave went to answer but Claire got in before him. "Probably," she said smoothly, "though we can't guarantee it. Ask for him anyway." It was far more likely, she considered shrewdly, that members of this crowd would remember Dave's name than her own for oh so many reasons. She deliberately ignored Dave's pained expression. "And now, in anticipation of help received, maybe you'd let me buy you a drink."

There was another general muttering, this time of grudging approval, and a move to the bar of rather more of the men than she'd anticipated. Drinks were ordered and passed round, thanks given, and then there was an all but complete redirection of attention from Claire back to Dave. Inspector Summerskill leaned back on the bar, toyed with the peanuts and sipped her second tonic. *Okay, let him do the hard work for a bit. But I'd be the one pulling in a dyke bar.*

Phil was standing beside her, picking up the pint he'd ordered. *At least he didn't order a double scotch like Andy did, cheeky sod.* On an impulse she pulled out the photo of Jonathan that she had and held it out to him. "Sure you don't recognise him now, Phil?"

He glanced at it but didn't take it from her. "I told you, inspector, I don't."

"Just as well Andy did, then."

"Yeah, it is. But I was assaulted or whatever you want to call it at least a couple of weeks before Andy. It was dark, and the kid was wearing one of those hoodie things. I couldn't see his face properly." He elbowed his way through the group round the bar to go and stand next to his friend Mikey again. Mikey was staring anxiously at her, his eyes as round as his face. She had a feeling that was the way Mikey had faced the world for most of his life. She noted the way Phil spoke to him gently, noted Mikey's obvious gratitude and adoration. *Yeah, more than just friends.* Mikey had been lucky. *We should all be so lucky.*

God, is it possible to get maudlin in a pub on tonic*?*

By the time they left, Claire felt she and her sergeant had both undone some of the bad impressions someone back at the station had created, and made a step forward in the case, albeit in a puzzling and unexpected direction. As they were leaving, one of the crowd, an unfeasibly thin lad in a tight Lycra top and his twenties, called out to her, “Oh, and by the way, those shoes and that jacket. Fabulous.”

“Okay,” said Claire once they were on the outside again. “That went quite well, I think. Something new to work on and some positive policing to boot.” She adopted a deliberately jaunty air “And you’ll notice they liked my jacket.”

There was a sudden burst of laughter from inside the pub.

“They were taking the piss, ma’am,” Dave said as they made their way back to the car.

Chapter Eleven

Jonathan Wilson's father wasted no time. "Have you found him yet? The bastard who killed my son?"

Claire braced herself. "No, Mr Wilson. I'm afraid it's early days yet, but I assure you that we are doing everything in our power..."

"Then what the hell are you doing here?" They were standing once again in the morning room of the Wilsons' home and Mr Wilson was gesturing explosively to his windows and the world outside. "Why aren't you out there, trying to find him? God knows I..." He trailed off.

Silently Jonathan's older brother Simon had stepped to his father's side and was now laying a calming hand on his arm. Mr Wilson said nothing but subsided, grabbing fiercely at the glass that never seemed far from his side and drinking deep from it. "Hello, inspector," Simon said. He nodded at Dave. "Sergeant."

Claire flashed Simon a small, grateful smile before addressing his father again. "With your permission, sir, we'd like to go through your son's room, to see if there's anything there that might give us some more leads in our investigation."

"What the hell are you hoping to find there? He's hardly been in the damn room for the past few months."

"Yes, I know. That is, we know about his bedsit and we've done the same there. Please understand, this is purely routine but it could reveal important evidence that would help us in the search for his killer."

"I'll go with them, Dad. It'll be all right."

Mr Wilson drained the glass and slammed it down on the bar top before turning his back on all of them. Simon gestured to them, indicating the door, and they left. Simon paused to murmur something to his father, who was already pouring himself another drink, before joining them.

"Sergeant, if you and, er, Mr Wilson would take a look in Jonathan's room, I was wondering if I might have a word with Mrs Wilson," Claire said.

Simon looked momentarily puzzled, then his expression cleared. "Sorry, I'm not used to being called Mr Wilson at home."

I'll bet you're not.

"Please, call me Simon." He paused. "You want to see Mum? But, well, why?"

"Again, Simon, it's purely routine. I'd just like to take the opportunity to get to know a little bit more about Jonathan. It helps. I'd have talked to your father but, well, perhaps he's not quite ready for that yet."

Simon nodded. "I understand. And perhaps a little woman to woman talk...?"

Claire nodded, though with less conviction. "Yes. Something like that." She couldn't help thinking that this chat with the mother would normally be something for the sergeant to do. *And if Jenny had got the job...* She cleared her head of pointless speculation, with a small effort.

"She's in the conservatory. If you'd like to wait here, sergeant, I'll show you to her." He hesitated. "Inspector?" Claire watched as Simon worked to choose his words carefully. "Mum's always been a bit..."

Claire thought back to the thin, nervous woman she had seen so briefly on her last visit. "Highly strung?" she suggested.

"Yeah."

Simon's gratitude for her supplying the word sparked a rush of sympathy for him in Claire. She was beginning to suspect that although Mr Wilson senior was undeniably the titular head, it was on Simon's young shoulders that the burden of holding the family together had come to rest. She pitied him. *Not that you weren't doing much the same sort of thing when you were even younger,* her more hardnosed, practical side reminded her. "I understand," she said.

The woman Simon took Claire to, sitting silent, unmoving, in the stifling heat of the enclosed glass annex of the conservatory, could have been ten years or more older than the one she had seen for the first time only two days previously. Mrs Wilson sat in a cane chair, her hair scraped back, no make-up, hands limp in her lap. Her face was turned to the garden outside though Claire doubted that she saw anything there, any more than she heard Claire's approach. Only her son's gentle touch on her shoulder roused her from her memories. "I'll get Liz to bring you both some tea," Simon said, leaving Claire and Mrs Wilson alone.

"I am so terribly sorry, Mrs Wilson," Claire began.

"I know. You said." The words were simply spoken, not bitter or abrupt. Mrs Wilson appeared beyond most things, beyond the statement of simple facts, as if the strength for anything more had been ripped from her by her loss. Claire thought of the gruff, abrupt Mr Wilson. Only two kinds of woman could share a life with that kind of man: the strong woman who stood up to him and held her own ground, and the one who surrendered from the start. She thought of the little she had seen and of Simon's tentative description, and was pretty sure already which kind of woman Mrs Wilson had been. Never strong from the start, a blow like the murder of her youngest son must have nearly broken her.

Claire sat, waiting for an invitation to do so obviously being pointless. She knew the questions she wanted to ask, that she *had* to ask, but was unsure of how to begin. She briefly thought of echoing the platitudes the principal of Jonathan's college had given her, but couldn't bring herself to repeat empty statements that hadn't even fooled her. But what could she say about a boy whom their interviews had suggested had had no real connection at all with anyone around him? "He was a very good looking boy, Mrs Wilson," she said finally. Mrs Wilson turned large, grey eyes on her but said nothing, then turned them back in the direction of the garden. "You were a very close family?" Claire ventured. So close he had moved out months ago when he could have lived very comfortably indeed, had he stayed.

"I loved my son," said the soft voice.

"Of course. I was wondering, though..." Claire sighed inwardly. *Give me a no-brain thug to interview any day.* "I was wondering, why did Jonathan choose to live in a bedsit when he had such a lovely home here?"

"He was growing up."

Claire nodded as if the answer had given her all she'd been hoping for. "I suppose all young men want their own freedom."

Mrs Wilson turned her eyes on Claire again. "It was best for the family."

* ~ * ~ *

Upstairs Simon was sitting on the side of Jonathan's bed watching Sergeant Lyon move around his brother's bedroom.

"Has anybody moved anything in the room, do you know, since the last time we were here?"

Simon shook his head. "I came in a couple of times, just to, you know, remember, but I don't think anyone else has. I don't suppose Mum could bring herself to, and Dad—well, that sort of thing just isn't Dad's way. Liz, she's sort of a cook-cum-maid-cum-cleaner, was told to leave the room alone. Not that she ever came in here anyway, really. Jonathan didn't like that."

"Pretty neat sort of a lad."

"You could say that."

"I think I'd have loved having someone paid to clear up my

things when I was his age. Though maybe I wouldn't have been too keen on them finding some of the things I used to keep in my bedroom then." Dave smiled and waited to see if Simon would respond to that comment.

"Jonathan was like that. A place for everything and everything in its place. He was like Mum in that way. I take after Dad more. You should see my room." He stopped suddenly. "You don't, do you? Want to see my room, that is?"

"No. No, that shouldn't be necessary."

Dave worked his way along the shelves, taking in the precise numerical organisation of the tapes and DVDs that he'd already seen in Jonathan's bedsit, noticing the gaps in the sequences. He made a note of the missing numbers in his notepad, intending to check them later against the numbers taken from the bedsit although he knew already there'd be no match. The bedsit numbers had been an uninterrupted run. "Did Jonathan bring many mates home with him?" he asked casually.

"Jonathan?" There was a note to that answer. *Amusement? Surprise?* "No. Jonathan didn't bring friends home." Simon hesitated fractionally. "And definitely not any boyfriends."

Dave waited, pretending to study an old poster—an original, he noted, of the Japanese anime *Spirited Away*.

"You knew he was gay, didn't you, sergeant?"

Dave turned to face him. "Yes. The college told us he was a member of the gay group there."

"Woggles." Simon pulled a face. Dave assumed it was of

distaste at the awful acronym. "Does that...does that affect things?"

"I'm not sure what you mean."

"I mean." Simon hesitated then the words came out in a rush as if he was forcing them out before he could regret saying them. "I mean will people think less of him because of that? Will they care less about what happened? Will you...?" The last question was left hanging.

"No," said Dave simply.

Simon nodded then looked down fiercely at the carpet. Dave walked over to another shelf, continuing his inspection, giving the lad time and space to deal with his feelings. "Had he been out long?"

"If you mean had he told the family, he only did that overtly about six months ago. I think some of us had known long before that. You do, don't you?"

"How did your parents take it?"

Simon threw his head back as he recalled events. "I think Mum thought it was a joke at first. Jonathan was given to those, you know—practical jokes. He didn't always know when to stop, actually. And then I think she thought it was all a phase . Something he'd grow out of if we all just left him alone and never, ever talked about it."

"And your father?"

Simon smiled, though there wasn't any real humour in it. "Dad was a bit more forthright. He'd not had any idea, of course.

It was a very ugly night, that first night when Jonathan told us."

"And is that why Jonathan went to live in a bedsit?"

"I don't know. Yes, I suppose so. He never really said. He didn't move out immediately. He certainly wasn't thrown out or anything melodramatic like that. He could have stayed on here. The place is big enough, and Dad is away a lot of the time. But he didn't. He just came back from college one day and said he was moving out. And he did. I guess it must have been more difficult for him than I realised. I should have known. Dad can be...hard to deal with. I'm older. I cope. Jonathan..." Simon cleared his throat. "I suppose I only saw him twice after that when he came here to pick up some clothes and things. And then he was...he was..." Simon again turned his face down, very deliberately hiding it from Lyon. Dave pulled a book from the shelf. He thumbed through it, hardly even aware of what it was about, and waited.

"And then I saw him again, yesterday. I had to do the formal identification."

"Your father...?"

Simon shook his head. "And there was no way Mum could have gone through with it. It was okay." He nodded, as if the gesture made the statement true. "It was a chance to say goodbye, I suppose. Did you grow up with a brother, sergeant?" The question was asked with a forced breeziness, as if it was changing the subject when really it wasn't at all.

"Yes, I did. Just the one."

"Are you close?"

Dave considered. "Closer than some, not as close as others, I suppose. We're very different. And we've had our...disagreements." He closed the book he was leafing through with a snap and replaced it on the shelf.

"And your father?"

"Fathers are...difficult." The two men regarded each other, and there was an unspoken understanding. "Did you have anybody with you, when you went to identify Jonathan?"

"There were some people there. They were very helpful."

"I'm sorry. If I'd known, I would have come with you."

Simon smiled briefly, gratefully, then looked down again at the carpet.

Back in the conservatory, Claire struggled on, trying to elicit responses from a mother apparently rendered all but insensible by grief. "Were there...any difficulties at home. Any arguments? Between Simon and Jonathan for example? Brothers often do fight. Or...between your husband and Jonathan?"

For the first time since the inspector's arrival, Mrs Wilson showed some hint of animation, a faint hint of colour in her pale cheeks. "What are you suggesting?"

"I'm not suggesting anything, Mrs Wilson. I'm just trying..."

"Then what is the point of such a stupid question? Of course there were arguments. What family doesn't have arguments? That doesn't mean anything. Jonathan and his father disagreed about...several things. He was more like me. Simon is more like his father. That was only natural."

"Yet Jonathan was living away from home."

"Many boys do that."

"Of course."

Mrs Wilson sank back into her chair, worn out by this brief exchange. "Do you have anything worthwhile to ask me, inspector?"

Many questions, and not one I can put clearly into words. Why do I feel like we're skirting around something significant? "I don't have any more questions at the moment, no, thank you."

"Then please leave me alone."

Claire stood and Mrs Wilson turned back to her sightless contemplation of the garden. Further words on either side were unnecessary. Claire left the room without speaking again. Back in the hallway she paused. Left in search of her sergeant and Simon? Or...? Pulling her shoulders back, she turned right and headed back towards the living room.

As she had expected, Mr Wilson was still there. And also as she had expected, so was the glass in his hand. "What do you want now?"

She noted the unsteadiness of the hand he wiped across his eyes, the weariness of his voice. The man was obnoxious and overbearing. He'd also lost his son. In some ways he reminded Claire of her own father, which, in turn, reminded her of what her mam would say about the pair of them. "Fire and fire," she'd say, when she was feeling charitable. This, Claire reminded herself, was not the time to let her own temper rise to the goading of his. "I'm sorry to have to intrude at this difficult time. It really is only because we want to find out anything we can to help us in our investigation." Mr Wilson said nothing so she pushed on. "I've just been speaking to your wife, and I thought..."

"What do you want to go bothering her for? Don't you think she has enough to deal with at the moment without you harrying her with a lot of pointless questions?"

The bluntness of the man's words was even more striking after his wife's anaesthetised detachment. Claire took a deep breath. *Okay, remember that course. The one with the terribly nice lady who taught you all about the public and grief and how to handle them.* The terribly nice lady she'd so badly wanted to punch before the course had been through. The thing about bloody counsellors, of course, was that they were never actually around when you needed them. Too busy running bloody rubbish courses for bloody wannabe inspectors. "It really does help us in our investigation if we can get as complete a picture as possible of what your son was like."

"Like? What do you mean, 'like'?"

Like with you, his family. "His friends. Acquaintances. College mates," she said. "We'll have to check up on all these things."

"That'll do you no good."

She stopped, momentarily nonplussed by this man's absolute

conviction that what she was doing was useless. "Why do you say that, sir?"

"If it was that easy you'd have sorted it by now. Well, wouldn't you?"

Claire decided to ignore the rhetorical question. "Was there anything that had been bothering your son lately, sir? Anything on his mind?" The questions felt like blunt instruments, and part of her felt guilty for wielding them. But damn it, the man had driven her to it. Even from a distance, she saw Wilson's knuckles whiten as his grip on his glass tightened. "Was he happy?" she persisted.

"Happy? What the hell kind of question is that? How should I know if he was happy or not? What had he got to be unhappy about?"

"That's what I was hoping you could tell me, sir. But if he wasn't happy, then the reason could be important."

"The boy had everything he needed. And everything he wanted, too. No money worries. Time to waste on those ridiculous courses of his..."

"You didn't approve of the courses he was taking at the college?"

Wilson rounded on her. "No, inspector, I didn't. And I also agreed to fund him through them and pay for his board and lodgings while he did it. That's how much of a monster I am. I wouldn't have wanted to run around with a camera all day every day when I was his age, but I wasn't him and he wasn't me." He took two unsteady steps forward from the bar, closer to her, the alcohol on his breath plain to smell. “Just what are you getting at? Are you trying to find out more about Jonathan or more about me? Asking me stupid bloody questions as to whether my son was happy or not is going to get you nowhere. If you want to find out who killed him…” He stopped.

“Sir?”

The silence hung in the air between them for a moment, then, “Get out there—” again the gesture to the world outside the leafy confines of the Wilsons’ comfortable home “—and leave me and mine to do what we have to do.”

Claire met Dave back in the hallway as Simon was showing him down the long stairway to the front door. She noted the way the boy was talking easily to her sergeant as they descended together, noted the way he stopped when he saw her. They made their goodbyes, and Claire saw how Simon stood in the doorway watching them all the way down the drive until their car had turned a corner and was out of sight.

Chapter Twelve

"He's in trouble again," Ian growled.

"What is it this time?"

"Geography."

"Well, there you go. You know he doesn't like the teacher—what's his name again?"

"Short. Barry Short. And whether he likes him or not is beside the point."

Claire massaged her eyes and wondered whether really not giving a damn at that moment, and wanting a drink considerably more than a report on her son's progress, made her an unfit mother. She thought it probably did, but she didn't especially care right then so it all kind of evened out. "So what's he done, or not done, this time?"

"Seems that practically all of his homeworks are missing."

"Hang on, hang on." Claire tried to force the mental changing of gears that had to take place every evening when she got home from the station. *A wife not a WPC. A parent not a policewoman.* That had always been the mantra. Except now it was *a family member not an inspector*. And that only made the gear shift harder. The buck stopped with her now. But apparently it also followed her home.

Thoughts of Jonathan Wilson, his father and mother circled in Claire's brain, as did thoughts of the tensions building in what had hitherto been a pretty tight unit at Foregate Street because of her new sergeant. And there were thoughts of Simon Wilson, too.

She brought a stop to the circling thoughts and focused instead on her eldest son's latest transgressions. Sometimes she was irritated that Ian couldn't cut the lad a bit more slack. He'd been a teenager once, hadn't he had his share of scrapes? Well, actually, from all that he and his family had told her, she didn't think Ian had. He'd been pretty much a model student. It was she who'd been in trouble more often than not back at Pontypridd Comp. Tony took after her, for understandable reasons. And then she was thinking of the Wilsons, of Jonathan, like his mother, and Simon, like his father, apparently. And then she was annoyed with herself for drifting off the domestic subject again, and for being ratty with Ian when he was only trying to do the good parent thing. *God, I need a drink.* "He's done some Geography homework," she declared. "I know he has. I remember printing out some maps or something for him at the station when our printer went bust."

"There's more to Geography than a few maps and things, Claire."

"I know," she insisted, though if pushed she'd have had to admit that she didn't. "There was some writing as well." *Just don't ask me what it was about.*

"Yes, well, I know Barry can go a bit over the top sometimes."

"Wasn't he the one who gave Tony an E grade in his report?"

"Yes..."

"And then he went and got a C in his end of term exam?"

"Yes, but there's more to it than end of term exams these days, Claire."

"Okay." The correct facts and figures coming back to her, Claire felt happier. Maybe after all it was a matter of treating family problems as just another part of her caseload, rather than as something completely separate. And, as in this case, the prime suspect was still out playing football, or whatever it was he was always doing when she got back from the station... "I'll talk to him about it later."

"You always say..."

"I *will* talk to him later." Then she was sorry, because she worried she'd played the ranking officer role when she'd meant to be the supportive partner. And it wouldn't have mattered if maybe Ian had stood up to her just a bit more on this one, but he didn't and he wouldn't, would he, because of the thing that no one tried to hide, but no one talked about. Tony was her son, not Ian's. Oh, in every sense that mattered they were both Tony's parents. But Ian wasn't the biological father, and now Tony was growing up, still the bright, loving son he'd always been, but fast becoming a man, testing his strength, pushing the boundaries. And out there at the edges was that simple fact. She didn't know how Tony felt about it, had never spoken to him on the subject, and she and Ian had never talked of it either—at least, not for years—but she knew how he felt. It was there in the silences, the moments when he pulled back, like now, as if fearing that he had gone further than was his right, and at times like that she wanted to hug him, or slap him, and tell him it was all right, he *was* Tony's dad. But she never did, because that would have meant talking about it. So instead she said, "How's Sam?" then really could have groaned aloud, because her attempt to tactfully change the subject might just as well have been translated: *Enough of my son, how's yours?*

She glanced quickly at her husband to see if that was how he had taken it, but he had his back to her. "In bed." There was an accusation there, it was true, but the reason was probably simple enough. She'd been late getting back home, again. "I'll go up and tuck him in, in a minute."

Ian said nothing and his back was still turned to her, but she heard the clink of glasses and the hiss of a bottle being opened.

Oh, thank God for that.

* ~ * ~ *

"So, who do you think did it?"

"It's not like that, Richard."

"Oh come on. You must have some ideas. Run me through the list of suspects."

Dave pulled out a piece of deep crust pizza—ham and pineapple, extra ham—from the Pizza Palace delivery box, closed the lid to keep the rest warm, and sighed longingly over it. All he'd looked forward to for the past hour was this pizza, a can of beer and maybe something completely brain-dead and relaxing on the telly before he fell into bed. And now Richard was giving him the third degree about his day. “That would hardly be ethical. Tell me about your day,” and he took a big bite of his Hawaiian. He wasn’t interested in the slightest in what had gone down at Richard’s school that day, but he hoped maybe the hint would be taken.

“Same as yours probably, oh, except with nothing of any interest or variety added. So come on, you must have some suspects. How about motives? Isn’t that always a good place to start? No reason, no crime? Who had the most to gain from the victim’s death?”

In spite of himself, Dave found his mind wandering along the paths of Richard’s Agatha Christie-esque imaginings. “As far as I can see,” he admitted grudgingly, “no one stood to gain anything from Jonathan’s death. He was a kid. He had no money of his own. His dad’s quite well off, I suppose, but not *that* rich, not so as a kidnapping would have been worthwhile, and anyway I can’t see that any kidnapper would be so clumsy as to accidentally stave in the head of a potential source of money, even if he had put up a fight.”

“Were there any signs of a struggle?”

“Yeah,” Dave said vaguely, not willing to dwell on the mental image of the marks on Jonathan’s face and body. He didn’t like Richard’s ghoulish relish in the idea, but then all Richard had ever seen was pictures on the telly or cinema screen. How to explain that the reality was so much less colourful, and so much more depressing? "More like a beating, though. He wasn't a big lad. He wouldn't have put up much of a fight back."

"So, maybe he pissed someone off?"

Dave shook his head slowly. "There was at least one lad who didn't like him, but definitely not enough to want to kill him. Apart from that, Jonathan had so little to do with people it's hard to imagine him making anyone angry enough to want to kill him."

"So maybe he knew something he shouldn't have," Richard said with dogged persistence.

"About what? He was a college student."

"What did he study?"

"Art and media...." Richard trailed off. Media. The cameras. Jonathan was always filming. *Maybe. Just maybe.* He thought back to Jonathan's rooms, at home, at the bedsit. Where were the cameras that Tom Adams and others had referred to? He couldn't remember seeing them. "Or it could just have been a hate crime," he murmured, as much as anything to hide from Richard the new directions his thoughts were taking, reluctant to let him see that he might actually have sparked off a useful idea. It was a mistake.

"Hate crime? What, you mean he was black or something?"

Dave swore inwardly. "No," he said, having seen too late where this was going to go. "He was gay."

"He was gay? You never told me."

"I'm not supposed to tell you anything. And besides, what difference does it make?"

"What difference? C'mon, darlin'. Wake up and smell the

coffee."

"You have got to stop watching so many American shows."

Richard went on, oblivious to Dave's criticism. "I think that's pretty damn important if that's the reason he was killed."

"We don't know that and..."

"And how come that wasn't mentioned on the news or in the papers?"

"It might have upset his parents."

"What, you mean they don't know?"

"Yes, they know, but..."

"So what, like it would have been hugely socially embarrassing if everyone found out that their one and only son was gay as well as dead?"

"He was not their only son, and yes, it might have been. Not everyone is as liberal as you and me, and we're only liberal in this because we have no choice. And why should the media make a big thing about his sexuality if it was nothing to do with his murder? They might just as well have told the world he had blue eyes or...or black hair, or was a member of the Thomas the Tank Engine Fan Club or something."

"You are being politically naive."

"And you are just being naive," Dave snapped. "There could be a hundred and one reasons why Jonathan Wilson was killed, and not one of them might have anything to do with the fact that he was gay." And he stuffed his mouth again with an unfeasibly large piece of pizza to prevent himself from saying anything about the second death, only yards away, of a second lad whose sexuality hadn't been so much something to hide or take for granted as something he appeared to have made a living from.

Richard toyed with his own slice of pizza, dipping it carefully into one of the small pots of sauce Pizza Palace provided. Dave couldn't tell if he'd hurt him or not with his outburst. They hadn't known each other long enough yet to be able to successfully read each other's silences. He hoped he hadn't. He also hoped that was the end of the subject.

"Is that why you were brought into the case?" Richard said finally. "Because you're gay?"

"No," said Dave shortly. "And if you'll excuse me, I'm going for another beer."

Chapter Thirteen

They knew something was up the moment they walked through the door the next day. Rudge was pointing the remote at the television, and there was that vacuum of silence always left behind just after someone has turned a set off. And both he and Cortez were smiling, grinning in fact, though Cortez at least made something like an effort to rein it in as Summerskill and Lyon entered.

“So, what’s up guys?” Claire asked suspiciously. “Morning TV? Chavwatch talk shows? Or spot of footy on company time?”

“’Fraid not, love,” said Rudge. “Different kind of ballgame altogether.” Cortez sniggered. “And how’s your first case going, then?”

“All right,” Claire said cautiously. “And yours?”

“Funny you should ask. Terry?”

Cortez cleared his throat and held up a Scene of Crime report. “We’ve lifted six separate clean sets of prints from the room, apart from the dead lad’s.” He held out a typewritten report with a row of prints prominently displayed across the top. “And one of them belongs to your boy.”

Claire took the report quickly and scanned it. “So they did

know each other."

Cortez guffawed and tried, none too convincingly, to turn it into a cough. Rudge laughed outright. "Oh, they knew each other all right, m'darlin'. Cop a load of this." He waved the remote at the television again and switched it back on.

After less than a minute, Claire said, "All right. I get the picture. You can switch it off now."

"You sure? Goes on for another—" Rudge squinted at the machine's digital read-out "—forty-two minutes. That's the thing about young lads. Plenty of staying power."

"So I see. Off, please."

"Yeah, but if you hang on for about, oh, nine minutes, forty-seven seconds, it all gets a whole lot more graphic." He turned to Dave. "You'd like to see that, wouldn't you? More up your alley really, isn't it?" He turned to grin at Cortez who turned away, though his own grin was readily visible.

Dave inclined his head, as if to get a better angle on the energetic action on the TV screen. "No, not really," he said. "Cute, but not really my type."

Rudge turned and switched the set off again. "Whatever. Pretty ugly stuff all of it, if you ask me." He walked over to the TV, ejected the disc, walked back and tossed it onto Dave's desk. "Homemade. There's three of them."

"All of Sean and Jonathan?"

"Near as we can tell. We haven't actually sat down and watched all of them all the way through. Not my idea of fun.

And—" he added with a note of triumph, and a quick smile at Cortez "—not my case any more."

"What do you mean?"

"I'd say these murders are obviously linked, wouldn't you, Inspector Summerskill? Two—" Rudge hesitated, making it very obvious he was searching for the right words "—gay men, who were shagging each other and filming it, and then both turn up dead, killed within yards and probably hours of each other. Madden says to turn it over to you. So congratulations. You might even have a serial killer on your hands."

Dave picked up the disc that had been dumped on his desk and spun it thoughtfully between his fingers. "Two killings don't make a serial killer."

"True, *sergeant*. But maybe you'll get lucky."

"Were these discs filmed by a third person?"

"Doesn't look like it." It was Cortez who spoke now. "One fixed angle throughout, from what we've seen, except for what you might call natural breaks when one of them—always Jonathan, in fact—reaches up and adjusts the camera. Oh, and he has some sort of small handheld device for close-ups during...certain parts. Except he seems to have forgotten to use that very much."

"Mind on other things?" Dave suggested. "Hands full?"

Rudge grunted but Cortez nodded. "This, however," he said, "is a different kettle of fish."

Claire inspected the fourth disc the sergeant had held out. The title on this one was printed, not handwritten. "*Banging Bedsit*

Buddies. Copyright Stand Up Productions."

"I hate titles like that!" Dave muttered.

"Pretty low budget stuff," Cortez explained, "but not filmed in Flanagan's bedsit, despite what the title suggests, like the other three were, and definitely involving at least one cameraman in addition to the...actors."

"Sean and Jonathan?"

Cortez nodded.

"So our boys are would-be porn stars?"

"Your boys, Claire," Rudge said, tossing her the remote and heading for the door. "Enjoy."

Cortez followed him, pausing in the doorway. He pointed to a folder on Summerskill's desk. "That's all the info we've gathered so far. We didn't spend much time on it." He gave a meaningful glance over his shoulder at his fast-retreating superior. "Lad's name was Sean Patrick Flanagan. Background's all there. Cause of death, strangulation with some kind of ligature. That wasn't found at the scene of crime although the handcuffs he'd been in were, along with a variety of other 'toys', in a box under the bed. We're pretty sure they were the cuffs used because they were the only things absolutely clean of prints." He darted another quick look back down the corridor, obviously uncomfortable at the thought of lagging too far behind Rudge. "At first glance there aren't any straightforward links between the two lads, school, home or work."

"Flanagan wasn't at the Tech?"

Cortez shook his head.

"And has the boy's DNA been cross-referenced with what they found on Jonathan?" asked Dave.

"Not that I'm aware of. Not yet." Cortez eyed the disc Dave was holding. "Pretty safe bet it'll be a match."

"Maybe. Sounds like another visit to Dr Aldridge." Claire rolled her eyes.

"Sorry." For a moment they thought Cortez was going to say more, but in the end all he came out with was, "Good luck," then he, too, was gone.

Claire sank into her chair and ran her fingers through her hair. "Great!" She indicated the folder that Cortez had left them on the way out. "So c'mon, what's the news on Flanagan?"

Dave picked the thin file up and skimmed through the details. "Not much. Like it says on the tin, he's from Ireland. Large family, but all of them based in or around Dublin. Flanagan moved here about a year ago and hasn't had any contact with the old country since then. Did some work at supermarkets, stocking shelves, rounding up trolleys, that kind of thing. Brief stint as a garage attendant, but for probably at least the last year seems to have been making a living as rent."

"Clients?"

Dave ran his finger down the page before answering. "About all we've got to go on at the moment are the descriptions of his 'friends' from his old dear of a neighbour. Vague to say the least. Doubt there's enough to go on, but I'll post them up and see if we get any bites."

"And no little black book of names?"

Dave was still skimming through the report. "A future pension plan, you mean? Not that's turned up yet, no. Not even any useful numbers stored in his mobile. Besides, I don't think a lad like that, in a place like that, was going to be pulling in the sort of diplomats and politicians who might be scared of blackmail later on, do you? No flashy possessions and no bank account that we can get a hold of." He paused for a moment in his read through the report. "He may have been thinking about a career with us, though."

"With the police. You're kidding! What makes you say that?"

Dave was po-faced "He did have several sets of handcuffs in that box under the bed."

"Tools of the trade?"

"Presumably." Dave ran his eye down the list of what exactly had been in the box. "All fairly run of the mill, actually."

He held out the report and Clare scanned the section he was pointing to. Her eyebrows shot up. "Run of the mill, you say?"

Dave took the folder back. "Yes, well, to each his own." He closed the folder and handed it to her but she shook her head. She'd got all she needed for the moment. He let it drop onto the desk in front of them. "Do you want me to call Aldridge?"

Claire grimaced. "No, I'll do it. I'm sure Jim left that little perk for me specially, the bastard." She leaned forward on her own desk, massaging her temples vigorously as she thought through what they had learned so far. "Still no indication anywhere of how, somewhere along the line, a downtown kid like Sean meets and teams up with a rich kid like Jonathan, and the two of them settle down to make home porn movies?"

"My guess would be a gay club or bar out of the area, probably Birmingham. Bit livelier than round here for a lad like Sean; bit less provincial for a lad like Jonathan. You get a good social mix at places like that: catholic with a small and very bent 'c'.

"Great."

"Well, at least we've got one more lead to follow up. I mean, I assume you'll want to question someone at—" he cleared his throat "—Stand Up Productions?"

"Of course."

"All right. But I have a feeling it won't have a direct bearing on why they were killed."

Claire regarded him incredulously. "You're joking, right? This is porn!"

"Porn doesn't lead automatically to death. It doesn't even carry a government health warning."

Claire's lips thinned. "Jim knows the score. All that crap about serial killers was just a wind-up. This is shaping up like two lads who got into something nasty over their heads and ended up paying for it. This is the key we've been after. And if porn doesn't have a health warning on it maybe it should. I did two years with vice. It's a nasty business."

"Okay, agreed. By and large. But you're talking mainstream straight porn, right? This—" and he waved a disc at her "—is just boys doing what boys do. With other boys. We know Wilson was a camera freak. Boy with camera and willing boyfriend. Wouldn't you? Just once at least?" He paused, inclined his head slightly. "Haven't you?"

"No! Definitely not." Then, because she couldn't resist it, "Have you?"

Dave hesitated, marginally. "Twice, actually. Once out of curiosity, once when I was...drunk. Didn't work."

"Pressure to perform?"

"Camera memory too short. Couldn't get it all in."

"Yeah, right. And no wide-angle lens either, I suppose. Nice to see gay and straight men boast about the same things. And maybe it is different for boys..."

"That's boyz with a 'z'."

Claire continued, not really sure what that meant and unwilling to admit it. "But this wasn't just a one-off experiment. It was three times, that we know to, plus *Bedsit Gangbang* or whatever the hell it's called. Which was done, we have to presume, for money."

"Why be an amateur when you can get paid for doing something you enjoy?"

Claire adopted a shocked expression, uncertain herself how genuine it was. "Are you actually condoning this?"

Dave chose his words carefully. "I just think that maybe there's a difference between the way gay and straight people see their respective porn. And maybe the connections you're making between these two deaths and the discs the boys made may not be quite...appropriate."

"Not quite appropriate." Claire arched her eyebrows. "It's all exploitation, sergeant. Treating people like meat. And whenever you start doing that you get a lot closer to being able to use them like objects, hurt them, kill them even."

"Meat is murder, eh?" Dave toyed with the disc in his hand, gazing into the rainbow colours of its silvered side. "I still remember the first time I saw two men kiss in a film. It was a porn film. Men don't kiss in any other kind, and never on telly. It was a real turn-on. Just a kiss. It was really exciting. But it was more than just that. It also made me feel...normal. I'd thought I was the only person who wanted to do that."

"Yeah, well," Claire rose and crossed the room. "These two were doing a whole lot more than just kissing."

Dave slipped the disc back into its case. "I suppose kissing is pretty much what you'd call a gateway activity."

"And all higher thoughts of empowerment aside, I repeat, they were doing it for money."

"Pays the tuition fees, I suppose. Beats lap-dancing, and you know how many nice, young, straight college girls are doing that these days to pay the bills."

"Neither Jonathan nor Sean, for very different reasons, had to worry about college bills."

"True," Dave admitted. "In fact, given his parents I don't suppose Jonathan had to worry much about any kind of bills at all." He piled the four DVD cases neatly on his desk. "Which makes these all the more labours of love."

"Right, well, since you're such a big fan, the first thing you can do is have the pleasure of going through them, thoroughly, to make sure there isn't anything beyond the bedroom gymnastics we've seen so far that we need to know about. Reckon you're up to it?"

Dave eyed his boss carefully for signs of innuendo. "I think I can be," he said, with a face as commendably straight as hers.

"Good. And then you can find out where the hell Stand Up Productions is based."

"They're fairly local. Brum, I think."

Claire did the eyebrow manoeuvre again. "Good detective work, sergeant. And there isn't even an address on the disc. You wouldn't happen to be familiar with the output of this particular studio, would you?"

"I've...seen their adverts in the gay press."

"Right."

"And given what we've seen here, I think we need to see what's on the tapes and discs Jonathan had at home and in his bedsit, too."

"There's hundreds of them!"

"I know," said Dave glumly.

"You think there might be more boy-on-boy action?"

"Maybe, and maybe with someone other than Sean, though probably not in the stuff left at home. Anything like that I should imagine Jonathan would keep fairly close to him. Or there could be other stuff altogether. Jonathan used his cameras the way other people use diaries. Could be all kinds of leads there. It's funny..." Dave's words trailed off pensively.

"What?"

"Jonathan seems to have been a bit of a control freak. His recordings are all very neatly numbered and organised. I wondered why there wasn't anything from recent months in his bedsit and if they had stuff like this on that could be the reason. But there were recordings missing from his home as well, but from all over the collection."

"I don't see your point."

"Well, if he'd taken them away with him because they were full of his home sex movies, and the recordings are all arranged chronologically, our Jonathan must have been a very precocious lad and have started his sexual adventures at a very tender age."

"Like I said before, great. All right, I'll sort out the warrant and, if need be, I'll even go over to the Wilson house myself and deal with Mr Wilson. I can't imagine that he'd let us help ourselves to his family's empty milk bottles let alone his late son's possessions without a fight."

"Simon Wilson will help if he's there."

Claire regarded Dave. "Yes. I suppose he will. But that's all to come and we might not even have to do it. Before any of that I want to find out more about the people behind this professional disc. I tell you, sergeant, I think this is the lead."

Chapter Fourteen

Claire's expression was one of mingled distaste and surprise. "So do you reckon many major Hollywood stars get their first breaks in places like this?"

"Probably not, though rumour has it that one or two got their first boyfriends from places like this."

"Yeah? Who?"

"Well, believe it or not–"

Dave was interrupted by the entrance of a balding man in his late forties, with a threadbare jumper and a suspicious attitude. "Can I help you?"

The police officers duly held out their IDs. "We hope so," said Inspector Summerskill.

The 'studio' of Stand Up Productions turned out to be more of an office than the sort of place you would expect to find lights, camera and action. And not so much an office as a small, dingy room with a battered desk and one chair. At the least Claire had expected to see posters or cover work from the *Amazing Range of Stand Up Productions* that the DVD they had brought with them promised. There was nothing like that, unless the calendar with the picture of a handsome young man in very tight speedos and an improbable tropical setting was a Stand Up product. She took a step closer, purely in the spirit of thorough investigation, but there was nothing to suggest it was. She did notice that the calendar was still turned to February, making it several months out of date. *Presumably Messrs March, April et al just don't fill their trunks as convincingly.*

"Mr...?"

"Arras. Len Arras. What can I do for you?" There was undoubted wariness in the tone, but Claire was prepared to concede that was hardly unusual. She carefully placed *Banging Bedsit Buddies* on the desk between them. "I believe this is one of yours?"

Arras picked it up, took out a pair of glasses to inspect it, as if its luridly coloured cover wasn't clear enough, then handed it back. "Yes," he said. "It's all legit. The models were legal age and all proof of identity and age is on record." Claire recognised the quotation from the blurb all adult studios were obliged to tag on the start and end of their productions. "This is a legal business, you know."

"Don't worry, Mr Arras, I know that. It isn't you we've come about. It's the actors..."

"Models. They're technically models."

"Right. Models. You say you have their details on record?"

"Yeah," Arras conceded uneasily.

"Could you show us the records you have on the two boys in this DVD?"

"They're not boys," Arras said quickly. "Like I said, I've got their ages."

"The ages they gave you?" Dave said.

Arras literally paled. "You're not saying...?"

"We're not saying anything, Mr Arras. We'd just like to see what information you have on—" she hesitated "—Jake Studd and Shane Harder. Those are the names given on your DVD?" Arras nodded. Claire gave a small smile. "Though we're guessing that maybe those aren't their real names."

"Have you got a warrant?"

"Do we need one?"

Arras shook his head dumbly and disappeared through a door behind his desk from which came the sound of a filing cabinet being opened and the screech of metal dividers being pushed back and forth rapidly.

"He was paying you a lot of attention," Claire remarked while they were waiting.

"Probably thought I was the ranking officer. You know how it is."

"Or maybe his interest was more professional. Perhaps he knows your film CV."

"All in the past, ma'am," Dave said smoothly. "These days I don't get out of bed for less than a Service pension plan. Besides, I don't think I could compete with the likes of Mr February over there. And his friend, Mr Sock."

"Too modest, sergeant. I'm sure there must be a casting couch somewhere around here."

"Mr Arras might not even be gay."

"He makes gay videos."

"I buy the *Sun* now and again, it doesn't make me straight, believe me."

"You buy the *Sun*?"

Arras was back. Claire wondered if his speed was because his filing system was extremely well organised or his catalogue of models very small. He handed over two dog-eared sheets of paper.

"Thank you." Claire skimmed through them. The information they contained was rudimentary but apparently all correct, giving real names, ages and addresses. Claire noted that Jonathan gave his bedsit as his place of residence.

"How did you come to know these lads?" Dave asked. "Talent scouting?"

"They came to me."

"Together?"

Arras sank back down into the rickety chair behind his desk. "No. The taller one, him." He indicated 'Jake' on the DVD cover. Jonathan. "He came. Said he'd seen our ad."

"Ad?"

"In *Midzone*."

"It's a free gay newspaper. Given away at clubs and pubs," Dave explained for his superior's benefit.

"Yeah. He saw the ad there and came along with a DVD he'd made with his mate."

"Do you still have it?"

"Nah, he took it back."

"But you copied it, right?" Dave said.

Arras gave a small cough. "Yeah."

"We'd like to have a look, please. You can have it back when we've finished with it."

"Can I send it to you? It's not here at the moment. It's at home."

"That'll be fine."

"And you just went ahead and filmed them?"

"Yeah. It was simple. I mean they knew each other, so there were no problems of, y'know, chemistry. You've no idea how difficult it can be if two guys don't get on."

"Oh, I think I have," said Dave.

"I can imagine," said Claire.

"But they had it all, in buckets, and they had the story worked out."

"There was a story?"

"It's not just about two guys fucking each other in a bed, you know!" said Arras, his sense of professionalism blatantly outraged by Claire's open scorn. "Setting, style, pace, structure, all these things are important."

"A beginning, middle and end," Dave said.

"Right."

"In that order," he added helpfully.

It suddenly occurred to Mr Arras that he might be being

mocked. "Yeah. Yeah, well." He attempted to recover some of his ruffled pride. "If you two have finished making your jokes at the expense of my legitimate business, I need to get on. I have a film in production, you know."

"What, here?" Claire regarded the door to Mr Arras's filing cabinet with renewed interest.

"Yes, of course here. Where d'you think. Pinewood fucking Studios?"

"You mean, you film here?"

"Of course we don't film here," Arras replied scornfully. "Think I could get a bed in here? Most of our stuff is location shooting."

"People lend their flats or houses," Dave explained.

"Yeah, that's right."

"But that's pretty limiting, isn't it? I mean, what if you need other kinds of sets, or even external locations. You can't always..." Claire stopped. Both Arras and Lyon were considering her with something that could, uncomfortably enough, have been pity. "Ah. Right." It was unlikely, she realised, that a Stand Up Production ever needed any location other than a bedroom. Or at least anywhere that offered more than a room with a flat, empty surface.

"Can you tell us where *Banging Bedsit Buddies* was filmed?"

Arras shifted uneasily in his chair, causing it to creak loudly. "Do I have to?"

"Yes," said Dave simply.

Arras shoved across a piece of paper he already had to hand. "Thought so, only, can you manage to be...discreet? We like nice places when we come to film, something to add a bit of class to the proceedings, you know? So the guys who lend us their places tend to be the sort of people who don't like to have a lot of attention drawn their way, if you know what I mean."

Claire took the proffered piece of paper and unfolded it. "Yes," she said, after just a momentary hesitation. "I can imagine the church wouldn't be too pleased if it knew about this. Okay, we'll need to talk to the people involved in the making of this film." She inspected the back of the DVD. "The director, Jon England."

"That's me."

"Principal cameraman, Stu Sutton?"

"That's me, too."

"Right." Claire ran her eye down the rest of the credits. She didn't think it would be necessary to interview the story editor, though she had a shrewd idea now of where to find him if she needed to. "Sound engineer, Dirk Masters?" she suggested, not with much hope.

"That's Derek. Yeah, you can talk to him if you like."

"Good."

"Though he wasn't actually there at the filming."

"So what does a sound engineer do?"

"Well, in this case—" Mr Arras shuffled a little "—he sort of helps with the sound effects, if you know what I mean. Derek and I put them on later if the models aren't, you know, especially vocal." Claire pictured another man as unappealing as Mr Arras, imagined them sitting round a microphone, supplying the 'sound effects'. It was an horrendous image. "And the music, of course," he went on. "It's really important to put on an appropriate soundtrack."

"Usually Eighties electro pop for some reason," Dave murmured.

"So who actually recorded the sound at the time?"

"That'd be me as well," Mr Arras admitted. "Just a case of hanging a microphone up somewhere out of shot."

"Not always," Dave said. Mr- Arras glared at him.

"All right. Well, with your close involvement with 'Jake' and 'Shane' you must have got to know them quite well. How long were you working on the film?"

Arras pursed his lips as he thought. "I dunno. It was quite a long shoot. Six, maybe seven..."

"Days? Or weeks?"

Mr Arras looked to Dave who looked away. "Hours," he said.

Refusing to catch her sergeant's eye, Claire tried one last tack. "And I'm presuming there's been some contact since then. I mean, have there been any royalty payments, for example?"

Arras frowned as if suspecting more sarcasm, only answering when he understood that she was actually being serious. "We don't do royalties. Payment down and that's it. We haven't broken the television and cinema market yet."

Claire took in the room around them, its peeling walls, its

location over a laundrette. “Really?” she said. “It can only be a matter of time, Mr Arras. C’mon, sergeant.”

“Oh, by the way,” said Dave, turning as he left. “The DVD you’re working on at the moment. What’s it called?”

“*Hanging Out.*” Arras was instantly suspicious again. “Why? You going to make trouble?”

“No,” said Dave. “But I thought I might look out for it when it hits the shops.”

Back at the station, the connection to an underworld of organised pornography almost certainly trashed, Dave went to see how the final day’s interviewing back at the Tech had gone while Claire set about the protracted process of sorting out the warrant they’d need to get hold of Jonathan’s tapes from his grieving family. Bumping into Jenny was a welcome distraction for her, though not without its difficulties.

She knew she should have sat down with her friend before now, talked through her disappointment at not getting the promotion she deserved, and explained that it wasn’t her doing. But events had happened, and she’d been launched onto a case that barely left her enough time to deal with her own life, let alone Jenny’s. So she felt really grateful and even touched when the WPC greeted her with an open smile and a cheery, “How’s it going then?” Claire rolled her eyes to the ceiling and no more needed to be said. She missed that easy communication with someone she knew so well. “Got time for a coffee?” Jenny asked. Claire hadn’t. She said yes.

The only other person in the canteen was Terry Cortez, poring over some paperwork. Claire nodded at him, made sure she and Jenny chose a seat across the room from him, then immediately wondered why she’d felt she had to. What was Foregate Street getting like? And why?

“So how’s the first case going then?”

There were a great many other things Claire would rather have talked about over a coffee but she supposed Jenny’s curiosity was inevitable. “We are proceeding with our investigations,” she deadpanned in the official style, and Jenny laughed.

“Yeah, well, rumour has it that it’s all pretty much sewn up anyway.”

“Says who?”

Jenny waved a hand vaguely. “I dunno. Everyone. You know how it is. They reckon that once Rudge gave you the porno lead it was just a case of rounding up the usual suspects.”

Claire jabbed her spoon into her coffee and stirred swiftly and unnecessarily given her foreswearing of sugar that month. “Yeah, well, *they* are wrong, I’m afraid. The porno lead was little more than an amateur operation. I’ll double check it, of course, but I’m pretty sure we’re not talking links with big league, organised crime or with anyone with the reason or ability to carry out two murders.”

“Oh, right. So you’re back where you started?”

"We're proceeding with investigations." And this time there was just a little bit less of a joke about the reply. Claire wondered whether Jenny's bluntness had always been this irritating. She also felt reluctant to talk any more about the Wilson and Flanagan case with her friend, as reluctant as she was to put her finger on why. She made a conscious effort to control her annoyance. "Anyway, enough about that. How are you? I've hardly seen you these past couple of days."

"Oh, pretty busy. You know how it is for the rank and file. If you can remember, that is."

"Jenny, it wasn't my decision. I really wanted..."

Jenny laughed again. "It's all right, Claire, really. I do know how these things work."

Claire felt a welcome release of tension. "I know, but still..." She felt on the verge of saying sorry, sensed that for all her words of acceptance Jenny was kind of expecting that, but couldn't bring herself to say the word. It really hadn't been her fault. "It's going to happen soon, Jenny. You know it is and I know it is."

Jenny nodded. "I know. It's cool. This is only temporary, and in the meantime I get more of an eyeful of the rather gorgeous Sergeant Cortez than you ever used to allow me, so everyone's a winner in the long run."

Claire blinked, trying to deal with two rather disturbing pieces of information at the same time and not knowing which one to begin with. "Cortez?" she said finally.

Jenny gave a conspiratorial smile. "C'mon, he is very easy on the eye. Have you seen the arse on him? It's not like he's trying to hide it in those trousers of his. They say he works out for a couple of hours every day."

Again Claire found herself wondering about who 'they' were. "Yeah, well maybe if he spent a bit less time in front of gym mirrors and more on his work he'd get made up faster. And what do you mean temporary? You're not thinking of transferring, are you?" She blinked again as another thought hit her. "You're not thinking of giving up, are you Jen?"

"Me? No way! Giving up or leaving. Not me."

"Then...?" Claire shook her head, puzzled.

"Well, your new guy, Lyons..."

"Lyon," Claire corrected automatically.

"Whatever. He's not going to last that long here, is he?"

"Isn't he? Why not?"

Jenny regarded her friend over her coffee mug. Claire recognised the expression from countless discussions, chats, long talks at work, on stakeouts, in pubs and clubs. It was the invitation to confidences. For the first time she could remember, Claire felt herself resisting the call to share. "Rumour is that you two aren't exactly hitting it off. And, well, he's not exactly your type, is he?"

"What the hell has that got to do with anything? Whatever it means." Claire pushed her own half-finished mug away from her. "If people want to know how my team is doing, they ask me," she said firmly. "I know this place is a rumour mill, but the last I heard there was a reason why we fill in all those endless reports and evaluation sheets, and I have to say so far that Sergeant Lyon has made a very good start to his term at this station. However long that may be."

Jenny Trent flushed. "Sorry," she said, and for a moment the word hung there between them. Not *Sorry, Claire,* not *Sorry, inspector,* just *Sorry.* "I know you've got to support your team now."

Claire could have risen to that one, too, but held back. She badly wanted to know who exactly had said she and Lyon were not hitting it off (though she had a fairly shrewd idea) and why they thought that. Whatever else she thought about the situation, this was her first case as inspector, and she'd thought she'd got a handle on it. But here was her friend, probably her best friend at the station, telling her the general perception was the opposite. In the past she'd have pressed Jenny—not that it would have taken much pressure—and they'd have talked about it, sorting it out, at least to their own satisfaction. But not now. A gulf was opening up between them, for more reasons than the one Claire had thought she was ready to deal with.

Claire rose from the table. "It's *our* team, Jenny. Let's not forget that, eh? And now, if you'll excuse me, I've got to go and draw up a warrant." She hesitated. "Still up for that drink later in the week?" Even to her own ears the offer sounded horribly false, though she did mean it. Jenny smiled up at her, and Claire found herself seeing that smile and trying for the first time to work out what was really going on behind it.

"Sure. Give me a call, whenever. I'm not going anywhere."

Claire nodded and made her way to the door, suddenly jumping back to avoid Eileen the canteen lady, who swept past her bearing a tray with a plate of something steaming. "You keeping that new sergeant busy, inspector?" Eileen asked breezily, as if the question was of no uncommon interest.

"Work's a bitch, Eileen," Claire said shortly before exiting the canteen. Eileen's darting glance after her suggested she thought that work wasn't the only thing.

*

"Wasting your time there, Eileen," Cortez said as she deposited his spaghetti Bolognese on his table, and a dollop of sauce on his paperwork for good measure.

"What d'you mean?"

"Sergeant Lyon's a very PC PC." Cortez shoved the rest of his paperwork to safety on the far side of the table and unrolled the knife and fork from the piece of kitchen paper that Eileen thought, for some reason, she had to wrap them in. "That is, he's not a WPC PC at all."

Eileen frowned. "I don't know what the hell you mean sometimes," and she thrust the now empty tray under her arm and marched back to the canteen. Cortez grinned and plunged a fork into his spaghetti. *Al dente* was presumably something else she didn't understand the meaning of. Over a twirling fork he caught the eye of Jenny Trent. He smiled at her, holding up a few strands of pasta with a *well, what can you do?* expression. She smiled, got up from her chair, and made her way over.

*

Outside the canteen Claire was met by a speeding and slightly breathless Sergeant Lyon. “We’ve got the cameras,” he said before she could speak.

“Where were they?”

“In Jonathan’s locker at the college.”

“I didn’t even know he had a locker. How come we weren’t told about it before?”

“If anyone should have known about it I guess it would have been Miss Humphries, the pastoral care tutor.”

Claire’s lips thinned. “Bloody woman. She should work the hours we do then she could moan about overwork. So, what have we got?”

“A video and a still camera. And they’ve both still got cards in them.”

“All right. Get whatever’s been found down to the labs and dusted. I expect we’ll find Sean’s fingerprints everywhere but I want to know if there’s anyone else’s there, too. I want to know what’s on them and I want to know what’s in them.”

“Already on their way.” He hesitated. “It could be just another bedsit romp, you know.”

Claire bit her lip. “And it could be a genuine snuff movie. Who knows? Either way, I want to know fast.”

"There's just one other thing you might like to know. This locker that was suddenly drawn to our attention was in a media studio at the college where a Mr John Elijah teaches."

Claire ran the unusual name through her memory. "Isn't that Jonathan's Moving Image tutor or something?"

"That's right. The teacher on the only course that Jonathan could be said to have been succeeding at."

"We didn't see him when we went in, did we?"

Dave gave a meaningful shake of his head. "He was off ill. Apparently he's still off ill. He only came in to pick up some work to do at home and that was when he discovered the cameras. Oh no," he added, in response to Claire's suspicious expression. "The ever cheerful Miss Humphries was with him when he found them."

"Okay. Still, I think we'd better have a word with Mr Elijah. If only to find out what the hell a Moving Image tutor actually does."

Chapter Fifteen

John Elijah's house wasn't in the same league as the Wilsons' by a long chalk but was still a surprisingly large detached house on the Battenhall Road, residence of choice of many well-to-do families. "I thought lecturers were supposed to be on a pittance," Claire grumbled as they walked up the drive. "My husband's a teacher and even with my salary as well we could never afford something like this."

"Your husband's a teacher? So's...the guy I'm living with. Where does he work?"

Claire noted that hesitation and wondered why Lyon was so reticent to use either of the words 'partner' or 'boyfriend'. She thought back to what Jenny had said. Did he feel so uncomfortable with her that he couldn't be as open as he would with anyone else? Before she could say anything, the door was opened and standing before them was a large, middle-aged man, hair perhaps slightly longer than was typical for someone of his age and position, and beard a pleasant salt and pepper colour.

"Can I help you?" The voice was as deep as you'd expect from someone with a barrel chest like that, but surprisingly quiet. Summerskill and Lyon showed their cards and the door was opened more widely, Elijah stepped to one side. "Please come in." There was no surprise in his inflection, if anything, Claire detected just a hint of weary resignation. *And he doesn't appear to be ill now.*

Elijah showed them into his lounge, and the two police officers sat down on the capacious leather settee he indicated to them. Both perched on the front edge, it being hard to conduct a formal police interview while sinking back into luxurious padding. Tea was politely and automatically offered and just as politely and automatically declined.

"We've been conducting some interviews at the college, Mr Elijah," Claire began. "You would have been one of the people we spoke to as a matter of course, but you weren't in."

Elijah nodded. "Yes. A back problem. Recurring. The muscles go into spasm. Very painful, very incapacitating. Fortunately I appear to be in remission. I hope to return fully to work tomorrow." He'd taken a single chair facing the sofa, sitting back into it, though still managing to look stiff and not at ease. That could have been a legacy of his back pain, Claire supposed. "I presume you've come to talk to me about Jonathan, haven't you? One of my colleagues told me that was who you were asking questions about. And I suppose we should expect that, shouldn't we? What with his having been..." He trailed off.

"We understand Jonathan was one of your students." Elijah silently acquiesced. "What can you tell us about him?"

Elijah regarded the parquet floor as if gathering his thoughts.

"He was a good student." Claire tried to decide whether the words sounded guarded, careful, or whether that measured tone was simply natural to the teacher.

"Really? That's just a little bit of a surprise, if you don't mind my saying so, Mr Elijah. Practically every other one of Jonathan's teachers that we have spoken to has been somewhat more cautious in their estimation of him."

Elijah gave a small expression of mild disdain, presumably for the opinions of his colleagues. "Yes, well, even I can't say that Jonathan was one of my most diligent students, but from what I hear he did put more into my subject than he did into many of his others. He was genuinely interested in visual media, you see. I rather think he had thoughts of a career somewhere in that direction."

"Yes, we know that he always had a camera of some kind with him."

Elijah gave a curiously colourless laugh. "Oh, yes. Jonathan's projects. Some of them were part of his coursework, you understand. Some of the others were...more outré." The pace of his words picked up slightly. "He had a genuine flair and enthusiasm for the visual arts, you know. I really think he could have made it in some way in the field. And I suppose you'd have to say he did have something of a head start over the others."

"In what way a head start, sir?"

"Jonathan's parents don't lack money. I'm sure you know that by now. Jonathan was very well kitted out when it came to cameras and equipment. State of the art, almost all of it. Most of it better than the antiques the college supplies."

"And did that cause any resentment among other students?" Claire asked. "Or among the staff, for that matter?"

Elijah's lips made a moue that suggested he really didn't care. "Possibly. It would have been hard to tell. He wasn't really..."

"...there enough for you to see," she concluded for him. "Yes, we've heard."

*

Dave listened carefully to the questions his boss was asking but also took the opportunity to let his attention wander a little around the room they were in. That seemed to be coming instinctively to him these days and he wondered, half amused, whether that was the policeman in him or the gay man. He'd always quite liked that game of being asked back to someone's flat or house and taking the few minutes that almost always ensued while the other guy put the coffee on, put the dog out, hurriedly tidied up the bedroom, or all three, to try to work out his personality from the books, CDs, DVDs, and general bric-a-brac. Depressingly, he'd found with the majority of gay men you met like that, the fixtures and furnishings tended to be very similar. That was one advantage of living with Richard: not having to resign himself to the discovery of yet another collection of Madonna discs.

He didn't expect to find anything like that in Elijah's living room today, of course, but then it didn't much match the admittedly vague idea he had of a media studies teacher's home. He'd expected perhaps wall to wall books, tapes and DVDs, and definitely a large television, one of those surround sound, widescreen jobs, whereas the room they sat in now was spacious and bright, and conspicuously empty of the clutter such things would have brought. There was one shelf, tastefully backlit, containing some books, it was true, but all were large, and hardback, with not a single airport paperback to be seen. There was no visible television, either, unless the big lacquered cabinet in one corner was one of those disguised sets, something to suggest to the world that you were far more interested in antique furniture than soaps and sport. In the absence of a television screen, the focal point of the room was a large painting over the fireplace, a vivid, abstract piece in tones of red and flesh colour. It wasn't really the kind of thing that normally appealed to Dave but he had to admit the curves, lines and tones of this piece were oddly compelling, almost familiar somehow. He suddenly became aware that Elijah was watching him, noting his interest in the painting. "One of your own, sir?" he asked, as much as anything to cover his slight embarrassment at having been caught studying it so closely.

"No. I have no talent at all with the brush. It was a gift from a former student. He's gone on now to become quite well known in certain circles. You might have heard of him. Duncan Lewis?"

Dave counterfeited regret. "Sorry."

"Ah well."

That probably explained why he felt he'd seen the painting before: perhaps in a newspaper or magazine if this Lewis guy was getting to be well known. Maybe even in a poster shop. Dave wondered if it was valuable. Certainly everything about the house that they had seen so far suggested taste. A very masculine taste. He wondered if Elijah lived alone. It was certainly a big house for just one man. And that probably solved the mystery of the missing telly, too. Dave would bet Elijah had a room set aside for viewing. How the other half lived.

"Did you like Jonathan, Mr Elijah?" Claire asked suddenly, and, his attention focused back on the questioning, Dave couldn't miss the sudden, deep flush that spread beneath that splendidly variegated beard. A touched nerve, or just the reaction of a guarded man to what could be seen as an impertinently personal question? Inspector Summerskill waited pointedly for the answer.

"Like him? What an odd question to ask, inspector. Do you like the people you deal with?"

"It's a very different line of work, Mr Elijah."

"Possibly. In my job it really isn't relevant, you know. We all have to teach our students whether we like them or not. My feelings towards most of them are... fairly indifferent."

"But for this one in particular, Mr Elijah," Claire said with cool persistence. "Did you like him or not?"

Elijah's eyes lost their focus for a minute, presumably as his thoughts turned to whatever memories of the lad he had. "Yes," he said, "I suppose you could say I did like him."

~~*

"So, what do you think?"

Dave inserted the key and started their car. "I think we've actually found someone outside the family who liked Jonathan. Is that progress?"

"D'you think he's gay?"

"Are you going to ask that about everyone involved in this case?"

"Deny you considered it."

Reluctantly Dave conceded that. "But I thought I'd already said my gaydar's about as reliable as cut price GPS. Following it has led me up all kind of blind alleys. And does it matter anyway?"

"I saw you giving the room a once over," said Claire, redirecting the conversation along less controversial lines, "like you did with Jonathan's. I thought maybe you might have, you know, picked up a few clues."

"You'll have me starring in makeover TV programmes next," Dave muttered as he pulled out into traffic. "'Sergeant Lyon will transform your house in next to no time for next to no money. Want that cop shop feel? Lyon's your man. Trust his exquisite taste. He's gay."

"Touchy."

"Sorry," Dave said automatically. "There's something...I don't know, at the back of my mind, niggling away, and I can't get it out."

"About Elijah?"

“Yes. No. I don’t know.” Dave deliberately focused on the slow moving cars outside to avoid having to see his boss’s wry amusement. “Probably nothing.”

“Great. Some unhappiness about Mr Elijah’s décor, perhaps, but otherwise no reason to suspect him of any involvement with the murders. Quite the reverse, in fact, as Elijah’s the only one of Jonathan’s teachers who’s given him a positive report and his subject was the only one Jonathan was doing well in.”

“This isn’t going well, is it?”

“It’s a pile of shit, sergeant.”

They hadn’t expected conviviality or even politeness from Jonathan’s father when they turned up at his home again, warrant at the ready should it be needed. But this time any semblance of restraint on Mr Wilson’s behalf seemed to have gone out of the window. He wrenched the front door open even before they had a chance to knock and immediately laid into them. “What the hell are you doing here again? Are you doing anything at all to find the bastard who killed my son? What have we got to do, take the law into our own hands?”

Claire held her ground in the face of an instinctive reaction to back away from Wilson’s forceful tirade. “I assure you, sir, we are doing everything in our power to—”

“Which means you are doing fuck all, right? The pair of you and every other idle sod back at that fucking station are sitting around on your arses or coming here to pester me with stupid questions when whoever did this is laughing in your faces."

"Mr Wilson, I—"

"I know you've been up the college. Do you honestly think one of those limp-wristed tossers could have done anything to my boy? What about that good for nothing layabout who was sponging off him? He's your most likely suspect. Where the hell is he?"

"Do you mean Sean Flanagan?"

"The little Irish queer! I don't know what the hell his name is."

"Sean Flanagan is dead, Mr Wilson."

That at least brought a temporary halt to the Wilson tirade. "Same way?" he said finally.

Claire shook her head. "No, but I can't say any—"

"Jesus! How many more people have to die before you'll get up off your arses and do something useful? Are there any men at your station, inspector, who'll actually get out there and get their fucking hands dirty?"

"You knew about your son's relationship with Sean Flanagan, Mr Wilson?" Dave said.

"What do you mean, relationship?"

"You said Sean was 'sponging' off your son. What did you mean by that? Did Jonathan lend him money? Did he...help with the rent?"

Wilson glared suspiciously at Dave. "Flanagan was another one of Jonathan's projects. He'd have got tired of him sooner or later, he always did. And he'd have learned the hard way that you can't trust any damn bastard in this..." He stopped, turned from the police officers momentarily, then turned back to them, the effort to control himself plain on his face. "In this life," he concluded.

"Inspector. Sergeant." Simon Wilson had appeared from somewhere behind his father and was now standing to one side of him, one hand protectively on his father's arm as he greeted the two officers. "I...heard you were here."

I'll just bet you did. Claire regarded him levelly.

"Dad, would you like me to deal with Inspector Summerskill and Sergeant Lyon?" Simon addressed Claire and Dave. "You'll have to forgive us. As well as...everything else that's been going on, my mother... My mother has had an accident."

"An accident?"

"The stupid bitch only tried to go and kill herself!" Wilson spat.

Claire regarded Mr Wilson with genuine shock. "Kill herself?"

"We don't know that, Dad," Simon said with a hint of pleading in his voice.

"My wife has never been the strongest of women, inspector," Wilson said grimly. "She's just lost a son and you're running around like a bunch of headless chickens getting nowhere in finding out who did it. It's no bloody wonder she was tipped over the edge again."

"Dad." Dave saw the gentle pressure Simon applied to his father's arm, the almost imperceptible tug backwards, into the house. “Let me deal with this. Okay? I’ll fill you in afterwards.”

For a second Claire expected Mr Wilson to bark at Simon, too, to snap his head off and continue his storm of protest. He didn’t. He nodded, just once, and went to move off back into the house, turning to fire one last shot at Summerskill and Lyon. “Get him. Get him quickly. Because if you won’t...”

“I’ll be with you in a minute, Dad.”

Father nodded once more at son, and slowly withdrew back into the house. Simon waited until he was out of sight before he spoke again. “I’m sorry about that,” he said. “As you can imagine, it’s been a hell of a strain on all of us. Dad talks a good fight, but underneath it all...”

Underneath it all he’s a total bastard. Claire respected Simon all the more for loving his father enough to stand by him and try to protect him at this time, and also for knowing how to deal with him. She wondered if the apparently unsociable, aloof Jonathan had been able to do the same thing. She suspected not, probably another reason why it was the older Simon who had stayed at home while the younger Jonathan had moved out almost as soon as he could.

“There’s nothing for you to apologise for,” said Dave quickly.

“Simon, I’m sorry if this is painful for you to talk about, but your mother...?”

Simon shook his head, and Claire was surprised to see the ghost of a smile on his face. “Mum didn’t try to kill herself. Dad can...fly off the handle sometimes, say things he doesn’t mean, or at least that he'll take back later. Mum had an accident in the car. Ran it off the road. Obviously she's been upset. Well, you saw her, didn't you? She shouldn't have been driving at all. God knows where she was going. And she'd... Well, she'd..."

"Been drinking?" David suggested softly.

Again that ghost of a smile. "No, no. That's definitely Dad's thing. No, but she had been on pills, I don't know what. Something to help her sleep, to help her cope. You know the kind of thing."

"That's...understandable," said Claire. "Was she badly hurt?"

"She was very lucky. She hadn't gone very far and wasn't going very fast. Not even anything broken that they can find. She's being kept in hospital overnight, just to be on the safe side, but I think–" he hesitated "–I think that has more to do with the state she was in before the accident. And I thought...*we* thought it would perhaps be a good idea to get her out of the house for a while."

Away from her husband, Claire noted, but she simply nodded. "That's probably for the best."

"Simon, we really are following up every lead we can," Dave said.

The young man nodded gratefully. "I know you are, sergeant, and I think Dad knows it, too, really, only he feels so helpless. He's not used to feeling that way."

"One thing that was obviously very important to Jonathan was his filming."

Simon laughed shortly. "You can say that again."

"Could you tell us what cameras he actually had?"

"To be honest, I'm not sure I can. There were several, probably starting with one of those instant ones Mum bought him when he was little, only seven or eight I think. He wore the damn thing out in about six weeks, wasted a ton of that expensive self-developing film. So Dad bought him a 'proper' camera, non-digital, you know? I think he thought that would slow Jonathan down a bit, waiting for the pictures to come back from the developers, and that he'd lose interest and move onto another hobby."

"Another project?"

"Yes. But it didn't. It was the one interest in Jonathan's life that he never lost. He actually went and learned how to develop films himself. And then of course he moved onto digital models and then video. Over the years he got through quite a collection of cameras, old ones, new ones, using one model for weeks on end before chucking it aside in favour of another." Simon smiled sadly. "That much was true to character. Towards the end, I'd guess he had maybe four still cameras. Don't ask me why. I think they did different things but I wouldn't have a clue what. I think one of them is in his room now."

"And video cameras?"

"Two, I think. Neither of them is here, I'm pretty sure."

No. One of them is at Foregate Station. And the other is still missing.

"It would really help us if you could see your way to letting us have a look at the material Jonathan left here," Dave said. "Pictures, but mainly video."

"You don't really think that will do any good, do you?" Simon said swiftly, quickly adding, embarrassed by what had really been only a very mild outburst, "I... I'm sorry. It's just I never thought anyone else would be going through Jonathan's things so soon...so soon after..."

"I promise we'll take very good care of them and they will all be returned to you."

"Thank you," Simon said to Dave, though it had been Claire who had spoken.

"Tell you what, how about if I go and wait in the car while you go and get the films?"

"Good idea, ma'am," said Dave.

Claire said goodbye to Simon and returned to the car, shaking her head slightly as she walked. *Am I taking this too seriously? Am I taking it too lightly?*

* ~ * ~ *

In Jonathan's room, Simon and Dave collected together the tapes, discs and a small tin of memory cards from the shelves, and Simon dug out a large cardboard box into which they could be put for ease of transport. "You've got a lot of watching to do," he said dryly.

"I may have to get some help."

"Inspector Summerskill?"

"Oh, she's far too important for that."

Simon gave that small smile of his again. "What's it like

working for such an attractive woman? I mean—" again he shifted embarrassedly "—if you don't mind my asking."

"No, no, that's fine." In fact, Dave had found it an odd, even a difficult question, but he forgave the boy the minute he saw that abashed face. It really made him seem very young. "Is she attractive?" And as soon as the words were out, he knew that hadn't been the right thing to say.

"Oh, go on. Tell me you haven't noticed."

"I can honestly say it has never crossed my mind. But then I have only been working with her for a few days now."

Simon sat down suddenly on Jonathan's bed, his face turned away.

"What's the matter?"

He shook his head. "Sorry. It just, just hits me every now and again. Jonathan's gone. And it doesn't feel right to be laughing and joking about something when he isn't here. Dad'd have a fit if he knew."

Dave sat down next to him. "I think," he began awkwardly, "that's what he'd want." *And what a load of crap that is.* For all he knew Jonathan would have wanted Simon to be bawling his head off for the rest of the year. But that was the sort of thing you said, wasn't it? If Simon had been a young woman he'd have put his arm around her, just briefly, to comfort her. But he couldn't do that with another man. Could he? *Bloody stupid.* "We all deal with things like this in our own way. You in yours, and your dad in his."

"And Mum in hers."

"Yes. I'm sorry."

Simon studied his hands, clasped in his lap. "Mum's never been strong."

"Were she and Jonathan very close?"

"Jonathan was...never really close to anyone. But I suppose he was closer to her than to Dad."

"Did they get on, your dad and Jonathan?"

"Is that important? You're not suggesting anything, are you?"

Dave shook his head quickly. "No, of course not," he said. "Truth be told," he added after a minute, "I was thinking more of my own dad there. Father-son relationships can be tricky at the best of times, all things being equal. And straight."

Simon looked levelly at Dave. *His eyes really are astonishingly dark*. "You mean, did Dad mind that Jonathan was gay?"

"Yes."

"Do you think he'd be this upset now if he did?"

* ~ * ~ *

In the car, Claire winced at the size of the box that Dave eventually returned with and loaded into the boot. "That's going to keep you busy."

"Oh, I've nothing else to occupy my time with, apart from a case of double murder."

He climbed in, started the engine up and pulled away from the Wilsons' house.

"You might like to be careful, you know," Claire said eventually, as casually as she could manage.

"What about? Lugging huge boxes around or getting eye strain from watching all this lot?"

"No, I mean about Simon Wilson."

"What?"

"You can get too close to families involved in cases. Too...sympathetic."

A few seconds passed before Dave answered, his eyes fixed fast on the road in front of them. "I know that, inspector."

"Right. Course you do."

They drove on in silence for a couple of miles. "Drop me off at my place," Claire said. "I've had to put my car in for servicing and the damn thing's not ready yet."

"Sure. Where do you live?"

* ~ * ~ *

Ten minutes later, Dave was driving off and Claire was receiving a peck on the cheek from Ian and an amused, quizzical grin. "What?"

"So that's your new sergeant."

"Yes."

"Good looking, isn't he?"

"I can honestly say I haven't thought about it," she said dishonestly. Because of the expression on her husband's face she couldn't resist twisting the barb just a little bit further. "Do you really think he is then?"

"Hmm." Ian sat back down to a pile of exam coursework he was sorting through, and Claire watched him file the same one three times before he finally said, "So when are we going to have him round for dinner?"

Later that night, and having dealt with his own quota of examination work and administration, Richard sidled up to his boyfriend on the living room settee. "Starting without me?"

"What? Oh, no. This is work."

"Ri-ight." Richard poked around among the pile of DVDs Dave had in a haphazard pile by the side of the sofa. "Oh, you're joking! Couldn't you have spent your promotion money on something a bit racier than this? You know Stand Up stuff's a joke."

"Actually, I quite like the homemade feel to it," Dave said vaguely, not really taking in what Richard was saying. "Buffed muscle gods on sunny beaches are all very well but they're just not very realistic, are they?"

Richard squinted at what was happening on the screen. "And that is? My God, the size of that! You're not telling me that's all flesh and blood." He sidled up to Dave. "Now if you're after something truly homemade..."

Dave untangled himself from Richard's arms. "I really am working," he said. "The case we're on is connected with these. We had to go round to their studio."

"Really? What was it like? Hundreds of gorgeous, scantily clad men draped all over chaises longues, peeling grapes for each other?"

"More like an old newsagent's that had crawled off and died. And the most gorgeous man there was me."

"I can believe that."

"Gratifyingly prompt, but you didn't see the competition."

"Which still doesn't explain to me what you're doing with this lot."

Dave used the remote to switch the screen off and tried not to be irritated, and that wasn't just because of Richard's interruption. It was partly because he himself wasn't sure why all he wanted to do right then was watch these videos, when he had an attractive, definitely willing and undeniably real man literally to hand. But somehow he felt so...restless. "I dunno, Rich. The job's so hard sometimes, you know. Every now and again you just need a bit of fantasy, I guess."

"Well, if you want fantasy..." Richard leaned over still further, and Dave sighed, and went with the flow.

Chapter Sixteen

"Morning. You look bad."

"That's, 'Morning, you look bad, *ma'am.*' Although I prefer, 'Good morning, ma'am. How do you manage to look so fresh after only three hours' sleep in a night spent dealing with your youngest son's nightmares?" Claire slumped down behind her desk.

"My version has more punch," said Dave. "Here, I've brewed up already."

"Thanks. God that smells good, what is it?"

"Don't ask me. Richard gets it. Don't know what it's called, I just know it's better than the rotgut you were percolating here before."

Claire sipped gratefully on the mug he had handed her. "You should have tasted the foul brew Rudge used to have on the go before I arrived. And talking of arriving, what time did you get in?"

"A while ago," Dave said diplomatically. "Now, are you ready for the good news or the bad news?"

Claire closed her eyes. "Start me off with the good news."

"Ah. Wrong answer. Strictly speaking, there is no good news. The first piece of bad news, however, is that all of Jonathan's equipment has been thoroughly wiped of prints. None of his, none of anyone else's. A very thorough job."

Claire grimaced. "No surprises there at least. And what's the less bad news? Or is it less good?"

"Well, it is certainly more interesting. The recordings recovered were mostly of friends and family. Or maybe that should be *acquaintances* and family. It's just as we've heard: Jonathan filmed anything and everything, whether people were ready for him or not. You can tell it didn't please everybody. It would have driven me up the bloody wall. There were gaps in the recordings, though. Not necessarily unusual given the pretty tame stuff around them, but the lab techs are going to see if they can recover anything, though they're not holding out much hope. However—" he paused slightly for dramatic effect, but Claire forgave him because of the coffee. "It's the mobile phone that was interesting."

Claire perked up. "I didn't know there was a phone in with the cameras. Call record?"

"No. He hardly used it for that at all. What calls were logged were to Sean's phone. No, it was the pictures on it, which, if you think about it, was always going to be more important for someone like Jonathan."

"Yeah, but you're hardly going to get the quality of picture on a mobile that you could get on some of Jonathan's expensive stuff, are you? So what was the point?"

"Ah, but sometimes the medium is the message, isn't it? Yes, well," Dave admitted quickly, in the face of Claire's baffled and unimpressed expression, "I've been skimming one of Jonathan's media studies text books. Anyway, the point is these." He handed across a sheaf of papers. "Recognise anyone?"

Claire flicked through the photocopied enlargements. "Phil. And Mikey."

"Plus one or two of our other new friends from The Old Navigator, yes. All in the act of being whopped round the face by a mysterious figure in a hoodie. Your classic happy slapping."

"So it *was* that, at first, and Jonathan Wilson and Sean Flanagan were doing it. The little bastards. But why?"

"Art," said Dave simply.

"What do y'mean?"

Dave half closed his eyes. "I went to the library once when I was a kid."

"I'm impressed."

He continued, ignoring his chief's ironic interruption. "And they'd set up a screen showing this continuous film of feet walking. That's all it was– endless feet, walking, walking, never getting anywhere. Gave me bad dreams for a month, it did. And that was art. I know it was because one of the librarians told me."

"Well, I can sympathise with your poor mother if she had to deal with your nightmares," Claire said with feeling. She paused. "This was still while you were a kid, wasn't it?"

"Ish. Anyway, I'd guess that's what Jonathan's justification would have been if we'd ever had a chance to catch him at it. I doubt Sean would have been so hi-falutin', though. I'm guessing he was just in it for the laughs."

“And maybe he would have been the more honest one.”

“We could always talk to Mr Elijah again. If anyone’s going to understand this kind of thing it’ll be him.”

“I have a feeling we will be talking to Mr Elijah, but not any sooner than I have to. And anyway, you seem to be fairly up on these matters. Your artistic side, sergeant?”

“I can just about manage paint by numbers, ma’am.”

“Well, you’re certainly doing a good job of getting under Jonathan’s skin.”

“I think talking to Simon has helped me there. It’s just a pity—” Dave added after a fraction of a beat, with obvious suspicion that he might have been lured into saying something it would have been better he hadn’t “—that we haven’t got anyone like that we can talk to about Sean.”

“Isn’t it?” said Claire bluntly, draining her mug and putting it down on the desk. “Well, anyway, art or sheer bloody assault, what those two idiots did was nowhere near motive enough for a double killing, was it?”

Dave shook his head. “I wouldn’t have thought so.”

The door to the office swung open and Rudge leaned in. “Morning, inspector. Sergeant. You’ve got visitors.” He directed his attention at Dave. “Bit of a fan club starting already? Eileen will be jealous.”

“What do you mean, Jim?” Claire asked wearily.

Rudge stood back, ostentatiously well back, to reveal Phil Evans and Mikey Henderson standing uncertainly in the doorway.

"I'll let you get on, shall I? Claire, want to come for a coffee and leave these boys to it?"

"Thank you, Inspector Rudge," Claire said, getting up to show the two men in. "But I'll be staying here. Please, sit yourselves down."

"What's his problem?" said Phil bitterly after the retreating Rudge. "Was really keen at first to show us up here himself and then he starts with all that 'boys' crap."

"His boyfriend's thrown him over," said Dave. Claire shot him a look. "Well, that's what I always tell myself when someone's acting like they've got a bee up their—"

"What can we do for you gentlemen?" Claire swiftly interrupted. She stopped, finally noticing the appearance of the man in front of her. "Mikey?"

"It's nothing," Mikey flinched away from her inspection, but Claire reached out, took his chin lightly in her fingers and turned his face fully to the light. The bruise on his eye was a recent blue-black.

"By the canal," said Phil bitterly.

"But..." Dave began, but Claire silenced him. She knew what he was going to say. With Jonathan and Sean dead, the happy slapping should have stopped. But it hadn't. Indeed, judging from the evidence of Mikey's face it had got significantly worse. Although, on the other hand, he wasn't dead. "Okay, tell me what happened, Mikey."

Mikey sat wringing his hands. "I... I really don't... Can't we just..."

"Mikey." Phil's voice was strangely gentle, such a contrast to his appearance. "We've been through this. You have to tell them. It's not right and it can't be allowed to go on."

Mikey's hands were twisting endlessly in his lap, his attention wholly fixed on them. Without warning, he began speaking, and both Summerskill and Lyon had to draw their chairs in as unobtrusively as possible to be near enough to hear the softly spoken, hesitant words. "I... I was going home from the Navigator and this man jumped out at me. Started hitting me about. And then he left."

"Was that all? Didn't he say anything?"

Mikey shook his head.

"Well, can you describe him?"

"I...I couldn't see well. I'd had a bit to drink and it was dark." The man was close to tears. Phil knelt down by the side of his chair and reached out to hug him. Mikey leaned into him and buried his face in his chest.

"All right." Claire sat back. "Mikey, I'm sorry to have to put you through this but you really need to make an official statement."

Mikey was instantly frantic again. "Wasn't that it?"

"No, I'm sorry. We need to have an official written account taken that you can verify and sign."

"Phil!"

Phil soothed him, stroking the side of his face with one large, calloused hand. “I’ll stay with you. That is okay, isn’t it?”

Claire nodded. “Dave, can you set that up?”

“Yes, ma’am.”

Phil suddenly guffawed and all three of the other people in the small office turned to him, startled by the unexpected sound. He looked instantly apologetic, but also still amused. “You have to call her *ma’am*?” he exclaimed.

Dave shuffled awkwardly. “Well, yeah. It’s what we do.”

“I thought people only used that with the Queen.” He indicated Claire. “And she’s the only one here who isn’t.” He nudged Mikey, waited until he’d teased out the faintest hint of a smile. “Jesus. Why don’t you just call her *mistress* and have done with it.”

Dave quickly made his excuses and went to find a recording officer. “Actually,” Claire said to Phil while they were waiting, “I think I could live with mistress.”

With Phil and Mikey shown to the interview room, she and Dave considered what they’d heard. “So what the hell is going on?”

“Someone else picking up where Jonathan and Sean left off?”

“Wilson and Flanagan never actually hit anyone hard enough to mark them, let alone bruise them the way poor Mikey’s been belted.”

“So maybe the murderer?”

“But what’s the motive?”

“I don’t think Mikey’s telling us everything,” admitted Dave.

“That much is obvious. Go along after Kelley’s finished taking the statement. See if you can't get a bit more out of him."

"Oh, like one gay man to another? All members of the same club?"

"Like one good looking guy to a gay man. If he was straight I'd play the charm game myself but he's not, so you go and flash your knickers for a change and stop being so prickly."

Dave stood nonplussed for a second, considered and quickly recovered. "Fair enough."

Less than a minute after he had left, Jim Rudge sauntered back into the office. "Suppose we've got to get used to the Village People conventions around here now."

"What do you mean, Jim?" Claire asked, knowing the answer already.

Rudge cocked a finger at the door. "That one, dressed like a trucker with all the tattoos. That his thing, is it? All macho when really he's a—"

"He is a trucker, Jim. Or a long distance lorry driver as we call them in this country, on this planet. And at the moment he's helping a frightened mate give evidence about a nasty assault. And maybe helping us get to the bottom of a double murder."

"Yeah. Right. *Friend.*" Rudge left, laughing knowingly.

When Dave came back twenty minutes later, he shook his head. "Mikey's a wreck. It was as much as he could do to get through the interview. He'd never have made it without Phil there. I doubt he'd even have come in the first place if Phil hadn't made him. He didn't have anything else to add."

"All right." Claire stood up and reached for her jacket. "Too much to think the day was going to start with a gift from heaven. Time to get down to some basic plodding." Distractions over for the moment, at least she hoped, and her system charged up nicely on Dave's coffee, Claire mentally recapped the agenda for the day as she'd seen it setting out that morning. And there was the one item at the top of the list that she'd thought best to get out of the way first, wasn't there? She paused a moment, couldn't help glancing to the door to see if anyone was there—Jim Rudge specifically—and was annoyed with herself for doing it, so that when she spoke it was with a defiant volume that gave a curious formal stiffness to her words. "Oh, and by the way, are you doing anything tomorrow night?" She hurried on before Dave had time to put words to the startled expression on his face. "My husband thought you might like to come round for a meal." *Christ, now I really do sound like the bloody Queen.*

"Oh, right. No. I mean, no, I'm not doing anything."

He was less tongue-tied dealing with Jim!

"And yes, I'd...love to come," he added, just a beat too late.

Yeah. And you look like you'd rather swallow nails. "Good." *Shit!*

They headed down the stairs. Claire pressed on, resolute in her determination. "And not just you. Bring your boyfriend."

"He's... Right. Thank you. I will."

"Great."

Summerskill and Lyon left the building, both looking as if they had been summoned to a disciplinary hearing.

Chapter Seventeen

"So what do I call her?"

"I dunno. Claire, I suppose. Follow her lead."

"And what are you going to call her? You're not going to say *ma'am* all evening, are you? It'll be like an audience at Buckingham Palace."

"Yeah, that has been pointed out to me, thank you very much." Dave gripped the bottle of wine they had grabbed at the last minute from their corner shop as if it was a talisman. "I've not really thought about it. This is the first time I've been invited to dinner with a boss—well, I mean without other coppers around. And all my bosses before have been men."

"Well, like I always say, you know where you are with men," said Richard. "You'll just have to follow her lead, won't you?" he added with false brightness.

"Right." Dave tapped the wine bottle he was carrying nervously against one thigh. He wanted to ask if Richard thought it was a good choice. Richard knew about wine like he knew about coffee, but Dave didn't want to give away how on edge he actually was about this evening meal with Claire Summerskill. It would be all right, he told himself, gripping the bottle even more tightly.

They'd been getting along fine these past few days, hadn't they? What could go wrong? He closed his eyes and, without realising it, grasped the bottle with his other hand, too. Now that was about the most stupid thing he could have thought.

In Claire's bedroom, the floor and bed were covered in blouses, skirts and trousers. Claire was changing her clothes. For the fourth time. "Sod it! How difficult can this be?" Meetings with sergeants, fine. Meals with friends, fine. But meals with sergeants? And their boyfriends? "Do you think this is okay?"

Ian didn't even bother to come into the bedroom from the landing to see. "I don't know what you're worrying about," he said in a peeved voice. "Given the nature of our guests, isn't it me who should be worrying about my appearance? Honestly, Claire, you could have told me."

"I did tell you," said Claire, struggling to get into a casual little number it had taken her ages to find and which had apparently gone and shrunk since last she'd worn it. Dave and Richard were due any minute.

"No, I mean more than half an hour beforehand."

"Why? What difference would it have made? Would you have whipped up something different for dinner? Is there some gay food code I don't know about?"

"You tell me. You're the one with gay colleagues."

"Haven't you heard what number one son has to say about Bob

Anthony in the drama department?"

"Wha's a gay kleeg?" said Sam running in under his father's arm and dashing up to his mother.

"Colleague, numbskull. And nothing for you to worry about," said Claire, sweeping him up and roughing his hair in the way that always made him giggle and always gave her an absurd rush of happiness and pride. "And you are supposed to be in bed by now." She looked accusingly at Ian. "I thought he was supposed to be in bed by now."

"Ah right, that must be the one hundred and first thing I haven't got round to yet. Hang on, I'll just go and finish dinner, lay the table and put out the cat and then I'll be right on it."

The doorbell rang. "Shit, that's them." Sam gave a squeal of delight at his mother's delicious profanity. Claire was too flustered to even attempt to rectify the damage to his young mind. "Thanks, love. You do that. I'll go and be the charming hostess." She raced halfway down the stairs, then stopped. "Where's Tony?" She upped the volume. "Tony? Where are you?"

"He's in his room finishing his homework," Ian said. "That is, he's in his room, wired for sound, sitting in front of his homework. He won't hear you. Don't worry," he forestalled her. "I'll unplug him and have him brought down for you in a minute."

"Thanks, love. Love you!" She stopped in front of the hallway mirror and gave her hair one last pat. *This is bloody ridiculous.* Then she opened the door. "Hello. Glad you could make it."

"Hi. This is Richard. And I think you know me. And this is a bottle of wine."

"Nice to meet you. Oh, very nice. Come in. Throw your coats down there." She took Richard's hand. "I'm Claire."

Richard shook hands and shot Dave a smug glance that made it clear at least he now knew how to address his boyfriend's boss through the evening, even if his boyfriend didn't.

"Come on through. Have a drink. Ian's just putting our youngest to bed."

"Already done," said Ian from the doorway. "Hi. I'm the husband." He shook hands.

"That was quick. What did you do? Cosh him?"

"Nah, Tony's putting him down."

"Tony?"

"Yeah. He's quite good at it, actually. Does it a couple of times a week for me now. Sam says he likes Tony's stories better than mine."

"Oh."

Dave couldn't have failed to note Summerskill's surprise at that, which she hadn't been able to hide. "Like the pinny." He nodded to the plastic pinafore with a picture of a French maid on it that Ian was wearing.

"Oh, right," Ian took it off, as flustered as if found wearing a real French maid's outfit. "It's Claire's."

"It's *ours*."

"Gift from the mother-in-law. She hates me."

"She loves you."

"Drinks?"

Claire slapped the bottle Dave and Richard had brought into Ian's hand. "Just as soon as you can get a corkscrew into that."

Ian lifted the bottle to better see the label. "Nothing fancy tonight food-wise, I'm afraid." Dave winced, as if he'd misjudged the wine. "Not that you have fancy food all the time, I expect," Ian added. "At this time of the week, I mean," he went on. "It being Wednesday. And all," he concluded.

"This one'll eat beans from a tin," said Richard indicating Dave. "But you're right, we generally neither of us have time for much fancy food during the week."

"You work, too, then?"

"Er, yes."

"You're not in the police as well, are you?"

"God no!" Richard gave a quick apologetic mile to Claire who gave a brittle hostess laugh. "I'm a teacher."

"Are you? Me, too. Claire never said."

"Dave didn't say you were, either." Dave and Claire exchanged vaguely apologetic gestures. "Where do you teach?"

"Monastery High. I'm an art teacher."

"Right. I'm at one of your feeders. Apple Orchard."

Ian, Claire was relieved to see, was actually relaxing slightly. Familiar ground had been found quite quickly after all. "What's your subject? You have to be pretty much all-rounders in the junior sector, don't you?"

Richard laughed with just the expected hint of bitterness.

"Yeah, pretty much. My specialism's languages but I get less and less of a chance to do any these days."

Ian nodded knowingly, professional to professional. "Squeezed out by the national curriculum, eh?"

Richard nodded. "Right, plus I got made deputy head last year and the admin takes up more and more of my time."

The smile that Ian had been relaxing into froze just a little round the edges. "Deputy head, eh? Gosh. Pretty young for that, eh?"

"Not that young," Richard said self-deprecatingly.

Younger than Ian, Claire couldn't help noting. "All right, now why don't you all go and sit down?" she said. "Dave, there's a corkscrew on the table. Put it to some use. I'll just go and see if Tony's finished and then we can get stuck into the food."

Claire left her husband with their guests and dashed up the stairs at her customary pace, only slowing when it struck her that perhaps it wasn't really the way a gracious hostess should behave. A quick peek into Sam's room showed that, miraculously he was already asleep. *Tony's good!* She offered up a silent prayer Sam would remain like that until at least six o'clock the next morning. She didn't know what Ian was letting him watch on the telly when she wasn't around but something had been giving him bad dreams for the last few nights. She moved over to her other son's room.

"Tony!" She rapped on the bedroom door. Not so long ago she'd simply have marched in and insisted that he tear himself away from whatever game he was playing or music he was listening to and come down for his food. But then there'd been the incident which had embarrassed them both hugely and reminded her that her little boy was fast growing up, and since then she'd always knocked before entering his room. She'd come across some pretty grim sights during her time on the force, but she never wanted to face what she'd faced that time. Mind you, they both knew she never waited long after having knocked, so whatever he was doing had to be tidied up pretty damn quickly or else. "Come on love, time for tea." There was an unintelligible muffled grunt from within the room. Fair enough, that was a signal she could enter. If Tony had really not wanted her in, his declamation would have been a lot clearer. She opened the door.

Her son was at his desk. And much to her surprise he did appear to be working. "What you doing, love?"

"History."

She waited for some development of that. There was none. "Sounds interesting."

"'S all right."

"Well, books away and come on down for tea. We've got guests, remember?"

Tony slumped forward over his books and there came a muffled exclamation that Claire chose not to hear clearly.

"C'mon, Tony."

Tony raised his head though his body somehow contrived to remain slumped. "Guests. A dinner party. This is so middle class, Mum!"

Claire reached over and switched off the anglepoise lamp on her son's desk. "What've you been doing in history? Marx? We are middle class, love. Hell, isn't it? "

Tony remained seated at his desk. "I'll never get this bloody essay finished if I have to keep coming down for guests every five minutes. And shouldn't it be dinner or even supper, not tea? Only common people have tea at this time of night."

"That's 'cause we're middle class *and* we're common. Think of it as a concession to our working class roots. And don't swear," she added with barely conscious maternal double think. She knew full well Tony would use worse language with his friends, and that she did with hers, too. The boy rose with deliberate reluctance from his desk. "And Tony," she added as she automatically dusted the shoulders of his T-shirt with one hand. She stopped, unsure of what to say. "Dave and Richard are gay, right?" she said finally. "It's no big deal."

Tony rolled his eyes, pushing back the unfashionably long hair that, frankly, still rather surprised her. "I know it's no big deal, mum," he said with teenage world-weariness. "I have told you about Mr Anthony, haven't I?"

"Yes. Yes, you have. Though I'm sure that's not true. Now get on downstairs with you. And be perfectly charming."

Tony squirmed past his mother's busy hand. "Why? Isn't this Dave your flunky? Shouldn't he be crawling to me?"

"If he does I'll get rid of him tomorrow. And he is not my flunky. You are. Now hop it."

"I'd hate to work for you."

"You already do, you just don't get paid for it. Move!"

Downstairs in the dining room, the wine had been opened and poured and conversation was occurring though Claire couldn't fail to notice the gratitude on her husband's face when she walked in followed, eventually, by Tony. "I'll just go and get the starters," he said, leaping out of his seat.

"This is my oldest, Tony," Claire said.

Tony bobbed his head and muttered something unintelligible before taking his place at the table. "Napkins?" he said with faint incredulity.

Claire turned to Richard. "So tell me all about yourself," she said, with a breeziness to cover her son's scorn.

"Can I have some wine?" Tony asked.

"No."

"Wow." Richard laughed. "Is this like a police interview?"

"If it was," said Claire, "you'd have been cautioned."

"Like I've been," Tony muttered.

"And I'd be operating the tape recorder," Dave added.

"You?" Richard snorted. "You can't even get the CD to change discs at home."

"Yeah, well, you've got one of those fancy multi-disc things. Mine only took one at a time. Classic, you see."

"Starters." Ian pushed the door open with his foot and entered bearing a large tray. "Hope you like soup."

"Great."

"Definitely."

"What kind?" said Tony suspiciously and more prudently.

Richard distributed the bowls and the company got down to the pleasant business of eating and making small talk. "So who's the good cop and who's the bad cop when you two are interviewing?" Richard asked.

"It's not like that," Dave said quickly.

"I bet you'd make a good bad cop, love," Ian said. "If you see what I mean."

"There are procedures, Ian," Claire said.

"I can't imagine you interviewing hardened criminals," Richard said half-jokingly to Dave.

Tony snorted into his soup and ducked his head quickly when Claire glared at him.

"I can't imagine you tearing strips off a class of naughty nine year olds."

"You're a teacher, too?" Tony said from his side of the table. It was clear from his tone of voice that the news was just another downward step into the middle class hell he'd imagined.

"So how are you finding Foregate Station?" Ian asked Dave.

Dave hesitated, soup spoon halfway to his mouth. "Interesting," he said.

"Interesting?" Now it was Claire's turn to pause in the act of raising her spoon to her lips.

"Challenging," Dave amended.

"Careful." Richard laughed. "That sounds like education

speak. *That child demonstrates challenging behaviour.* Translated means, *he's a right little sod.* You know what I mean, Ian?"

Ian nodded, reluctant now to discuss schools. "I'll just go and see how the beef's doing." He winced as a sudden thought struck him. "You're not either of you vegetarians, I hope?" Both men shook their heads. "Good. Claire didn't really give me a lot to go on so I'm afraid you'll just have to take what's on offer." And he was gone back into the kitchen before his wife could respond to that.

"So which school are you at?" Richard asked Tony.

Tony stared at him as if he'd been asked to enlarge on his sex life.

"Monastery Grove," his mother supplied quickly as Tony ducked his head again and focused determinedly on his empty soup bowl. "Same as Ian."

Richard nodded. "Good school." Then, after a pause, "Good headmaster."

"I've never met him."

"Good man. Bit tricky going to the same school as your dad, though?" he added to Tony.

"Ian's not my dad."

"Oh. Right."

"I'll just go and see if Ian needs a hand."

"Stay! If he needs a hand, he'll call for you." Tony subsided back into his seat and his mother smiled deliberately around the table. She lifted her glass. Now would be a good moment to say something welcoming and diverting. “Cheers,” she said finally.

Ian, Claire was pleased to note, had taken no chances with the meal. The rare occasions they had had people round for a meal—and, now she thought of it, they had almost always been colleagues of his rather than of hers—had always brought out the amateur chef in him, and armed with a selection of TV chef cook books, he’d often slaved away producing meals of a complexity that gave rise to much discussion if not actual appreciation. But tonight he’d served them up a simple roast that might have sat on their table any Sunday, when she wasn’t on duty. Both of their guests seemed to enjoy it anyway. It certainly put a hold on conversation for a while.

“All right if I go and watch telly now?” Tony said on finishing his meal, significantly ahead of the rest of the table, picking up the napkin from the floor where it had lain most of the meal, and beginning already to rise from his chair.

“There’s pudding yet, mate,” Ian said.

“No,” his mum said more pointedly.

“But it’s *Star Trek*!”

“Like you haven’t seen it a million times before. You should have set the video.”

“Don’t worry, Tony,” Richard said. “If you miss an episode, you can always ask Dave to lend it to you. He’s got all of them.”

“Not quite all of them,” Dave demurred.

“All of them, and they’re in order on the shelves,” Richard

corrected.

"D'you like science fiction?" Tony asked cautiously.

"Yeah, I guess so."

"So..." Tony was obviously struggling with his own assumed indifference. "What's your favourite TV science fiction?"

"Well..." Dave leaned back and Richard gave a pantomime groan. There followed an enthusiastic swapping of titles and opinions that quickly left the remaining three adults at the table way behind. Claire sat and watched her oldest finally talking reasonably and sensibly with an adult who wasn't a member of the family. And she watched Dave, too, who seemed no less relieved than her son to have someone he could talk to easily and openly. She remembered him in The Old Navigator, talking easily, making friends. He was good at it. Better than she was. Maybe she *was* the bad cop. Odd thought, that. Odd that she should compare his behaviour with her son to that with a load of potential suspects in a gay pub.

"I blame *Doctor Who* myself," said Richard when he could finally find a gap in the talk between Tony and Dave. "Single man, good sense of humour and own home. Travelled round the universe with a succession of beautiful women and never kissed one of them. He had to be gay. What?" Both Tony and Dave were giving him a pained expression. "What?"

"I always preferred westerns myself," said Ian.

"Did you?" said Claire with genuine surprise. "Do you?"

"Right. You still haven't seen *Brokeback Mountain* yet,

though, have you?" Tony guffawed. Dave raised his own hitherto neglected napkin to his lips to hide a smile.

"What?"

The ice cream out of the way, Tony was finally allowed to escape the table and return to his room. Claire had no doubt they would see nothing again of him that night. "I'll just load up the dishwasher," she said, rising herself, "and then we'll go and sit down in the living room."

"I'll give you a hand," said Dave. Together they carried the dishes and glasses through into the kitchen and Claire started loading up the machine. "He's a nice guy. Richard, I mean," she said.

"Thanks. So's Ian."

Claire hesitated fractionally as she arranged the glasses on their washer tray. "Thanks," she said, just a bit more shortly than she'd intended. "So how long have you been together?"

Now it was Dave's turn to hesitate fractionally, as if surprised by the question. "Getting on for a year, I suppose."

Suppose. "Getting on for an anniversary then?"

"Yes. Yes, I suppose so."

There it was again. "Try not to forget. If Richard's anything like Ian he won't let you live it down quickly. One thing teachers are good at is remembering dates."

"I guess I'll soon find out."

"Right."

Dave picked up a tea towel as if he meant to do something with it. "I suppose it's because I don't really think of us as being 'together' as such," he said quickly.

"You live together, don't you?"

"Yes. But that's sort of happened because of my transfer here. It made more sense to move in with him rather than rent until I knew... Well, you know."

Claire nodded. *Until he knew if things were going to work out for him at the new station.* She ought to say something encouraging at this point, she knew she ought.

"Ah, right."

Dave replaced the dish cloth. "Tony's a nice lad."

"Thank you."

"And you've got another?"

"Yes, Sam. He's four."

"Nice."

"He's Ian's son."

"Right."

Claire wondered why she'd felt she had to say that. She didn't normally make a point about her sons' fathers. Why did it feel as though she and Dave were tiptoeing through a minefield?

They both cast around the room for something, anything else they could load into the machine.

"I've been thinking about the case," Dave said quickly.

"Good!" Claire replied in a rush. "Me, too. So, share."

"The tendency's always to see the victim as—well, a victim, right? Especially when they're young guys like Jonathan and Sean.

And yes, okay, maybe I've been too ready to see the gay guys in the set-up as victims, too."

"But?"

Dave leaned back against the sink, more comfortable now than he had been at any other point of the evening, except when he'd been discussing sci-fi with Tony. "But the more we learn, the more Jonathan in particular seems to have been a pretty nasty little shit. Apart from his family, only his tutor, Elijah, had anything good to say about him."

"I wouldn't say that the family's attitudes are exactly straightforward."

"Except perhaps for Simon."

"Do you think Elijah fancied Jonathan?"

"Maybe."

"So, putting aside for a minute Sean's role in all this, what is a college kid like Jonathan going to have done that pissed someone off badly enough to want to kill him?"

"Or to have him killed."

"Possibly."

"What does it always come back to with Jonathan?"

"The filming."

"The filming."

"Maybe he filmed something he shouldn't have."

"Maybe."

"But then why Sean as well?"

"Perhaps they shared more than just bodily fluids."

"Could be. And thanks for that image just after supper. Or tea," she added, thinking back to her earlier conversation with her eldest. She gestured for Dave to move to one side so she could get at the fridge. "So what we've established is we've still not got any real idea who's done this and now we're even less sure about possible motives."

Dave nodded slowly. "That," he said, "is about the size of it."

"Great. Fill the kettle. I think we need a coffee after all that hard detective work." He dutifully did as he was told, and she saw his small expression of surprise as she took the packet of ground coffee from the fridge. "Yes," she admitted, "it's the brand you brought to the station."

"Richard'll be happy."

"Ian definitely is."

Dave smiled. "Suppose we'd better not be too much longer out here," he said.

Claire laughed as she ladled coffee into the cafetière. "Why? Ian knows you're not going to try to make a pass at me out here. Or are you worried he might make one at Richard?"

"Never let me stand between a man and his wish to experiment."

Claire pulled a face. "Oh, don't worry. Ian's hardly what you'd call the experimental type. Not," she added hurriedly, "after a full day of work and two glasses of wine."

"Ah, but you know what they say about the difference between a straight man and a bisexual?"

"No."

"It's about three pints of lager."

There was just a fraction of a second of confused guilt. This was her husband they were talking about. Dave was a sergeant and she was an inspector. But then she and Jenny had shared enough ribald comments about the men in their lives before. But then Jenny was another woman. But then... *Oh, sod it.* Claire laughed.

"Actually," Dave continued, "I was more worried about there being the most awful silence back there as they tried to find something to say to each other that wasn't about schools."

Claire paused in her coffee making. "I'm sorry," she said with brutal honesty. "Have I cocked it up? I'm not really very good at this gracious hostess crap. To be blunt, it was something I thought I had to do."

Dave nodded ruefully. "I kind of thought this was a line of duty sort of thing," he admitted. "But no, honestly, you have not cocked up. Not at all. It's been...nice, thank you. Trust me, a million times better than the evening I had to sit through a couple of weeks ago with Richard's colleagues. Three hours of sitting in a pub listening to a bunch of teachers talking about the National Curriculum and their workloads."

Relieved, Claire lifted up the loaded coffee tray. "We're not much better, are we? Hold the door for us."

As expected, Ian and Richard had decamped to the living room, but unexpectedly Ian had not made straight for the television as Claire had feared he would, and the two of them were not sitting in awkward silence as Dave had suggested. Indeed, their conversation sounded quite animated.

"Yes, well, if I'd let Claire have her way the whole room would be beige. I wanted to go for something with more of a Mediterranean vibe instead of feeling like we were living in a flour sack all the time."

Dave turned to Claire. "They're discussing décor," he said.

"I just said I liked the curtains," Richard said defensively.

"It's the art teacher in him," Claire said putting the tray down. She smiled sweetly at her husband. "Or is there something you'd like to tell me, love?"

"I just said..." Ian began, a little hotly, when the telephone rang. "I'll get it." He crossed to the phone and picked it up. Claire watched him even as she poured out the coffee, and wasn't surprised as, without a word, he held it out to her. "DCI Summerskill? When? Where? Okay, we'll be right there." She put the phone down and addressed Dave. "Mikey Henderson. He's in hospital. Assaulted as he was walking home."

"Again? How bad is it this time?"

"Worse. He's shaken up but he'll live. Heavy bruising, suspected broken rib."

"Attempted murder?"

"Don't know. But definitely not happy slapping." The pair paused, suddenly aware of their respective partners again. She felt like a schoolkid caught discussing something dirty. Ian and Richard were regarding them in startled silence. "We've got to go out," said Claire shortly.

Richard sat up, and Claire at least could clearly read his body language: he was waiting for Dave to challenge her peremptory assumption of authority over him when he was off duty. "I'll leave you the car," Dave said. "You're okay getting home by yourself?"

"Er, yeah. I suppose so." Richard shrank back down into his chair.

"You're going? Now?" Ian said with a slight touch of alarm.

"We have to."

"But surely..." Ian began.

"We have to talk to this man as soon as he wakes up, love," Claire explained patiently. She bent over him in his chair and pecked him on the cheek then strode out purposefully into the hall to find a coat. "I'll try to get back just as soon as I can," she called back to him.

Dave leaned down and kissed Richard on the lips. "Me, too. I'll come straight back to the flat. Shouldn't be too late."

"Right."

Ian sighed as the two police officers headed out of the front door into the drizzly night. "Claire always says that, just before she does one of those stakeout things. It usually means I don't see her until at least nine the next night."

Glum and bemused by the speed in which an evening out with his boyfriend had somehow turned into an evening in with a man he'd only met a couple of hours ago, Richard asked, "D'you reckon there's like an official book they get given? *Excuses to Give to*

Partners Back at Home?" He accepted the coffee cup that Ian handed to him. "If there isn't, maybe we should write it."

The two men settled back into their chairs, sipped their coffee and contemplated just how they were going to end this evening. "So, where did you get those curtains from, anyway?" said Richard eventually.

Worcester City Hospital was large, modern and almost impossible to park at. By the time Summerskill and Lyon had located Mikey in the ward to which he had been taken, Claire was all but spitting blood at the delays. Neither of them was surprised to find Phil at Mikey's bedside. The big man raised his head as they entered, nodded as if in acceptance of something he expected, then turned back to the figure prone on the bed. His big hands were knotted together, the thick gold rope chain round his bull neck glittering faintly in the dim light of the room.

"How is he, Phil?" Claire asked.

"Sleeping." Phil stopped, cleared his throat and continued. "The doctors've given him something to make him sleep. They reckon he'll come round by morning. They've taken scans of his head and things, but they say it's all good." He snorted—a bitter laugh that had nearly become a sob. He stared miserably at Mikey's beaten and already badly swollen face. "They kicked him. When he was down. I'd have killed them." *No you wouldn't*. Dave watched him sitting by his lover's bedside. *Not you.*

"*They*, Phil?" Claire probed gently.

"I don't know who," Phil said with weary anger. "I wasn't there, right? There's no point in asking me questions. If I had been there this wouldn't have happened, would it? But it's got to have been the same bastards who did this before. The same ones who killed those two lads." All the time he spoke his eyes were fixed on the unconscious figure in the bed.

"Why do you say that, Phil?" Dave asked quietly.

"Well it's got to be, hasn't it? Isn't that what you're thinking? Isn't that why you're here?"

"Do you know what happened? I mean, did you...find Mikey?"

Phil shook his head. "No. I got a call. From his parents, would you believe? They haven't spoken to him for years but they were the ones who got the call from the hospital. Not here, you'll notice. At least they called me. Didn't even know they still had my number."

"And he hasn't said anything?"

"Of course he hasn't said anything!" Phil exploded, subsiding just as quickly. "I'm...sorry."

Dave walked over and put a hand on his shoulder. "It's all right, mate. I think we can guess how you feel. It's just that we have to ask these questions. No matter how stupid they might seem." Phil just nodded, rubbing furiously at his eyes.

Claire rallied round. "Phil, how long have you been here?" The big man started to answer the question, but found he couldn't. "Right. If Mikey's not waking up till the morning there's no point in your staying here, is there?" Both Phil and Dave regarded her reproachfully. "Right. Sorry. Well, have you had anything to eat or drink? Have they given you anything?"

"I don't want anything," Phil said leadenly.

"Maybe, but you need something. Sergeant, hop to it."

"Wha...? Oh, right. Ma'am."

With just a quick glance to check that Phil had picked up on his use of title and a reassuring smile, Dave left the side ward in search of vending machines. Summerskill was right: it would be good to have a cup of something, but he'd kind of thought she'd let him stay and talk to Phil, gay man to gay man. He'd forgotten the lot of sergeants throughout the ages was to keep their bosses supplied with coffee and sandwiches.

Great play had been made of Worcester Hospital's newness, size and modernity when it had been built, and quite rightly, too. But as he toured the corridors and stairwells in search of anything resembling a drinks or snack machine, Dave became increasingly convinced the architects had been at least partly maze builders. Huge signs directed him firmly in directions that quickly became circles, and a helpful system of coloured lines painted along the floor directed him smack into gurneys, piles of furniture and even, on one occasion, into a darkened, unused operating theatre.

As he was walking down one corridor for what he was convinced was the third time in quick succession he was unexpectedly hailed by an uncertain voice. "Sergeant Lyon?"

He turned to see Simon Wilson standing by an open door. "Hello, Mr Wilson. Simon."

Simon walked towards him, smiling, but Dave noted the uncertainty of the gesture, saw how the cold white strip lights of the hospital corridor accentuated how thin the young man's face had become, how they threw the shadows under his eyes into relief. "What are you doing here?" Simon said "Or am I not allowed to ask? Is it official?"

"Actually, yes it is." Dave briefly considered saying it was connected to Jonathan's murder, lest Simon think that they'd already abandoned that, but then realised he couldn't. They still didn't know for certain if it was. "How about yourself?"

Simon bit his lip. "My mother," he said simply.

Dave could have kicked himself. He'd assumed that by now Mrs Wilson would have been released from hospital but obviously not. "How is she?"

Simon hesitated. "Fine. I mean..." He drew a hand through his hair. Dave noticed it was trembling slightly. "Physically she's fine. No real damage to speak of. It's just...the things she's saying."

"What things?"

Simon took a deep breath. "She insists that she wasn't...that she wasn't trying to kill herself."

"Well, that's good, and to be honest probably true. I don't mean to sound crass, but people who are trying to kill themselves don't normally do it by crashing their cars. Too uncertain."

Simon gave a brittle laugh. "And too costly. I think she knows Dad would never have forgiven her for ruining a car. Cars are the basis of the family fortune, you know. No, it's the way she talks about the accident. That it shouldn't have happened. She'd taken more of her pills than was good for her, she knew that, but she keeps saying not that many."

Simon stopped and Dave realised there was a subtext to the young man's words that he hadn't been picking up on. "I don't quite follow you."

Simon took a deep breath. "I think she's trying to say that it wasn't an accident at all."

"What, you mean that somebody did something? To the car?" Dave had thought Simon was worried about something when he'd first seen him tonight. Now, on closer inspection, he realised he was quite possibly scared. "Your mother's been through a difficult time," he said slowly. "She's very shaken up by what's happened to Jonathan and to her. You can't expect her to be..."

"And there are the men," Simon said in a rush.

"What men?"

"I think I'm being watched. Two men. I've seen them three times now. Outside the house, once when I was in town, and tonight outside the hospital. Just now." Again he ran his hand through his hair and this time there was no mistaking the tremor of it. Up until now Dave had thought of Simon Wilson as the rock of his family, the strength that his irascible father and fragile mother could draw on. Now Dave was forcibly struck by how frighteningly fragile the remaining Wilson son appeared himself. "I'm sorry but I don't know what's going on."

"You've nothing to feel sorry about, Simon." Dave caught himself in the act of reaching out to take the young man by the shoulders. Would that have been so wrong? It would just have been a gesture, a reassuring moment of human contact. There was no one about. He held his arms by his side, feeling unnaturally awkward. "You're in a bad place at the moment and it's our job to help you. I want you to come with me now to see Inspector Summerskill. But before that, what I really want—" he smiled at Simon, deliberately trying to lighten the moment "—is for someone to show me where the hell I can get a cup of tea or coffee." His ploy seemed to work. Simon gave a weak smile in return. "Come on then, lead the way." The two men moved off down the corridor side by side. "These men, did they follow you into the hospital?"

"No."

"How did you get here?"

"I drove."

"Okay, well, I'll get someone from the station to take you back home, so you won't have to worry about bumping into anyone then, and tomorrow we'll see about having someone keep an eye on your house."

"I don't think Dad will like that."

"We'll be discreet, I promise."

Simon stopped dead. "No, I really don't think Dad would like that. If he found out..." He didn't need to complete that thought.

Dave nodded understandingly. "Okay, well, let's see, shall we?"

"I don't suppose... I mean, would you be able to drive me home?"

"I... I can't. I'm sorry. Like I said, I am actually here on duty, pretty much until my boss says otherwise. Speaking of which, if I'm much longer finding this coffee DI Summerskill is going to tear...she's going to be very annoyed." He moved off again and Simon followed.

Simon gave Dave a shy grin. "Scared of a woman, sergeant?"

"Scared of an inspector," said Dave with feeling.

Simon swiftly and accurately led Dave to the nearest coffee machine which turned out to be only round the corner from where they had bumped into each other, which in turn was only a few feet from Mikey's room. "I swear they just installed this while I was talking to you," Dave muttered, while the machine, at great expense, poured out four cups of a brew that he just knew was going to be even more vile than the old station coffee he had insisted on replacing.

Claire Summerskill's eyebrows rose slightly when he re-entered Mikey's room with Simon in tow. "I bumped into Mr Wilson outside, ma'am," he said, adding quickly lest his boss should make the same mistake as he had, "his mother."

"Ah. Yes. Hello, Simon."

"And Mr Wilson thinks that he may have been followed."

"Two men, you say?" she asked once Simon had brought her up to speed with what he had already told Dave.

"Well, I only saw two men. There might have been more."

"Indeed. And can you describe them?"

Simon turned to Dave as if for support and he gave him an encouraging nod. "Not really. They were big men."

"Tall? Fat? Well built?"

"I... I don't know. I think one of them was wearing dark glasses."

"Can you lot take this out of here, for God's sake?" Phil hissed.

"Do these men sound like the ones who attacked Mikey the last time, Phil?" Claire asked.

"How the hell should I know? I wasn't there that time, either, remember?" Phil dragged his hands shakily across his face. "I'm sorry, mate," he said, directing his comment to Simon. "I didn't mean to snap like that. And I'm really sorry if your brother was one of... I am, I'm sorry. But this is...this is my friend, and he's been badly hurt. And right now I just want to sit quietly here and wait for him to come back to us. If that isn't too much."

"Of course not," said Dave.

Claire rose from her seat, putting her half-finished cup of coffee carefully to one side. "We'll be back in the morning. If anything happens before then, call us."

"What do you mean if anything happens?" Phil said quickly.

"I mean if Mikey comes round and wants to say anything."

Phil subsided into his seat. "Oh. Okay. Yeah, right. Good

night."

Dave held the door open for Simon and his boss. Just before it closed he saw Phil leaning over the bed to take hold of the unconscious Mikey's hand in a way he hadn't been able to while the others were there, too. Dave saw the big man's lips moving. He couldn't tell if Phil was talking to the comatose man or praying.

A swift call to the station secured a lift home for Simon and left Summerskill and Lyon free to make their way home. For a while they drove in silence, both wrapped in their own thoughts. Gradually, though, through his tiredness and gloomy thoughts, Dave began to sense something else in his boss's silence, seeping through the darkness. "Something wrong?" he finally asked.

Claire kept her eyes fixed on the road. "Bit of a coincidence, don't you think?"

"What?"

"Simon Wilson bumping into you like that in the hospital."

"Maybe. But his mother's ill and that's the main hospital. He had every reason to be there."

"Hell of a big hospital. Do you know what ward she's on?"

"We didn't get round to discussing it." With a conscious effort Dave reined in his irritation. "Are you trying to tell me something, ma'am?"

"I think," Claire said carefully, "maybe you could have a bit of...an admirer there."

Dave laughed, a short bark of a laugh. "Just because his brother was gay..."

"It's all genetic, isn't it? Isn't that what they say now?"

"Oh please!"

"I'm just saying be careful, Dave."

And do you tell the straight coppers to 'be careful' whenever they're interviewing pretty female witnesses? That was what Dave wanted to throw at Claire; it was on the tip of his tongue. And that was where the words stayed. Biting back at his boss would just dignify the idea she was suggesting. Simon was good looking, yes. And yes, Dave had picked up on that request, so casually made, for him to drive Simon home. But that's all there was to it. And he was being careful. Wasn't he? "Yes, mum," he said.

*

Claire signalled the turn into Dave's road. She could sense clearly enough the irritation he felt at her advice. Well, tough. He was her sergeant and would have to learn to take advice whether he liked it or not. It was important they should be upfront with each other. She thought back to the meal at her place that night, at her first sight of Richard. *And talking about being upfront...* "I've been meaning to ask you. About Richard."

"Yes?"

Now that was definitely prickly. Perhaps, after all, she had gone far enough for one night. "Nothing," she said, pulling the car up outside Richard's flat. "It'll keep."

Dog-tired, she drove back to her own home and a doubtless fast asleep Ian, reviewing as she did the conversation she'd just had with her sergeant. Had she gone too far? *Hang on a minute!* She jammed on the brakes at a nearly missed red traffic light. *Did he really call me* mum?

* ~ * ~ *

“Thought you’d be in bed by now.” Dave kissed his boyfriend as Richard held the front door open for him. “It’s what, two in the morning?”

“Three. But you know I can’t sleep when you’re not there.”

“You’ve got dependent quickly enough.”

“Yeah, well, you’re an addictive personality. So, what happened? Was it...okay?”

Dave felt Richard making an effort to curb his normal ghoulish interest in the darker aspects of his work. He should have been pleased, but in fact he was irritated. Maybe it was Summerskill’s patronising advice that had got up his nose. Maybe it was just because it was so late. Maybe it was because it felt like they were making no headway at all with this damn case. “It was okay. The guy who was beaten up was sedated. We couldn’t talk to him. But he’s got someone with him. He should be all right tomorrow. Well, he should be able to talk tomorrow.”

“Right.”

Dave could tell Richard didn’t know how to take that. ’Beaten up‘ was just such a vague and brutal thing to say. How did you cope with that? He knew he should have been more specific, more helpful. He threw himself down on the sofa and loosened his tie.

Richard stood uncertainly behind the sofa. "You coming to bed, then?" he said finally.

"In a bit. I feel a bit wired at the moment."

"You want some tea. Camomile. Help you relax. Or a drink?"

Dave shook his head. "You go on up. I'll be with you in a bit."

Without turning round to see, he felt Richard hesitate. "Okay." Richard bent over the sofa, Dave leaned back and the two men kissed. "Don't be long."

"I won't."

Dave reached for the remote and turned on the TV, muting the volume. He sat through quarter of an hour of some inane late night/early morning quiz show that only insomniacs or drunks back from the clubs would have watched, then quietly reached over to the pile of DVDs by the side of the set and slipped one in.

It was another hour at least before he was startled by the sound of the living room door opening and Richard standing blearily in his dressing gown. "If that was what you wanted you only had to ask."

Dave switched the set off. "It's work," he said.

Richard picked up the case of the video Dave had been watching. Without his contacts he wouldn't actually be able to make out the writing, but the pictures of the scantily clad lads on the cover made its contents clear. "Right." He tossed the case back on to the sofa, turned and headed back to bed without another word.

Dave sighed. *Right. Now I really am in the dog house.* But it had been work. *Mostly.*

He pulled a couple of cushions up and switched the TV back on. He pressed play. Two young men picked up from exactly where he had left them in a way he guessed you could if you were young and life hadn't yet started to get complicated, and you didn't have to worry about jobs. And relationships. And relationships *in* jobs...

* ~ * ~ *

"So, what did you think?"

There was a muffled sound from somewhere beneath the duvet.

Claire gave Ian a not too soft poke as she sidled up to him. "I said, what did you think?"

"An' I said I'm asleep."

"Well, you're not now."

With a weary sigh, Ian rolled over and faced his wife. "I presume you mean Sergeant Lyon."

"Yes."

"He seems nice. G'night." He made as if to roll back over again.

"Is that all?"

"What more do you want me to say?"

Claire lay back. Good question. She didn't know, though she had an obscure feeling there was something. "You got on well with Richard."

"He's all right."

"You have a lot in common, I suppose." Ian rolled over again and she could feel his eyes on her in the dark. *Got your attention now.*

"What's that supposed to mean?"

"Well, both being teachers and all."

Ian grunted "Right. Now go to sleep. This teacher's got a bloody full day tomorrow. Good night."

"Good night."

Claire lay back and listened to her husband's breathing settling into the softer, slower pattern that showed he had drifted off. The snores would probably come in a bit, but that was okay. She knew how to deal with them. She wondered if Richard and Dave were in bed now. Were they lying like this, side by side? Or were they wrapped up in each other's arms? She pulled the duvet around herself. There was a sleepy and involuntary protest from Ian which she ignored. Richard. Not at all what she had expected. But then there was a reason for that, wasn't there? She rolled over, back to Ian, dragging still more of the duvet away from her husband, and was asleep before he could even begin to protest.

Chapter Eighteen

"So, what do you think?"

"Sir?" Claire prevaricated, momentarily nonplussed by the open-ended nature of Superintendent Madden's question.

"About Sergeant Lyon. Still hankering after WPC Trent?"

"That isn't quite the way I would have put it, sir."

Madden leaned forward. "How is he shaping up, inspector?"

This, Claire realised, was more than just a casual, *what a lovely day we're having* kind of chat. "Well sir," she said, sitting up slightly more straight in her chair as she delivered what was essentially a report. "He's a good officer. He's bright. He's committed." She was on the verge of saying she couldn't have asked for a better new sergeant then remembered Jenny and her previous insistence, and bit her tongue. It wasn't really letting Dave down. She had only known him a short time. *Time to be glowing later. Maybe.*

"No problems among the men?"

She thought of Cortez and Rudge, as she knew Madden would have. "Nothing we can't handle."

Madden sat back "Good. I'm glad to hear that. Because from everything else I'm hearing, the case you're in charge of is dying in the water."

Right, so now we get to the real point of this call for a little chat. "We have several leads we're following up, sir. We..."

"Claire, don't give me bullshit." Madden spoke calmly. There might even have been the hint of a smile in his eyes. But this was reprimand. She knew it. And she knew she deserved it. She'd hated coming up with that spiel, so sitting still and keeping her mouth shut now was something of a relief.

"You are in a dead end, inspector. And what do you do when you're in a dead end?"

"You turn back, sir."

"Right. And reassess where you're going. Could it be you've let yourself get just a little too close to the picture? Maybe got yourself caught up in some of the more personal details?"

"Sir?"

"Talk to Chief Inspector Rudge. He might have something to tell you."

"You've been talking to Rudge about my case?" The words were out of her mouth and Claire was out of her chair before she had time to consider.

Madden remained unmoved and unmoving behind his desk. "I talk to all of my officers, Inspector Summerskill, as I am talking to you now. And I listen. Contrary to what some say, it's a good way to get on. Try it."

The first person she saw when she stormed back into their office was Dave Lyon. He was leaning over in his chair, retrieving something from the waste bin. She'd put money on its being his picture again. He opened his mouth to speak but quickly shut it again as she stormed past him to tower, as much as she could manage, over Rudge's desk. "What the hell have you been doing talking to Madden about my case?"

Rudge stopped his conversation with Cortez in mid-sentence. "Inspector?"

With an effort, Claire kept her voice as low and steady as she could. "Superintendent Madden said you had information that might prove useful to my case."

Cortez sidled back to his desk and chair with exaggerated discretion. Rudge didn't wink at him. Not quite. Claire felt the telltale rush of blood to her face and neck that had always given away her anger since childhood, and damned her temper even as she damned Rudge for provoking it. Behind her, she could sense Dave silently watching what was going on, in the dark as to the reason for his boss's outburst.

"First," Rudge began portentously, "I didn't go and talk to Superintendent Madden. We were discussing cases generally as you will find happens once you get to your rank, inspector. Second, I happened to mention something that I felt might have a bearing on the case which you and your sergeant—" he didn't bother to look across at Dave though Cortez did, and Claire couldn't decide if his expression was one of sympathy or was a downright smirk "—might have missed. You've got too close to the case, Claire. Sometimes you have to stand back a bit to see the wood for the trees."

Right. You haven't been discussing this, but you both happen to use the same turn of phrase when talking about it with me. She quickly pushed to the back of her mind the thought that this might have been because they were both, in fact, right. "So maybe you'd like to let me have the benefit of this important insight so that I can better go about my job?"

Rudge gave a nod to Cortez who rose, picked up a manila folder from his desk and handed it over to Claire. It had one name on it: *Robert Wilson*. "Jonathan Wilson's father is not exactly the clean-living businessman you may have been led to believe."

Claire flicked through the sheets of paper in the folder before handing it over to Dave. "Shady links. All right. He's a used car salesman made good, so what? I'd be surprised if he didn't know some dodgy people in that business."

"It's a bit more than that," Dave said softly as he, too, skimmed the slim dossier. He raised his head, caught Claire's glare and ducked his head back into the folder.

"As your sergeant says, inspector," said Rudge, not bothering to keep the amusement out of his voice, "Wilson has done considerably more than sail close to the wind for the last twenty years. He's been implicated in fraud, car theft, insurance scams and may have links to some of the biggest crooks this side of London."

"No convictions, though."

"Not yet," chimed in Cortez, "though London says that's only a matter of time."

"London always says that."

"Maybe," growled Rudge, "but there's evidence to suggest that his early retirement to our neck of the woods was just a cover for an actual acceleration of his dodgy dealings. Our man wasn't settling down, he was moving up."

"All right. So he's going to get nicked himself sometime in the future. Time comes we'll do it. Right now he's got a dead son. You saying we treat Jonathan Wilson's murder any differently because of who his dad was?"

"Don't be so bloody naïve, Claire," Rudge barked.

*

Under cover of studying the papers in his hand, Dave studied the two inspectors before him. He thought he was starting to get a handle on at least some of his new boss's moods. He'd quickly twigged what the flush in her face and neck meant, knew already the signs of her short temper. What surprised him was her reaction now to Rudge. She was red, her eyes were sparkling, but it wasn't fury. And that note in Rudge's voice. It wasn't anger, wasn't even the contempt that Dave himself was learning to accept as routine from his superior officer. It was genuine disappointment. He sighed inwardly. Relationships. At work and at home. Why were they so sodding complicated? "So, you're saying," he interjected, "that Jonathan's killing at least was connected to his father's criminal background? Maybe some 'business' rival trying to get back at Wilson senior?"

"You were right, then," said Claire, turning her whole body to Dave and deliberately away from Rudge. "You said this was all about someone being pissed off."

That wasn't quite what Dave had said and they both knew it. *A small repayment for a small intervention?*

"That still doesn't explain Sean, though."

"But if we are saying now that these killings were more premeditated than perhaps we've been assuming..." Dave pushed his chair back and jumped to his feet. "I'd like to have Mrs Wilson's car checked."

Claire frowned. "What?"

"Something Simon said, that his mother's been insisting she wasn't doped up enough to have come off the road. Maybe she wasn't."

"Another go at Robert Wilson, through his wife this time?"

"Or maybe even at Robert himself. Wrong car? Who knows?"

Claire gave a tight smile. "Do it."

Dave was out of the office without a backward glance.

*

"*Simon*, eh?" said Rudge, picking up a pen from his desk and toying with it as if he were just making casual conversation. "Like I said, Claire, sometimes you can get too close to a case. Too *involved*."

Claire abruptly leaned over Rudge's desk, fists balled on its surface, ready to tell him exactly what she thought about his insinuations and innuendos. And the words caught in her throat, because he'd not said anything that hadn't crossed her own mind, nothing she hadn't tried to suggest to Dave herself only the other day. "Thanks," she said, the word thick and difficult in her mouth. "For the help." She glanced across at Cortez, who would almost certainly have done the donkey work. He had the grace to turn to his computer screen rather than meet her eyes, though she was certain he had been smiling.

Inspector Summerskill stalked out of the office to find her sergeant.

~~*

Robert Wilson sat as if carved in stone in that same living room where they had first met him, and glared at Summerskill and Lyon like a basilisk. "I know you still haven't found out who killed my son, so why are you here again? And what the hell were those men doing round my car earlier this morning?"

"Dad?" Simon Wilson was at the door. He'd appeared again, without warning. *Almost like he comes running whenever he catches a glimpse of Sergeant Lyon*, Claire thought uncharitably.

"We've come to discuss something with your father," Dave said.

Simon closed the door and walked over to Robert Wilson, whose cold gaze remained fixed on the two police officers. He looked to Dave as if for further explanation.

Dave in his turn looked to his boss, and Claire knew what he was thinking. It was time for some plain speaking, and Simon might possibly be about to learn things about his father that Robert Wilson would have preferred him not to. *Well, tough,* Claire decided. "We wanted forensics to check out your car because we had reason to believe it might have been tampered with," she said.

"Reason to believe?" Wilson snorted. He turned to his son. "Do you know anything about this? You were the one who let them poke around it without telling me."

"We had to, Dad," Simon said quietly.

Wilson rounded on Claire. She could practically see the effort it cost him to address his comments to her rather than to her sergeant. She wondered briefly if that might be different if Wilson knew that her male colleague only fancied his other male colleagues. "So? Did you find anything?" he challenged.

"Yes, sir, we did." Claire said, and she couldn't deny to herself the pleasure she got from saying that. She nodded to Dave who opened his notebook. It was a bit of police showmanship, really, designed to remind everyone who was dealing with whom here. The facts had been simple and easily memorable, but Dave read them deliberately from his notes.

"There was clear evidence of tampering with the brakes. Connections had been loosened. By the time of our inspection the system was bled almost completely dry of hydraulic fluid. Anyone attempting to drive it would have noticed straight away that something was wrong. But at the time your wife took the car out, presumably only just after the interference had taken place, the leakage was less significant, enough though to affect the braking sufficiently to lead to your wife's accident." Dave snapped his notebook shut again. "Not enough, fortunately, to kill her."

"Tampering!" Robert Wilson snorted, though for the first time Claire thought she saw something other than belligerence. Was that a flash of anxiety? Worry? Fear even? "You talk about tampering, but it could have been a simple leak. Wear and tear. Nothing so out of the ordinary there."

"You are, I think, sir," said Dave, "not a man who takes his cars lightly. I don't believe you would have let any of your vehicles get to such a state that they would threaten the lives of your loved ones. And," he fixed Wilson squarely in the eye, not perturbed in the slightest by the cold glare he received in return, "our forensic boys are quite sure in their findings and very good at their jobs. Your car had been tampered with, sir. We can only assume with the intent to cause damage, injury or—" and he couldn't prevent a quick glance at Simon "—death. Your wife was lucky." Dave continued over the incredulous sound exploding from Wilson. "She must have driven out just after the loosening had occurred. It could have been a lot worse."

Claire upped the pressure. "And we understand your son has been followed recently by two men. Isn't that right, Simon?"

"What?" Wilson seemed genuinely startled. He turned to his son. "You...you never told me about this."

Simon fidgeted uncomfortably. “I didn’t want to worry you, Dad. I...”

“But you told the police!”

Claire saw Simon dart a hurt look at Dave, as if her sergeant had betrayed a confidence. But of course he hadn’t, and Simon couldn’t have expected Dave to keep quiet about something like that, could he? Although he probably wouldn’t have expected Dave to pass it on to Claire for her to use it as a weapon against his father. Robert Wilson might be a shit of the first water, and might yet turn out to be a crook to boot, but to Simon he was still his father.

“Who...? Who is doing this? Why?” And it was there again, the difference in Robert Wilson’s voice. *You’re not asking yourself who. You’re asking yourself who exactly.*

“Well, really, Mr Wilson,” Claire said with a calmness designed as much to provoke as soothe, “we thought you might be able to help us with that. Our inquiries are beginning to suggest there might actually be a large number of people who feel they have a grudge against you.”

“You’re supposed to be investigating my son’s death, not poking your noses into my...”

“Business rivals?”

Robert Wilson subsided. “I don’t... I don’t know...” There was a new expression on his face that Claire struggled to read, words on his tongue that Robert Wilson couldn’t bring himself to speak in front of strangers. *Or in front of his son, perhaps?*

Simon stood up suddenly as if eager to leave the room. "Sergeant Lyon, if...if you've got a moment I think I have some things that might be of use to you."

"I would like my sergeant here," Claire began, "to..."

"And I would like my son not to be present while I discuss this matter with you, inspector," Wilson said. It was presented as statement. It was, she saw, the closest he could get to a request and still save some face in front of Simon.

Claire weighed the options and finally nodded. "Okay. Meet me back in the car in ten minutes," she added as Dave went to leave with Simon. She faced Robert as the two young men left the room. He was still defiant, still angry, but some of that crest was more fallen than she'd seen it before. "Now then, Mr Wilson, I think it's time we were completely honest with each other, don't you?" *Well, it's a start even if neither of us believes it will actually happen.*

* ~ * ~ *

Outside in the hallway, just far enough away from the room they'd left to ensure they wouldn't be overheard, Simon abruptly stopped. He was pale. Dave thought he might almost have been trembling as if fighting with something inside himself. When he spoke, his voice was barely above a whisper. "I know, of course."

"Know what?"

"About Dad. Not everything. I mean, I know he's done more than just sell cars. It's obvious, really, isn't it?" He raised his hands slightly, his shoulders in a semi-apologetic shrug, as if indicating their surroundings: the house, its furnishings, its grounds. The sort of home that didn't come from flogging off cars, no matter how classic, from a parking lot. Yes, it was obvious, really, Dave considered bitterly. So obvious that it had taken Rudge to rub his and his boss's noses in it. How had that happened? Whatever the cause, he wasn't about to let that happen to either of them again. "But, well," Simon was continuing, "that's what happens, isn't it? I mean, in the real world. In business. It's just sharp practice, that's all. Hard to keep your hands absolutely clean. And it's not like he's killing people or anything. Not like he's a real criminal, like whoever...like whoever..." He stopped, took a deep breath. "He's a good man, sergeant."

"Dave. You call me Dave, yeah?"

Simon nodded, and instinctively Dave went to reach out, just to put a hand on his shoulder, a reassuring squeeze of the arm maybe. He really wanted to. He held back.

"Thank you. Dave." The two men stood for a moment in the hallway facing each other, caught in the bright light of the morning sun as it streamed through one of the windows. It was Simon who broke the moment. "Well, this isn't what I dragged us out here for," he said with a brittle levity. "As I said, I've got something for you. Do you want to come with me—" he gestured up the wide, sweeping staircase that led upstairs "—or...?"

"I'll wait down here."

"Right."

Simon ran quickly up the stairs and out of sight, leaving Dave to contemplate his surroundings and the last few minutes. He took in the many car prints, the artificial flower arrangements, the framed photographs—mostly of Robert Wilson in the company of people presumably famous in some field or other, hardly any of Mrs Wilson, none of either Simon or Jonathan after the age of about ten, and none at all of the family as a group—the china statuettes, the thick, bright red carpeting like that of a car showroom and one gold-plated model of some car or other from, he guessed, the 1930s. It was, he decided, all quite revolting.

As assiduously as he'd tried, Dave had been unable to completely avoid the plethora of 'style' programmes on the telly, hosted by mincing queens who would descend on some hapless household with exaggerated screams of disapproval and proceed to remodel it in a hellish version of their own concept of 'good taste'. As a red-blooded, card-carrying, completely committed gay man without a single style-conscious bone in his body, Dave had never been able to understand how it had become axiomatic that meant he should know instinctively about such matters. Richard had tried to explain it to him as postmodern irony, and he hadn't been able to understand that, either. To him, it might all just as well be the sort of stereotypical queer-bashing you could have seen in any Sixties or Seventies sitcom, only now the queers were bashing themselves. But maybe, he admitted now, he was finally getting the point. Certainly this house made him feel sick, but was that just because of what the style queens would have called the *ambience*? Was it the crushing unhappiness created by Jonathan's murder? Or was it down to something that went back further: the stifling malaise created by Robert Wilson's heavy-handed rule, maybe? What must it have been like growing up here? How had Simon managed? *And Jonathan*, he reminded himself. How had Jonathan managed?

He was brought out of his sombre thoughts by the sound of Simon's return down the stairs. He was carrying a small cardboard box, and Dave had a feeling he knew what was in it even before Simon said. "I found these," he said, placing the box carefully into Dave's arms.

As he'd thought, a small number of DVDs, maybe a dozen in all. "Jonathan's?" Simon nodded. "Where did you find them?"

"Out in the garage."

Dave gave the collection a quick once over, picked out one of the DVDs and examined the case. Yes, there was Jonathan's neatly printed numbering, and the number was a low one. So why had they been kept away from the rest? He dug down to the bottom of the box. No memory cards. Nothing in the format that Jonathan's latest cameras had used. Still, he was anxious to get them back to the station and in a player. "Thank you," he said.

"I'm just glad I can still help in some way."

Claire Summerskill burst through the door. "Ready to go," she said as she strode past Dave. It was a statement not a question. She threw a goodbye to Simon over her shoulder as she went.

"And how was Mr Wilson?" Dave asked when they were back

in the car.

"In something up to his red, leathery neck," she spat. "When we get back to the station, I want to find out everything we can about that man—where he's been, what he's doing and who he knows."

"We've got the info from Rudge," Dave ventured. Claire glared at him and Dave wisely turned his attention back to the box Simon had given him, taking out cases at random and examining them as if he could get some idea of their contents just by inspecting them, leaving his boss to her driving and apparent dark thoughts about station politics.

"Nothing. Twelve DVDs of nothing."

Dave shoved the now empty box that Simon had given him to one side of his desk.

"What were you expecting? A taped confession from the murderer?"

"Helpful, but no. I don't know. Something more than just home movies," Dave said bitterly.

"And that's all there is?"

"Pretty much." Dave thumbed the remote, and muted pictures of Mrs Wilson sitting in a chair in the garden bloomed on the screen.

Claire moved a little closer to the screen. From her appearance, she'd guess Mrs Wilson to have been about five or so years younger than she was now. Happier times, she presumed. And, inevitably, the woman didn't have that shell of frozen grief she'd had last time they'd met. But she still wasn't exactly a bundle of laughs. The camera work was busy, lots of bobbing up and down and zooming in and out, the work of an as yet inexperienced Jonathan, she assumed. She peered at the date on the tape. How old would he have been at that time, thirteen? Fourteen? Claire watched his mother's lips move and could clearly get the sense of the words even though the sound was off. "Go away, darling. Do stop fussing. Leave mummy alone for a while, dear." Something along those lines. It was all in the face and body language. A young boy suddenly walked in from the side of the picture and the camera wheeled with dizzying speed to focus on him. Claire had time for a quick glimpse of Simon, incongruously formal for a teenager, in shirt and tie, a brief flash of an irritated expression hidden first by quickly raised hands then by the burst of black and white static that played until Dave stopped the machine. "End of disc?"

"Yes and no," Dave said. "There's nothing else on the disc, but there's a good deal of it left unused." He juggled the remote thoughtfully. "Kind of like the cards we got back from Elijah. Jonathan seems to have been quite happy to waste space on cards and discs."

"I guess he never had to worry about finding money for new ones."

Dave snorted. "Right. And yet..."

"What?"

"Everything else about Jonathan has suggested a really organised, almost obsessively organised, personality. It doesn't seem true to form that he'd be so wasteful like this. And they're not quite the same. These just end with blank space. The cards had gaps in between recorded material."

"It's easier to edit cards, isn't it? Even I could manage it. Probably. With my lad's help."

Dave nodded. "Yes, it is. I'm probably making too much of it. I'll get the boys on these right away, though I'm guessing they'll have no more luck than last time. That'd just be too damn easy, wouldn't it?"

"Worth a try, anyway." Claire paused. "Lucky for us Simon found it."

Dave grimaced. "Not that it's done us a lot of good."

Claire regarded the blank television screen thoughtfully. "Good of him to let you have it. Wonder if he'd have passed it on to me if I'd turned up on my own."

"Course he would," Dave said immediately.

"Maybe," said Claire. "Maybe."

Chapter Nineteen

"So how's the case going, then?"

Claire was jolted from a reverie over a cup of tea by the sudden question. She'd faced questions all day from superiors, colleagues and press about how the case had been going. This was the one direction from which she hadn't expected to hear more, the one from which she never received questions about her job. She stared across the kitchen table at her eldest son, who promptly took refuge behind his fringe of hair and a pretended interest in the music magazine he had out in front of him. "Fine," she said, immediately realising her vague answer was precisely the sort of unhelpful and annoying reply she got from Tony whenever she asked him about school.

"Really?"

She swirled the remains of her tea as she considered how to deal with this unexpected turn of events. "Actually, no," she said. "We're stumped. Nothing is coming together."

"We? That's you and Dave?"

"Sergeant Lyon, yes. There are actually a heck of a lot of other people working on this, you know. It's not all solved by two people sleuthing like on the telly."

"You mean like Inspector Rudge and, what's his name, Cortez?"

Claire did a small but genuine double take. She'd honestly never realised her son had taken so much of an interest in what she'd said about her job in the past. Had she ever told him Jim and Terry's names? Had he just picked them up by listening to her conversations with Ian? Christ, what else had he picked up from sitting quietly in the background and listening? Discretion had never really been one of her bywords, doubly so when in her own home. Maybe that was something that needed changing. "Well, yes and no," she concluded. "They're not exactly involved in the case, but there are lots of others."

Tony nodded as if his mother's evasive answer made perfect sense. "I liked Dave. Sergeant Lyon," he said. "He's cool."

Claire did another double take. She couldn't help it. That had to be the first time ever that her son had described one of her friends or colleagues as 'cool'. Why Dave? What made him cool? What made him more interesting than say…? She racked her brains trying to think of a friend or colleague that Tony might have known well enough to describe as cool or not. Shit, there had to be someone in her life that her son knew.

"Takes more than liking bloody *Star Trek* to make someone cool," said Ian shortly as he walked into the kitchen.

Claire gave a small laugh as if to agree. And instantly felt nettled. And then wondered why.

"It wasn't just because of *Star Trek*, actually," Tony said, drawling slightly in a way calculated to irritate anyone over thirty.

"So what did you like about him?" Claire asked with forced brightness.

"I didn't say I liked him," Tony protested, pushing back his chair with a calculated screech on the kitchen tiles. "I just said he was cool, that's all. Jesus!" He stomped his way out of the kitchen.

Claire finished her drink. "Remember when he used to laugh all the time?"

"Do you think he's cool?" Ian said.

"That's not a word I use a lot, and definitely not in any staff evaluations." Ian just stared back at her blankly as if she hadn't answered his question, which she hadn't. "He's a good officer, though."

"Nice to have one you can finally invite round to dinner."

It was only half an hour later that Claire thought, *Hang on. You were the one who said we had to have him round!*

* ~ * ~ *

"God, you're not still working on that case, are you?"

Dave bit his lip and continued to stare at the screen. "It's not like the telly, I've told you before. It takes more than a couple of 'tecs interviewing a handful of guest stars before finding out the name of the killer in just under two hours. Minus the advert breaks."

Richard came round the sofa and sat down with a harrumphing sound that could have conveyed contempt, disbelief or just at the annoyance of getting up again at two in the morning to find his lover not in bed. "Maybe Morse and Columbo get their cases solved more quickly because they're not spending all their time watching endless gay porn. What are you hoping to find anyway?"

Dave picked up the remote with half a mind to freeze the picture. Instead, he let it run. "I don't know," he said. "I'm not sure."

"Right." Richard stared at the screen in bitter silence for one minute. Two. "You know, if this really turns you on," he said finally, "I can do it. I mean, I can watch it with you."

"No. It's not like that."

"It'd be okay. I mean, it doesn't do a great deal for me. Too many young, perfect bodies. It's like a sugar-loaded meal, you know? I end up feeling a bit sick after a while. But I know some guys—well, it's kind of like a starter for them, yeah? Paul, my ex..."

"You've told me about Paul and I am not like him, okay?" Dave snapped. He wiped a hand across his eyes. It was late and he was tired. But he didn't want to go to bed. Didn't want to chat idly about his day with someone who just couldn't begin to understand what it was really like. Didn't want to hear about the latest gossip in the staffroom. Didn't want to make love. Didn't want to think about why he didn't want to do any of those things. "I'm sorry," he said dully, and carried on staring at the screen.

They sat side by side for a further two minutes, three, four, the vivid colours of the TV screen washing over their faces, the ghastly dated electronic music muted, playing away heedlessly. Richard stood up stiffly. "I'm going to bed. Don't wake me when you come. I don't suppose you will." He walked out of the room, not bothering to close the door behind him. Dave sighed. He'd been a shit, he knew he had. And he couldn't see how he could have avoided it. He sank back resignedly into the settee and let the images flow over him, about as stimulating now as the CCTV surveillance tapes he'd had to sit and watch when he'd been the short-straw rookie. "Lucky sods," he murmured to the knot of writhing flesh on the screen. It wasn't their bodies he envied, not even the apparently spectacular sex they appeared to be effortlessly having time and again. It was the way they could swap partners between tapes, between scenes even, without any of that messy *it isn't you, it's me* nonsense. So laughably unreal. As unbelievable as the bloody wonderful apartments and houses they supposedly lived in, even the ones who could only have been about eighteen and wouldn't have stood a hope in hell of earning enough to buy something like...something like...

Dave lurched for the remote, scrabbling around for it where it had slipped between the sofa cushions in that way it had, like it was a living thing forever trying to escape his grasp. He froze the picture, rewound it. "Not that, not that," he muttered angrily as he tried to get past the two faces filling the screen with their mouths open wide in simulated ecstasy. "That!" He froze the picture into a flickering rectangle of light and leaned in close.

"Well hello," he said, and he wasn't talking to either of the twinks on the floor.

Chapter Twenty

"Am I under arrest?"

"No, sir, just helping us with our inquiries."

"So why are you recording everything we say?"

"Just routine, sir, I assure you, and as much for your own protection as anything else. Now, as I said, if you would please give us your full name."

The figure across the table from Summerskill and Lyon took a deep breath, but the voice when it came was low and steady. "My name is John Sebastian Elijah."

"Thank you, Mr Elijah. Now, if you would be so kind as to give us your age and current address."

With a pointed sigh, Elijah provided the information requested.

"Thank you." Claire shuffled the sheaf of papers she had in front of her. They were mostly meaningless requisition forms, with little or no bearing on the case, but she liked the impression they created. All the information she had was in her head, passed on by her sergeant at her side. "Now, you are a Media Studies tutor at Severn Valley Technical College."

"Yes. As you very well know, inspector. And yes, I was tutor to

Jonathan Wilson." He made a sardonic expression. "Well, this is what this is about, isn't it?"

"Yes, sir, it is, though it's not Jonathan I want to talk about first."

"It isn't?" Elijah's almost confrontational attitude gave way to something, not surprisingly, more puzzled. "Then what...?"

"Do you know a Mr Len Arras?"

Dave scrutinised Elijah's face, trying to read its expressions. Was that genuine bewilderment or not?

"No. I don't think so. Is he a student? Or was he a student?"

"I very much doubt it. Although perhaps I do the man a disservice. You could say he works in your field."

"What do you mean? If you want me to help you, inspector, you are going to have to be less elliptical and tell me just why I have been brought here."

"Invited here, sir, I think that would be a better way of putting it. Len Arras is...a film producer. Do you know many film producers, Mr Elijah?"

Elijah's broad forehead wrinkled. "Yes, inspector, I do. As you say, it is my field. Many of my friends from university went on to become producers and I have been instrumental in forging links between the college and several independent producers. It comes in useful for securing work experience placements for the students."

"But you don't recall having...forged links with Mr Arras."

"I've already told you no."

"Yes, well, perhaps it would be a bit odd for Severn Valley to be getting into bed with Mr Arras. So to speak," Dave said.

"So you are not familiar with the work of—" Claire hesitated, and Dave was pretty sure that, even under the decidedly serious circumstances, it was because she was having difficulty keeping a straight face as she spoke "—Stand Up Studios."

And there it was. So far Elijah's responses had seemed natural, unforced, but for the first time there....

"Familiar might not be the right word," he said carefully, "but I am aware of them. They are a small company specialising in gay interest videos. Very much the cheaper end of the market, I believe."

"I'm impressed."

"You shouldn't be. Again, it's part of my job to know about media distribution in this country. The market for erotic material is one of the healthiest areas of growth."

"Quite," Claire said, all trace of amusement killed. "Well, I wonder if you would indulge us with a little critical appreciation of something from that particular studio."

Dave waited for the protest at this surely unusual request, but Elijah turned without demur to face the screen of the television that Claire had just switched on with the remote, reaching into his jacket for a pair of glasses. "I'll look at whatever it is you want to show me, inspector, if it means I can get out of this cell the quicker."

"It's an interview room, sir," said Dave quickly, "not a cell."

"But I would appreciate it," Elijah continued as if Dave had not spoken, "if you didn't try to dress up your request with poorly thought out irony."

Claire just nodded at Dave who thumbed the start button. "Sergeant Lyon," she said for the benefit of the recorder, "has started tape number CV52." She cleared her throat. "*Muffin Stuffing*. The tape is approximately ten minutes into its playing time. Do you recognise either of the two young men you can see here, sir?"

Elijah stared stonily at the screen, his features completely unreadable. "That would be rather difficult from this angle, inspector," he said. "The camera is not exactly focusing on their faces."

"Ah no, you're right. Please bear with us, sir, I think that in a minute they—yes, there you are. Please pause there, sergeant."

Dave obliged, freezing the picture at exactly the spot he had held it last night. He'd had practice since then in finding the precise moment.

"Recognise them now, sir? The camera has pulled back somewhat."

Elijah was staring fixedly at the screen. His face was undoubtedly pale, though maybe that was just the reflected light from the television. *Maybe*. Dave saw him swallow once. "No," he said, and Dave had to give him credit, his voice was as steady as ever. "I do not recognise either of the young men."

"But perhaps you recognise something else?"

Elijah twisted round in his seat. "Of course I recognise something else. You know perfectly well I do. Why do you persist in this ridiculous archness?"

"For the record, sir," Claire said calmly, "could you tell us what it is that you recognise?"

Elijah took a deep breath. "I recognise the picture hanging in the background. I recognise the room in which this...this film is being shot."

"And the room is...?"

"The room is the living room in my house. As you damn well know. You've both been there, for God's sake. Now will you please switch off that travesty of a film? There is only so much bad film-making I can take in one day, and I have plenty more to see from my students before the day is through."

Claire nodded and Dave switched the tape machine off. The image of the large abstract painting he'd admired during that first interview in Elijah's house, an original as the teacher had so obligingly informed them, winked out. "Now, Mr Elijah. I'd like to ask you again: do you know Mr Len Arras?"

Elijah cleared his throat as if himself auditioning for some screen test. "I tell you again, I do not know a Mr Arras, and neither, for the record—" and he directed the comment pointedly at the machine silently recording their every word "—do I know either of the boys you have just shown me in that video."

"The two boys having sex in your living room?"

"My sitting room. Yes."

"You didn't seem particularly shocked."

"Should I have been? I'm sorry, but I wasn't. I have seen considerably worse, or considerably better depending on your point of view."

Dave leaned forward. "So can you explain for us, Mr Elijah, how this gay porn movie came to be filmed in your...sitting room, without your apparent knowledge?"

"The question isn't how, sergeant, it's why, and the answer, as is so often the case in these circles, is glamour, or rather, the illusion of glamour, as again, is so often the case. The two lads we have just seen are, in all likelihood, unemployed and probably unemployable. In five or six years, their happy lifestyle of drink, dance, recreational drugs and casual sex will have eroded their fresh-faced attractiveness, and their careers as film stars will have ground to an inevitable full stop. For the moment, though, the enthusiastic use of their bodies is something some gentlemen will pay money to watch. But although the more realistic setting for it would be a squalid bedsit or even their parents' house when mother and father are out, it is felt that the experience is enhanced if we can forget the mundane and imagine for at least thirty minutes or so that we have been invited into a pornographic *Hello!* moment to observe beautiful people in their beautiful home doing what comes beautifully and naturally. Hence the use of my house, and countless others, loaned out to friends and friends of friends who happen to live not too far from the studios concerned. It's common practice. It cuts down on set costs and can add a false veneer of—" he hesitated before adding with obvious irony "—sophistication."

"Which still begs the question, sir," Claire said levelly, "of how the makers of this film, comprising in this case, presumably, its two stars, a cameraman, sound man, maybe one more—"

"Fluffer," suggested Dave, before quickly turning back to his notepad.

"—managed to get into your house without, as you say, your knowledge and use it to make a pornographic film."

"I think, on the whole, I'd rather my living room was immortalised on film as the setting for two young lads enjoying a spot of healthy and mutually beneficial recreation than, say, have it prostituted on some *Through the Keyhole*-type programme. And it did not happen without my knowledge, inspector."

"Friends of friends, Mr Elijah?"

"I did not lie when I said I did not know a Mr Len Arras. I am, however, aware of a Mr Alan Harris. He has used several names during the course of his career. I appear not to have kept up with the latest."

"A touch disingenuous of you, wouldn't you say, sir?"

Elijah made no answer to the implicit accusation.

"Aware of Mr Harris, sir," Dave pursued. "In what context?"

"Film-making of course, sergeant. I have many contacts within the industry locally. It is part of my job. And as I have already told you, I use them to secure placements for our students."

"Did you secure these placements, sir?" Dave picked up the box from which he had taken the DVD they'd just watched. "For—" he cleared his throat "—Dirk Strong and Chad Chadwin."

"Not even under their real names."

"How about placements for Jonathan Wilson and Sean Flanagan?"

They both watched as John Elijah sat, eyes cast down, obviously considering his next answer very carefully. *Give the man credit, he's a cool one.* When he spoke again, his voice was as calm and apparently untroubled as ever, though maybe quieter. "I believe I introduced Jonathan to Alan—that is, Mr Arras. It might even have been when Alan was arranging the loan of my house for his filming, which he has done on at least two other occasions. My bathroom became quite a talking point in some circles for a while a year or so back, you know. It was not, however, with the intention of getting Jonathan a role in any film. It was a social occasion, nothing more."

"A social occasion?" Claire said.

"Like a party?" Dave pressed.

"Yes, sergeant, like a party."

"Do you often invite your students to parties, sir?" Claire asked.

"I often arrange meetings for my students with media contacts, inspector. I keep telling you this. It's networking."

"But you've also said this was a social occasion. That doesn't sound like networking. Was it at your house, Mr Elijah?" Elijah did not answer. "We can check with Mr Arras, Harris or whatever name he's using this week."

"Yes, yes, it was."

"And did you often invite your students to your house for these 'networking' sessions?" Claire persisted.

"No."

"Then why...?"

"Jonathan Wilson was my lodger."

"Your lodger?" She tried to keep the surprise from her voice.

"Yes."

"I see. And did you have a sexual relationship with Mr. Wilson, sir?"

Claire had expected a violent reaction to that one. Between them, she and Dave had pushed and teased and bludgeoned and had finally broken through the evasions and crap to the truth this man was trying to hide. And with this question she should have got the payoff: the outburst, the anger, the unbalancing emotional loss of control she could use to finish off this game of half-truths and lies. Claire was disappointed. Elijah's answer was clear and steady. "Yes, inspector. We had had a sexual relationship for nearly two months prior to his murder." He regarded them both steadily in turn. "Jonathan was clearly over the age of consent. It was not illegal."

"Not illegal, no, but clearly unethical given that he was one of your students," Claire pointed out. "And something you obviously felt sufficiently uncomfortable about not to mention during your previous interview with us. Surely you can understand the kind of impression that must have created?"

"Of course I can. But my conscience was clear. I had nothing to do with Jonathan's death. There was nothing I could say that would have helped with the matter. If anything, it would have merely clouded the picture with prejudice and false suspicion, as I can see it has now."

"You'll let us be the judge of that, sir, please. It's our job, and will be carried out without prejudice and to the best of our ability."

Elijah sighed disgustedly. "What can you know about it?"

"Nothing, unless you tell us."

Elijah considered, and when he spoke again there was an edge of resignation to his voice. "Jonathan was a remarkable boy," he said. "Not a genius, don't get me wrong. I wasn't blinded by...by love or his youthful beauty or anything puerile like that. He had an energy, a different way of seeing things. He was exactly what one hopes for as a teacher but so signally fails to find: the student who questions, has fire, wants things on his own terms, not one of the endless stream of flaccid, placid, sheep that troop through the door only interested in the right grades so they can get the right job at the end and stop thinking about anything for the rest of their lives."

"And when did this admiration for his work translate into a sexual relationship?"

Elijah laughed bitterly. "Oh, now that was very subtle, wasn't it, inspector? Is that all it comes down to for you, the sexual relationship? Everything else just a means to a base end? Or is it your job that makes you think that way? How sad for you." He carried on, not waiting for an answer. "The sex was an aspect of it, inevitable perhaps, but not at the core. We spent more of our time together talking about film and art, his work, listening to his plans. He had such plans. And I felt invigorated, refreshed by it again. My own work picked up after years of being depressed by the administrative boredom of that pit of a place."

"The college?" Dave said.

Elijah ignored him. "I could see he was unhappy, so I invited him to move into my spare room. That was the reason."

"Unhappy?"

"He didn't fit in with the rest of the students. How could he? They were just paying lip service to their subjects. Film studies actually meant something to Jonathan. And he was unhappy about something at home as well, so I offered him the use of my spare room. The relationship had not been sexual until then. It became so soon afterwards, as opportunity arose. As I said, almost inevitable, I suppose."

"Inevitable that he should make a sexual advance or that you should?" Dave asked.

"Inevitable that there should be a mutual recognition of compatibility."

You make it sound very cold."

"I'm trying to explain it in terms you can understand."

"You say he was unhappy about something at home. Did he

ever say what?"

Elijah shook his head. "The usual, I assumed. Artistic son stifled by the petit bourgeois opinions of his parents. Even his brother had done law or some such."

"History," Dave corrected automatically.

"Jonathan didn't fit in anywhere. He was struggling to find himself, held back by everyone and everything around him. All I wanted to do was give him the space he needed to become himself."

"Very poetical. And did you know he'd used the contact you'd made for him to make a porn film?" Claire asked.

"No. No, I didn't. Oh, yes, I am surprised, inspector. But not shocked, which I'm sure is what you'd hoped for. I've just told you, Jonathan's unpredictability was what made him stand out from the rest. He was always wanting to explore, to challenge others and himself."

Claire picked up the empty DVD box on the desk in front of them. "Like Dirk and Chad?"

Elijah laughed softly, and Dave saw how Claire struggled to conceal how that made her blood boil. "Motives, inspector. I thought as a policewoman you could at least have understood that. Jonathan's motives would have been very different from those of 'Dirk' and 'Chad'. And I'm sure the end result would have had an ironic subtext well beyond that of your average skin flick. I don't suppose I could see it by any chance?"

"It's porn, Mr Elijah," Claire said bluntly. "Plain and simple, and it's not up for a public viewing right now."

Elijah nodded slowly. "How lucky for those who were able to watch it." His gaze lingered on Dave who kept his own expression fixedly neutral. "Pornography versus erotica. Art versus commercialism. We could debate that one till the cows come home, inspector. I suspect our points of view are very different and unlikely to ever converge. Are you familiar with the work of Robert Mapplethorpe?"

"This wasn't the only sex film he made. You knew about the others, the private ones he'd made?"

"Yes." Elijah's answer was noticeably more reluctant.

"And I suppose you spent the time discussing camera angles and zoom lens technique?" There was no response, and Summerskill didn't bother to press for one for the machine. "Did you make a sex film with Jonathan Wilson, Mr Elijah?"

"No!"

"An artist like yourself not tempted to make a little...art with someone so obviously keen on the idea?"

"No, inspector."

"Either as cameraman or performer...?"

"I know my limits," Elijah said coldly. "All artists should. I did not make any such films with Jonathan Wilson."

"We'll need a full description of all of the films you watched with him."

"Oh for God's sake, inspector!"

"No, Mr Elijah!" Claire slammed the plastic case she was

holding down onto the table with such force that even the imperturbable John Elijah jumped in reaction. “You will listen to me. I don’t know about the links between art and pornography. I don’t care about them. I do know about the links between pornography and crime—drug dealing, prostitution, murder. And guess what? We’re investigating a double murder. So I will allow you your professional opinions—” and she managed to hide none of her contempt for these “—if you will allow me mine. If you did care anything for this boy, you will not presume to hold back information that might very well lead us to his killer. And may I remind you that although you are not currently under arrest for that crime, any further reluctance to aid us in our investigation can only make me question my decision on that matter. Am I making myself clear?”

Elijah took a long moment to consider what had been so forcefully presented to him. “Perfectly, inspector,” he said finally. “There were only two films—no, maybe three. Yes, definitely three that I can recall. And they were all of Jonathan and one other boy. He said his name was Sean. I...I assume that he was the other boy who died?” Neither Claire nor Dave spoke or made any sign, so Elijah continued with his description of the films he and Jonathan had watched together. His voice was as even and controlled as ever but throughout he kept his head down. The descriptions matched the tapes that Summerskill and Lyon had already seen. There was nothing new here.

“Thank you, Mr Elijah,” Claire said at the end of his account.

"That was most helpful." Elijah nodded and pushed back his chair as if to leave.

"What was Jonathan like, sir?" Dave said quietly.

Elijah reluctantly pulled his chair back to the table. "He was beautiful." He gave a dry laugh. "I'm sorry. Does that embarrass you, sergeant, one man calling another beautiful?" Dave met his question impassively. Elijah's expression was dismissive, as if he didn't care anyway for the policeman's opinion. "I don't mean just physically, although of course he had the sort of beauty that only youth can give men. But he had a beautiful mind, if you'll forgive my plagiarising a third rate film. He was restless, frantic almost. He didn't know what he wanted out of life but he was determined to get it." Elijah's voice softened as his thoughts went back to the time he had spent with Jonathan. "That could make him...difficult to be with."

"Difficult? Did you argue?" Claire asked.

"Argue? You appear determined, inspector, to reduce us to your preconceived roles of heterosexual marital bliss. He challenged me. Constantly. And I liked that. It's what youth should do. It was exciting."

"He used you. You were a meal ticket. You were a way to better grades."

"Oh, so now it's another stereotype: the deluded older man being duped by the grasping, manipulative youngster. You didn't know him at all, did you?"

"Of course we didn't, sir. By the time we met him he was dead,

Murdered. But through you and everyone else we're interviewing, we are getting to know him better day by day. Where were you on the night of November 23rd?"

"From stereotype to cliché in just over one minute. Congratulations, inspector."

"Well?"

"You'll have to forgive me. Even I am somewhat surprised by just how potent that question is when you realise the rest of your life depends on how you answer it."

"Does it, Mr Elijah?"

"I can see you have never been on its receiving end, inspector. As it happens, I can answer your question even without consulting my diary. November the 23rd was...is an anniversary of sorts. I was with a friend that night in Manchester, celebrating."

"All night?"

"All night."

"And will he be able to vouch for you, this friend?"

Elijah smiled. "*She* will, yes. She's my ex-wife. We remain on very good terms, although our lives have long since followed very different paths."

"It was you who put the cameras and phone back into Jonathan's locker, wasn't it, sir?"

Elijah nodded at Dave's interjection. "Yes. I thought they might be of some use to you. You see, I am as anxious as you are to know who killed Jonathan, though for very different reasons."

"But you cleaned them first, so we couldn't know you'd had

them."

"Of course. I didn't want to give you a—what do you call it—a red herring?"

"They only call them red herrings in bad detective fiction, Mr Elijah. In the real world it's called obstructing the course of justice. You also wiped significant portions of those cards. I want to know what was on them."

Elijah shifted uncomfortably in his chair. "Nothing."

"Please. Don't insult our intelligence, Mr Elijah," Dave said. "Nobody goes to the trouble of erasing nothing."

"Jonathan filmed everything."

"We know."

"No. You don't know. He filmed absolutely everything. It was an obsession, a mania. I could see it might one day make him a great film-maker. In the short term though, even I had to admit it could be...irritating. He particularly liked filming emotion. Strong emotion. His films, I think, would have been very passionate." Elijah's voice trailed off, his focus lost for a minute as if contemplating that future, now gone forever.

"So what was on the films, Mr Elijah?" Claire said.

With obvious reluctance and some sadness Elijah returned his attention to the there and then. "Arguments, inspector."

"Arguments. So you did argue with him?"

"Yes, inspector, we did. That is what I have just said."

"Violently?"

"Passionately. But never with recourse to physicality. I never hit him, if that's what you're wondering. Never."

"And what did you argue about, Mr Elijah?" Dave asked. "About Jonathan's seeing Sean, maybe?"

"No, sergeant. Not about Sean. I was not about to insist that Jonathan devote his formidable energies to me and me alone. We argued about films. For all his potential brilliance, Jonathan was still inexperienced. He actually believed that Stanley Kubrik was a director worth watching. Incredible, don't you think?"

"Incredible," said Dave tonelessly.

"And you didn't want us to see these arguments?"

"It seemed...prudent."

Claire glanced up at the interview room clock. "Just one more thing, Mr Elijah, if I may. Just to clarify something for myself. How long did you say you and Jonathan were lovers?"

"*Lovers.*" Elijah snorted with a suggestion of the scorn he'd shown so clearly at the start of the interview. "What a ridiculously old-fashioned word."

"You had sex with the boy."

"He was not a boy, inspector. Hardly ever was, I should imagine, but legally most definitely not."

"Let me put it this way, then. When did you say Jonathan—Mr Wilson—moved into your house?"

"Towards the end of September."

Claire frowned deliberately. "And the college course starts when? At the start of September?"

"Yes."

"So you had known Jonathan—what, about three weeks, maybe a little less, before you invited him to move in?" Elijah nodded. "You seem to have recognised his talent very quickly."

Elijah's mouth opened, closed, then, "I think if we are going to continue, I really do need to call my lawyer."

"I think you do, Mr Elijah, though you can do it from the comfort of that lovely living room of yours. We don't need to continue here." Claire raised her voice as she addressed the machine by her side, "Interview concluded at 15.17." She pressed the off switch. "Good afternoon, Mr Elijah. We'll be in touch."

Slowly Elijah rose from the chair, as if expecting one or the other of Summerskill or Lyon to call him back again at any moment and put still more questions to him. Dave got up and held the door open for him. Elijah hesitated. "It seems we have been a lot more open with each other than I'd expected, inspector."

"I hope so, Mr Elijah."

"Given that is the case, it would perhaps be a good idea for me to mention something to you that has been...troubling me lately."

What the hell now? "Go on," Claire said.

"There have been... That is, I think..." Elijah gathered himself. "There have been men, outside my house. I think they have been following me."

Summerskill and Lyon exchanged looks. "How many?"

"Two, I think. That is, I've never seen more than two. Once there was only one."

"What do they look like?"

"I...It would be hard to say."

"I thought you were some kind of artist. Aren't artists supposed to have an eye for that kind of detail? And why haven't you mentioned this before?"

Elijah swallowed the barely disguised sarcasm. "You and I both know I am innocent of any involvement with the death of Jonathan Wilson. And the other boy. My concern up until now has been to keep as much distance as possible between myself and the whole sordid affair. I didn't wish to draw attention to myself."

"You've obviously drawn yourself to somebody's attention, Mr Elijah."

Elijah fingered the silk tie he was wearing. "Yes," he said quietly. "I fear I have."

"If you'll just go back to the waiting room, I'll see somebody comes along to take a statement about these men. Perhaps you can even work with one of our artists to draw up some kind of picture."

"I very much doubt..."

"Oh, they're very skilful, Mr Elijah. Perhaps not 'challenging' or 'invigorating' but they get the job done. I hope they can be as much help to you as you have been to us. Good day, Mr Elijah."

With a vague nod in their general direction, John Elijah walked out.

"Shall I send Simmonds to him?"

"Let him wait. Pompous bastard."

"Do you think he's our man?"

"For Jonathan? Maybe. Crime of passion? Jealous older man

kills younger lover who's about to leave him, something like that."

Dave looked doubtful. "Like the man said, bit of a gay cliché, don't you think? And our Mr. Elijah is far too full of self-belief to have been worried about the loss of one student body, even someone he considered as potentially brilliant as Jonathan."

"Actually, I agree. And far too up himself to feel the need to step down from his throne and dirty his hands with the likes of Sean. No, damn it." Claire shoved the useless notes across the table in disgust. "As soon as we found out for certain it was him who put that stuff back in Jonathan's locker, I knew we were wasting our time with him. If he'd really had something to hide, he would have just chucked all that stuff away somewhere instead of clumsily editing it and handing it over to us."

"Unless he's trying for some kind of double bluff?"

"Oh, get real!"

The door to the interview room opened and WPC Jenny Trent stuck her head round. "All right, Claire?" She turned to Dave, her tone noticeably changing. "Phone call for you, sergeant. Mr Wilson."

"Simon or his father?"

"The son by the sounds of it."

"What does he want?"

"Didn't say. Want me to tell him to call back?"

"No, no. I'll come and get it. 'Scuse me, mum."

*

Dave hurried from the room. Jenny walked in after him, letting the door close behind her. “Any luck?”

Claire sighed and ran her hand through her hair. “No, I don’t think so. What was that call about?”

“Dunno. Young Mr Wilson didn’t sound too upset but was very insistent that he wanted to speak to Sergeant Lyon. Sorry, Sergeant *Dave* Lyon. Did he just call you *mum*?”

“No, no. It’s his accent,” Claire said distractedly, her thoughts on Simon Wilson.

The door to the room opened again. Claire was expecting Dave but it was DCI Rudge who stood there. Jenny quickly got up from the edge of the table where she had perched herself in front of Claire. “I’ll get onto those reports right away.”

Claire nodded, simultaneously amused at her friend’s speed in coming up with a cover, and irritated at her apparent belief that one was needed. They’d only been talking. About Dave. That didn’t need a cover, did it?

Rudge let the door close behind Jenny, and without asking Claire, he strode into the interview room and sat down in front of her, straddling the chair in a way she couldn’t help feeling was a bit naff in someone his age and build. “So how’s it going?”

Claire sighed. Were they queuing up outside that door to ask her the same question? “All right,” she said defensively, acutely conscious of the very different account she’d just given Jenny.

“No, it’s not,” Rudge said matter-of-factly. “Talk of the bloody station. You’re going round in circles, girl.”

"Well, I'm sorry I couldn't manage the speed and directness of the great Inspector Rudge."

"Don't get cocky with me, Claire," Rudge said calmly.

"And don't call me girl."

"I've always called you girl, and always will. When I'm retired and you're superintendent, you'll still be 'girl', so get off your bloody high horse. You didn't mind when you started and you cannot mind it now."

"I'm older now than I was then."

Rudge grinned. "But bearing up well for all you're knocking on." He quickly sobered again. "Less snot, Claire, and listen to someone who's trying to give you some good advice."

Claire bit her lip, momentarily shamed. Rudge was an aggravating, sexist pain in the arse, but he'd always been good to her in the past. They'd worked well together. They'd worked *very* well together. But just lately they'd undoubtedly lost their way. And she knew as well as he did why. She forced herself to sit still and listen to what was coming, even as she wondered if this was how Tony felt when she had to come the responsible adult in the face of some new adolescent transgression.

"This is your first case as inspector," Rudge began, and he held his hand up as he saw the sarcastic response coming involuntarily to Claire's lips. "And it's not working out. There's no shame in that. It happens to us all. My own first case happened to be a brilliant success, but there's plenty of others as have cocked it up. Time to start learning how to play the game."

"What do you mean, play the game? I'm a girl, remember? I don't understand ball talk."

Rudge went on as if she hadn't spoken. "Two things. One, it's okay to ask for help when you need it."

Claire took a deep breath and let it out very slowly.

"And two," Rudge leaned across the table, "you have to learn where to place the blame."

"What?" She shook her head, genuinely puzzled this time.

"Shit is going to fly, Claire. The air's going to be so full of it, you'll think you're swimming in the Med, and Brass is going to be flinging it. That's what Brass is for, and what you're here for is to make sure as little as possible of it sticks to you."

"It's my case. I'm in charge. Who the hell am I supposed to...?"

"Use your head, girl. Shit falls on you, you drop it on the people under you."

Understanding finally dawned. "Dave."

Rudge nodded. "Sergeant Lyon."

A sick anger welled inside Claire, whether at this naked admission of dislike for Dave or the hateful cynicism of the attitude he was outlining she didn't know and didn't care. "You've never liked him from the first time he..."

"It's not about like or dislike, Claire. LIFO. Last In, First Out. He's been here two minutes. No one's going to miss him when he goes. Brass gets to pass the buck, you pass it on and then you get to start again with a blank sheet. And maybe this time they let you have the team you want."

Claire flushed. Did he know just how near the mark that one had hit? Of course he did. He was a right bastard and a dinosaur and a bloody good policeman who could read people like books. "I've got the team I want," she said automatically.

"C'mon, Claire, you're not talking to Madden now. It's me. We worked together before this. We'll work together after this."

This. What is this? The case. Or Dave. "This is all about Dave's being gay, isn't it?"

"No," Rudge said. "Though most of it is." He pantomimed surprise. "What? Expect me to say no, not at all? Come over all PC? Of course it's about him being gay. It doesn't work in the Force. People don't like it, no matter what they say. It's not good for a team. How can the guys work not knowing if the other guys fancy them or not?"

"The women manage."

"It's not the same. But more important than that, you can't trust his judgement. He'll always have an agenda."

"*He'll* have an agenda! He's here because of Madden's agenda."

"Fine, that's what I've just been saying. Madden passed the problem to you, now you pass it on."

"Dave's being gay is not a problem."

"It is as far as I'm concerned, as far as the majority of the Force is concerned, no matter what they'll say up top, and no matter what poxy quotas they'll push on us. From what I see, your sergeant is more interested in cosying up to all the gays who've come tumbling out of the closet since you started this case than he is in banging one of them up. Been on any more hospital visits lately, has he?"

"That was an official visit, and I was there, too."

"The first time maybe. And since then?"

"He's been back?" Claire damned herself for letting slip that she hadn't known.

"Whereas the dead lad's dad, straight I think we can both agree, has been well stirred up by your gay sergeant."

"You were the one who dug up the dirt on Wilson, and I think Sergeant Lyon and I can definitely both share the blame for rattling his cage."

"Maybe, but are you both making such good friends of his son?"

Claire felt a cold lurch in her stomach. "What?"

"I understand Sergeant Lyon has given Simon Wilson his extension number."

"I know that. It's hardly unusual practice," she snapped, wondering just how Rudge had come to understand that.

"And do you know how many times Wilson Junior has rung Sergeant Lyon over the last couple of days?"

Claire recalled that uncertain expression just a few minutes ago when Dave had been told he'd got a call from Simon Wilson. That was the only one she'd known about, and he hadn't looked too happy that she'd found about it. There'd been others? "Do *you*? And what are you saying? That he's behaving unprofessionally with someone involved in the case? Someone who isn't a suspect, remember. And who, for that matter, hasn't even admitted to being gay." She checked herself. "Hasn't *said* he's gay. Not admitted, *said.* All this, just because of a few phone calls?"

"So maybe he's not getting his leg over. Let's just say he's letting his more sensitive side get the better of him. It's still not the sort of detachment that he should be showing."

"Oh, you just want it all ways." Claire stormed to her feet. "I have seen nothing to suggest that Dave Lyon is any less professional or disinterested than you or me."

"Yeah? Well, you just tell me this. Why did you want Jenny Trent on your team?"

Claire stopped, hand on the door handle. "Because she's a bloody good police officer, that's why. You've said so yourself."

"Yes I have. And there are a dozen bloody good police officers in the station in addition to her that you could just as easily have chosen. But she's your friend, isn't she?"

"Oh, come on, now you really are going over the top."

"Well, why shouldn't you?" Rudge continued, ignoring her outburst. "She's a woman. Good to have another woman amongst all us rough and ready men, eh? Balance the scales a little? Bring in that different perspective? More accurately reflect the make-up of the real world? Can you honestly tell me none of that was in your mind somewhere when you put her name forward? Eh? That you didn't suggest as much to Madden when you were trying to push it through? And you say Lyon's as disinterested as you? I think that makes your pursuit of this case dangerously flawed from the start, inspector. Maybe it wasn't your fault it got off to a bad start, but it's my job to point out to you now that's what happened. And your job to do something about it."

The door opened and Dave Lyon stood there, immediately sensing the tension in the interview room. He cleared his throat. "We've got problems."

"Simon Wilson?" Claire snapped.

A brief frown shadowed Dave's face at his boss's tone. "No. No, I've dealt with that. Phil's here."

"You mean Henderson?"

"Yes. It's about Mikey," Dave said deliberately. "He's gone from the hospital."

Chapter Twenty-one

Dave led Claire to another interview room further along the corridor and there she found Phil. He was seated at a table in a mirror image of the one where she'd just interviewed Elijah, but the difference between the two couldn't have been more pronounced. The burly, shaven-headed man was slumped over the table, his shoulders shaking with dry sobs. When he raised his head at the sound of them entering, his eyes were raw. "Have you found him? Have you found him?"

"Easy, Phil," Dave said, moving forward and putting one hand easily on the other's broad shoulder. "You've only just told us, mate."

"You've got to find him. You've got to."

Claire took her seat across the table from him. Automatically she felt herself shifting into the interview mode she normally had to adopt in a room like this, and that was the last thing this man needed right now. "Tell us what's happened, Phil."

"They'd sent me home. The hospital had sent me home. They'd said there wasn't anything I could do and I needed a proper rest and they'd let me know if anything happened. Bastards! They just wanted me out of the way. Think they'd have sent me home if we'd been a straight couple?"

Claire said nothing. She could have pointed out that Phil and Mikey had been backward about coming forward when it came to identifying as a couple even in the gay sense of the word, but wisely she kept her counsel.

Phil glared bitterly at his meaty hands, clasped tightly on the table in front of him. "I was away five hours. Five sodding hours, that was all. And when I got back, he was gone."

"Hadn't the staff noticed that he'd gone?" Dave asked.

"Oh yeah, they'd noticed all right. Just assumed he'd checked himself out. Sodding covered in cuts and bruises and they just assumed he'd checked himself out. And they hadn't told me. The bastards hadn't even told me."

Dave came round the table and took a seat on Phil's side. "Did anyone see anybody else?"

"What do you mean?"

"Did Mikey leave with anyone else?"

"Who the hell else is there? There's only me, that's all he's got. Who'd go to that place...?" Understanding dawned. "You mean the guys who beat him up in the first place? Shit!" He grabbed hold of Dave's shirt with his huge paws. Dave instinctively took hold of Phil's hands with his own but, as yet, used no force to separate them. "You've got to find him, you've got to," Phil pleaded again. Dave kept eye contact with the big man, so close to him Phil's spit landed on the skin of his face, and slowly Phil let go and sank back down hopelessly into his chair.

“All right, Phil, listen to me. Listen to me,” Claire said. “We’re going to send men into the hospital, get them to interview everyone they can, every doctor and nurse and cleaner who was on duty. Find out what and who they saw. We’ll circulate a description of Mikey, that’s something you can help with. Sergeant Lyon here will take you to someone who’ll ask you to give them every detail you can. Are the clothes he came with gone?” Phil nodded miserably. “Good, that’s good. You can describe them, too. And then I want you to go home, you hear? There really isn’t anything you can do this time.”

“But...”

“No buts, man. You live together?”

Phil shook his head again. “But he spends most of his time round my place. Daft sod can’t really take care of himself properly.”

“Then you need to be there in case he comes back. I’ll have someone run you home. And don’t worry. We really will let you know what’s happening. All right? All right?”

She waited until he left off his despairing absorption with his fists and nodded. He got to his feet shakily. Dave put his hand on his upper arm and Phil automatically clasped it. He sniffed violently, made the effort to straighten. “She’s a tough one when she gets a mood on her, isn’t she?” he said to Dave with a watery smile.

“She is that,” Dave said.

“Don’t suppose she’s...?”

Dave shook his head quickly. “No, she isn’t.”

“Right. Didn’t think so really. You can never tell, though, can you? Okay, tell me which way to go.”

Claire opened the door and called out to a passing uniform, instructing him where to take Phil. She and Dave watched him shuffle off.

“Thanks for that,” Dave said.

“Thanks for what?”

“The way you were with him. It’s hard for a man like that to show his feelings about someone he loves. Don’t suppose he’s ever even said it to Mikey.”

“I do know a bit about people, sergeant, and I didn’t treat him any different from anyone else in his position. It’s our job, remember?”

She strode out, leaving Dave to wonder just what the hell he’d done to deserve that.

* ~ * ~ *

The search for Mikey Henderson got nowhere. Amid grumblings about large modern hospitals manned barely to minimum requirements by staff stretched to their very limits, it quickly became obvious that no one had seen Mikey leave his room, and that it was entirely possible for a patient to get out of the hospital without having to sign any of the forms and counter forms that had been so essential when he’d been trying to get in. The CCTV cameras would probably be of very little help, designed as they were to spot people trying to break into the building rather than to monitor them as they left, and it would indeed be entirely possible for two men or even more to have made their way unannounced into Mikey's room and taken him away with them. But of course that sort of thing didn't happen in real life, did it?

Nothing was overtly stated between Claire and Dave, but they both had the uneasy feeling that they were working against some kind of deadline, neither of them willing to voice what the consequences of missing that deadline might be. But then Inspector Summerskill seemed very unwilling to voice anything that day. Communication was at a minimum and the progress in their relationship that Dave thought they'd made over recent days now seemed to be a thing of the past.

Richard had been expecting him home at about six that night. At seven Dave rang him to say he'd be an hour late. At nine he rang again to suggest they meet outside the Indian takeaway round the corner from Richard's flat to get that night's meal. He said he'd be there for half nine. He finally made it for ten.

Richard, to give him credit, did try his best. No rolling pin, literal or metaphorical, no queeny fits. No, "What time do you call this and where have you been till now?" Which was just as well. Dave had wanted to call in on Phil on his way home, which would have made him even later, but Summerskill had vetoed that with decisiveness if no explanation. So, he'd decided instead he could maybe save the visit for first thing the next morning, before he clocked in at the station That way, Summerskill wouldn't even need to know.

In his own way, Richard had had a bad day, too. His head teacher, in perpetual fear of an imminent OFSTED inspection, was pushing her staff remorselessly in an impossible bid for perfection, plus he'd had an unsettling meeting with aggressive parents who'd verbally abused him for daring to suggest that their child could probably benefit from a few hours' extra tuition to help him cope with the learning difficulties they refused even to acknowledge he had. Dave knew he should let Richard talk to him about all this. He knew he should indulge Richard when Richard asked him what his day had been like. *That's what couples do, isn't it? What living with someone's all about.* And he was too damn tired to want to think about it. They hugged quickly outside the restaurant and walked in to order and wait for the food to be prepared.

"And you've had a load of phone calls, too," Richard said, after several failed attempts to bridge the all too obvious gap of silence yawning between them.

Dave put down the local newspaper he'd been faking interest in. "Yeah? Who?" Even as he asked, he raked his memory, trying to recall the last time he had spoken to his parents. It had to be them. Well, they could always call him again, couldn't they? And maybe they had. Although 'a load' hardly sounded like his mother's usual pattern of one call then a long and frosty silence as she waited for the response. Maybe his brother? *Yeah, that'll be the day.*

"A man," Richard said. "I could get quite jealous if I didn't know you better. Much better, I hope, than anyone else currently."

"Richard, just tell me who it was, will you?" Dave closed his eyes. "Sorry, that came out sharper than I meant."

Richard ignored the apology so it wasn't clear whether he had accepted it or not. "Simon Wilson," he said.

"Simon?" Dave sat up from his slouched position on the restaurant's velveteen couch. "Did you keep the messages?"

"No need. It was just the same thing over and over. 'Is Dave there, please? Could you tell him to ring me when he gets in, thank you,' or words to that effect."

What did Simon want? And how had he got hold of his home number? Why ring him there anyway when he had his extension at the station? Okay, he had been out and about all day coordinating the fruitless search for Mikey, but someone should have passed on any messages that had been left. Or they'd have been forwarded to Summerskill as his immediate boss. Summerskill, who had hardly been talking to him all day. Maybe the messages *had* got through, to the station at least, if not to him. What the hell was going on back there? "Did he sound scared?"

"Scared? Not that I could tell. It was just a bunch of messages. I...I'm sorry, I didn't think it was that important. I thought anything important would have got through to you at work."

Yeah, you would, wouldn't you? "I'd better get back to him."

"What, now? Wouldn't it be better left until the morning? Who is he, anyway?"

"He's someone involved in the case. The brother of one of the murdered lads."

"You didn't mention a brother."

"Didn't I?"

"Christ, I thought only teachers were supposed to bring their work home with them."

"Yeah, well now you know different. Oh!" The exclamation had been completely involuntary, caused by one of those unnerving moments of thought and reality suddenly and unexpectedly becoming one. He'd been talking and thinking about Simon Wilson, and suddenly the man was standing in front of him. "Simon," he said, rather unnecessarily.

"Hello, Dave." Simon radiated nervousness and uncertainty. His hair was stuck to his forehead by the light rain outside, the thin coat he was wearing unsuitable for the weather or even the time of year. "I... I hope you don't mind."

"Sit down." Dave gestured to the space at the end of the couch and Simon sat down. "You look cold. Would you like a drink? I mean a tea or a coffee. They're pretty good here. I'm sure they could make you one if we asked. We're waiting for a meal anyway."

Simon shook his head.

"It's no bother," said Richard, rather stiffly.

"Ah. Right. Coffee, then. Thank you."

Richard turned on his heel and stalked to the bar area.

"How did you know...?" Dave began.

"I'm sorry. I saw you. Ten minutes ago." Simon hugged

himself—whether from chill or some other reason wasn't clear—and his words came faster, so that he was almost gabbling. "I've been pacing up and down outside trying to decide whether I should come in or not. I know it's not right, you'll probably be angry with me, but I've been trying to get in touch with you and nothing seems to work. And I've seen those men again."

"Who? The men you told us about at the hospital?"

"Yes. I am sorry. I've been ringing all day but I either ended up in endless telephone queues or left messages that... Well, they didn't get any replies." Dave waved aside the apologies. "Dad's always said, if you want something, don't mess about at the bottom of the ladder, go straight to the top."

Dave smiled mirthlessly. "Yes, I can imagine your dad saying something like that. But I'm not exactly the top of the ladder, y'know?"

"You're...you're the one I've been able to speak to the most easily. And I was...worried."

Dave regarded Simon closely. He looked a lot more than just worried. "Where were they? The men who were following you?"

"I was out, in town, picking up some things for Mum, and suddenly they were behind me. They were walking quickly, heading straight for me. I just turned and ran. They followed. I didn't know what to do. I thought if I called out people would think I was mad and back away. If I asked for help it would slow me down and the men would reach me. I... I managed to get to my car and drove off. I've been at home the rest of the day, stuck by the windows, listening for the sound of cars in the drive. And telephoning the station. I only came out tonight because...because sometimes it's pretty hard to stay in these days."

Dave could imagine. He rubbed his hand across his face. He was going to fire some bloody rockets off at that station tomorrow morning. And if DI Claire Summerskill was still riding her bloody high horse, then she could cop some of the flack, too.

Richard came back with a single cup of coffee which he handed over to Simon. "Sorry if you take sugar. There isn't any. I think they'd much rather we'd had three Cobras while we were waiting."

"Yeah, well maybe you could get us a couple of those, eh? Just to keep them sweet."

It was obviously on the tip of Richard's tongue to point out that five minutes ago Dave had said no to precisely that suggestion, but for now he gritted his teeth, turned on his heel and returned to the bar to buy the beers.

"Who's that?" said Simon, cradling his coffee cup. "Your flatmate? Is he a policeman, too?"

"That's Richard. And no, he isn't a policeman."

"But he is your flatmate? Or your brother? You do look a bit alike."

"Do we?" Dave couldn't help his reaction to that one. He'd never thought that. He'd seen for himself how gay couples often started resembling their partners. Inevitable, really, when you fancied someone, liked the way he looked and had the chance to look the same. But he didn't look like Richard, he was sure of it. Had Richard started to look like him? Richard came back more quickly this time with the two beers. Halves, Dave noted. He stood there holding them both out in front of him like weapons. "This is Richard," Dave said. "He's my boyfriend."

Simon blinked, nodded expressionlessly.

"Hi." Richard went to shake hands, realised he was still holding the beer glasses so searched for a space on the low table covered in local newspapers in front of the couch. By the time his hands were free again, the moment for a handshake had passed.

"Richard..." Dave began uncertainly, unsure how he was going to explain that he wanted him out of the way again so he could sort out whatever the hell was going on with Simon. He saw already the glint of defiance in Richard's eye at that prospect and steeled himself.

Simon abruptly stood up. "I'd better go."

"What? But you've only just got here."

Simon swept round the sofa, nodding at Richard who nodded perfunctorily back. "I have to go. I'll be fine. I'll call you later. Tomorrow, I mean. At the station."

"Wait. What about those men?"

"It'll be all right."

"Wait!" Instinctively Dave reached out to take hold of Simon's arm.

The young man flung it off with a force that surprised Dave. "Fuck off!"

Dave snatched his hand back, shocked by his own stupidity in making unwarranted contact and by the vehemence of Simon's reaction. "Simon, I..."

"Just fuck off! All of you. You're bloody useless. Like Dad said. He's right. You want something doing, you fucking do it yourself!" And he was gone, slamming the door behind him, leaving a stunned silence in the restaurant.

Richard was staring at the carpet, mortified at suddenly becoming the focus of attention for the restaurant's staff and clientele, unable to raise his head and meet the astonished eyes of diners and waiters. "Christ," he muttered again and again, colouring deeply. Dave moved quickly to placate the management, which was moving towards them in the corpulent form of Rayheel, the owner.

"Okay," Dave said after a rushed conversation. "Rayheel's cool. It's sorted. Our food should be ready in a couple of minutes. If you take it back to the flat, I'll be with you as soon as I can."

"Where are you going?"

"I've got to go and find Simon."

"What the fuck for?"

"It's work, all right?"

"Everything's bloody work these days!" Richard exploded. "Is this what I can expect from now on? A stream of suspects and/or criminals accosting us whenever we're out? Aren't they supposed to stay in cells or something, or is that just another of those things that only happens on the telly? If I invited kids home for coffee and biscuits every day, I'd be out on my arse faster than you could say 'taking advantage'."

"Simon Wilson is neither a suspect nor a criminal, and I'm hardly taking advantage, am I?"

"*You* might not be."

"What the hell do you mean by that?"

"God, are you so stupid or what?"

"Why is it that everyone...?" The mobile in Dave's pocket trilled annoyingly. "Lyon?" He stood, phone pressed to his ear, glaring at Richard who glared back at him, then as the meaning of the words that were being spoken into his ear sank in, his expression changed. "Shit! What? Sorry. Yes, yes, I'll be there in—" he checked his watch "—five minutes." He switched the phone off but stood still, taking in what he'd just been told.

"What is it now?"

Richard's hard words snapped Dave back to reality. "It's Mikey."

"Who's Mikey? Another handsome non-suspect?"

"I told you who he is."

"I can't keep track of all the people you have to deal with. It's like a madhouse."

"Well, he's dead," Dave shouted. "All right? *Dead!* In the same canal we found Simon's murdered brother by. If you like, I'll put it all into a flow chart for you when I get back. Whenever that is."

He didn't slam the door on the way out. But it was a close thing.

Chapter Twenty-two

They hadn't had to tell him. Phil had known as soon as he'd opened the door to Summerskill and Lyon and seen their faces. "He's dead, isn't he?"

Dave stepped forward. "I'm sorry, Phil," he began.

It was frightening seeing the speed of the collapse of the man. In an instant all strength fled his large body as he disintegrated into absolute grief. "C'mon. Come here." Dave slipped his arm round him, bearing the dead weight of him. "Where's your living room? Is it round here? Ma'am. If you could maybe make us a cup of tea? I think the kitchen will be that way?"

Claire followed where Dave pointed and indeed found the kitchen. She set about making the tea. Yes, it was precisely the sort of thing she would have exploded big style about if Rudge had ever tried it on his watch. Yes, it was wrong that he, the sergeant, should be dealing with this man and not her. But she was so glad he was. It was right, for the moment. So she'd play the little woman, for at least the time it took to make a cup of tea, while Dave opened himself up to his more female side. Sometimes, she decided, as she spooned tea into the pot, irony was just a pain in the arse.

Walking back into the living room carrying the tray and an expression that made it clear this was the only time her sergeant would ever see her doing such a thing, Claire tried to find somewhere to put it. The room was small and cluttered. She shoved a pile of dog-eared motor and football magazines off the arm of an armchair onto its seat and balanced the tray on the space left behind. A glossy magazine open at the picture of an unclad and extremely excited young lad slid onto the floor, and without comment Claire stood the milk bottle on his evident enthusiasm.

She stood rather awkwardly to one side. Phil filled the single sofa and Dave was perched on the side of that, his arm taken from around Phil now, anxiously watching him take in the news that had just been broken to him. Phil was sobbing—huge soundless gulps that shook his burly frame. "That fucking canal," he gasped. "That fucking, fucking canal."

Yes, that fucking canal. Happy slapping along it. Jonathan's body found by it. Sean's bedsit overlooking it. That first assault on Mikey on its banks. And now Mickey's body found floating in it, face down this morning. It all came back to that fucking canal. Or almost all of it did.

"Had he...?" Phil's eyes were fixed on Dave, not on her at all. "Had he...? Were there any marks? I mean, had anyone...?"

Dave shook his head. "No. There were the marks from the last time, of course, but nothing new."

"It wouldn't have mattered," Phil said shakily. "Idiot couldn't swim. All they'd have had to do was push him in and...and watch and…" He leaned forward, pulled up his knees, a tight, foetal spasm of grief. She couldn't help herself; Claire wanted to run, to escape. The emotion was too raw, too overpowering. She hated this. She made herself stay, as she had before. Running didn't make it better, and that was what she was supposed to do, wasn't it? Make it better. She regarded her sergeant. Did men feel it the same way, straight or gay? Did it matter? His face was unreadable. But then so was hers. Part of the job.

"I'm sorry Mr… Phil," she said, in a voice barely above a whisper.

Phil said nothing, regressed to a leaden mass of inescapable misery.

"Phil? Phil?" Dave spoke softly. "Do you have anyone? Is there anyone we can call?"

Phil uncurled slowly, effort written in every movement as he struggled for some measure of control. "Oh yeah. Loads of friends. Loads of 'em. I'll be okay. Just go away, will you? Go away now."

Claire nodded once, and Dave reluctantly rose to stand by her. "I'll be back later," he said. Phil made no reply, just sat on the sofa, eyes closed, waiting for them to be gone.

~~*

Outside, Claire asked him, "Was that true about no marks?"

"From a quick once over, yeah. Pathology will have the details by now but I don't think we'll find anything else. Like Phil said, all anyone had to do was push him in and stand back."

"Okay, but they'd have had to have known that, wouldn't they? What were the chances some stranger would have known Mikey couldn't swim?"

"So maybe it was an accident. Maybe they didn't mean to drown him."

"Just scare him? Like they did before. Which means someone thinks he knows something. But what?" Claire glared at him as if he held the answer to the maddening question.

"Whoever did it," Dave said, as if reluctant to voice it, "has been following Simon Wilson again, too. Possibly."

"How do you know that?"

"He told me." She waited. "He bumped into me last night outside a restaurant."

"Bumped into you?"

"It was a coincidence."

"Oh, don't be so bloody naïve, Dave." She took a second to gather herself again. "What did he say?"

"He just said he'd been followed again."

"What, and that was it? No descriptions, nothing else?"

"He...he left. I think... I think he was a bit freaked at meeting Richard."

"Great. A real get-together. Why should he be bothered by Richard? He's a pretty unscary sort of guy."

"I think it was about his being my boyfriend."

"Oh, so you had time for a bit of personal chat first, did you? How cosy."

"The guy came up out of nowhere. I was on my own time, I was with someone else, he asked. What was I supposed to do? Lie? Why should I? I stopped doing that years ago and I'm not starting again now. What if it had been you and Ian? Would you have introduced him as your friend? Your brother, maybe?"

"It's not the same!"

"No it isn't, but it isn't that different, either."

"All right!" She ended the subject with a sweeping gesture of her hand. "Well, at least that's knocked one problem on the head."

"What do you mean?"

"At least now Simon Wilson knows you're unavailable, doesn't he?"

"He isn't... I don't think..." Dave gritted his teeth. It was pointless to take that one any further. "Yes, ma'am, I guess he does."

They drove in icy silence back to the station. When they got there, Jenny Trent was waiting with papers for them. "Final report from path on the guy in the canal."

"His name was Mikey Henderson." Dave took the folder from her and passed it to his boss. "I'll be back in five."

"Someone's got his knickers in a wedgie, hasn't he?" said Jenny, sitting herself down across from Claire as soon as Dave had gone. "Got that to look forward to every time we get a dead gay guy?"

Claire opened the file and flipped through it. Nothing there she hadn't been expecting to find. No evidence of violence against

Mikey, apart from the blows he had received earlier, and the fact he was now dead. She slapped it shut and let her mind run back over events of the last couple of hours. “Did Simon Wilson call the station yesterday?”

“I think so.”

“You’re on operations, Jenny,” Claire said calmly, deliberately keeping her eyes fixed on the file she had just closed. “You should know.”

Jenny’s lips pursed as if she’d found something tart in her mouth. “Yes. Yes, he did.”

“More than once?”

“Several times, actually.”

“And did he say who he wanted to speak to?”

Jenny sat up straighter in her chair, a growing awareness of the unexpected formality of these questions making her apprehensive. “Yes, he did.” Claire waited. “He was calling for Sergeant Lyon.”

“And did you pass these messages on to Sergeant Lyon?”

“Sergeant Lyon wasn’t here and was unavailable.”

Claire sighed heavily, rested her elbows on the desk and shoved her face into her hands. “Knock it off, Jenny. There were a hundred and one ways you could have got the messages to him before he came off duty. A hundred and one ways you should have.”

“I didn’t think it was our job to fix up dates for station police.”

“That is out of order!” And now Claire’s eyes were flashing fire.

"It is not your job to screen calls for senior officers without their knowledge or consent."

Jenny squared her shoulders even as she struggled to find new footing on the shifting ground of this old friendship. "You know the way it's going, Claire. Lyon's on his way out. You don't want him making you look...well, any worse, do you? You could say I was doing you both a favour."

The two women sat on opposite sides of the desk, and to Claire the expanse between them had never felt wider. "Thank you," she said finally.

Jenny frowned uncertainly. "For...?"

"The file." Claire tapped it. "Thank you. You can go now."

"Right. Okay." Jenny got up uncertainly, crossed to the door, opened it then stood, hand on the handle. "You still up for a drink later this week? Couple of the girls going over to the Anchor."

"I'll see. I'm very busy at the moment. As you know."

"Right. Okay." Jenny jumped back as the door was pushed from the other side and Dave bowled in.

"There's been a call from Elijah," he said breathlessly. Jenny left, unregarded by either Summerskill or Lyon.

"What now? More men outside his door?"

"Bang on. Only this time he was ready for them."

"Don't tell me he's gone and done something stupid. He hasn't shot one or anything, has he?"

Dave grinned and she was surprised how good it made her feel to see that grin again. It had been a while. "In a manner of speaking. Let's not forget the type of people we're dealing with, eh?" He paused, just long enough to give the boss time to frown and open her mouth to say something sharp. "He had cameras lined up. He's taken several photos."

"Okay. So get over there and pick them up."

"Mum, sometimes you are so Twentieth century. No need. Mr Elijah has very obligingly emailed them over and I've printed them out." Then his grin and boyish enthusiasm faded, and Dave gave a puzzled frown. "Only that's where it gets a bit strange. Elijah insists that this is one of the guys he's seen hanging around his house for the last week or so. Only..." He held out the three printouts he'd picked up.

Claire took them. Elijah was good, no doubt about it, but then his equipment had to be better than anything she could ever afford to take the holiday snaps with. The quality of the prints was excellent. Very nicely framed, too, if she was any judge. And there was absolutely no doubt who was in the centre of each one. "Phil Evans?"

Chapter Twenty-three

Phil wasn't in his flat when they got to it, but the door was open.

"Careless," Claire murmured.

"I don't think he's exactly thinking straight at the moment."

The two of them went in. "Phil? Phil." Claire scanned the room; saw the clutter, the tray she herself had left on the arm of the chair. "Okay. We don't touch anything, remember? That way we're not searching."

"Not even this?" Dave picked up the one thing that was different from their last visit, the sheet of paper on the sofa with the large uncertain handwriting on it. "*I'm sorry*. Oh, shit!"

Claire reached for her mobile. "Okay, we're putting out a call. I want everyone who's free on the streets after him. I'm damned if we're going to end up with another body on my watch. Especially not of the prime suspect."

"You think...?"

"Oh, come on. Don't you?"

Dave stood in the small room, amid its tangle of contents. He shook his head slowly. "No. No, I don't think he is. But I do think I know where he'll be."

* ~ * ~ *

It was cold by the side of the canal. The late afternoon sun was setting and the shadows of the cut were already deep. They were almost upon him before they saw him standing, staring sightlessly into the water. It was Dave who spoke, cautiously, wary of startling him, making him do anything rash. “Phil?”

The figure on the edge of the canal didn’t stir. He could have been carved out of stone. Or already dead. They moved a step closer and only then did he move: a slumping of the shoulders, a strangled sigh. The two police officers held back. “Couldn’t do it.”

“What was that, Phil?” Dave asked. “Phil, we didn’t quite hear what you said. Could you repeat it for us, please?”

“Couldn’t do it.” The voice was no stronger the second time round. Phil stood gazing bleakly into the water that had claimed his lover not so very long ago, and when he spoke it was as if the words were coming from the water itself rather than from his own lips. “Couldn’t kill myself. Had to help the daft bastard all his life to do everything, but in the end he managed it and I couldn’t do it. He’ll be laughing somewhere. That’ll make him right proud, that will.”

“Why, Phil? Why do you want to kill yourself?” Claire threw the words carefully into the gathering darkness like a lifeline into the shadows. She couldn’t let him stop speaking, frightened of what he might do if he did.

“I killed them. I killed those boys.”

"No, you didn't, Phil," Dave said. "You've not got it in you, mate."

Phil turned. They couldn't even see his face in the gloom now but they watched as slowly, slowly he crumpled to the ground, facing away from the cold water. Summerskill and Lyon carefully kneeled down by him, one on either side, each just slightly behind, to be between him and the blackness of the canal. "Tell us what happened, Phil."

"He was a fool. He was a stupid, trusting, gullible prat. And they took advantage of him. And I let them."

Dave frowned. "Them? Do you mean...?"

"The dead lads. Sean, and that other one."

"Jonathan?"

"Aye."

"So you knew them?"

"Course I knew them. Well, mainly knew Sean. Mikey had a soft spot for him and Sean never made fun of him. S'pose part of his job, really, wasn't it? Not making fun of people. Making them feel good about themselves."

"You mean Mikey paid for Sean. As rent?"

They saw the slope of Phil's large shoulders in the darkness. "Might have done. I was never really sure about that. Sean was...well, it wasn't all hard and fast with Sean. He just liked doing it, you know? If he got money for it, so much the better. He was a nice lad. I liked him, I really did. Helped him out a bit when he first arrived on the scene. Bought him a few drinks."

"Had sex with him?"

Claire's words hung in the air. *After all, it's irrelevant now.*

Phil went on, her question unanswered. "And then Sean hooked up with this other lad. Different kettle of fish altogether. College lad. Not on the game as far as I could tell. Mikey was upset. Thought he was changing Sean. Thought it was spoiling their friendship. Daft sod. I don't think he ever really understood just what it was Sean did with his life. It just made him all the more eager to please. And then he started talking about the films."

Dave sat up slightly. "Films they watched or films they made?"

"Couldn't make out what he was saying at first, but then it turned out to be films as he was making, that other one, Jonathan. Thought the daft bugger had got it wrong at first, but he'd got it right, hadn't he? The lads were making their own home grown porn films, though Mikey was too thick to see it. Kept saying as Sean and Jonathan called it art and a way of hitting back, some such crap. I'd heard it all before, wasn't interested. And then there was the night when Mikey came home as white as a ghost and on the edge of bloody breaking down. And he said he'd killed someone."

"Who'd killed someone?"

Phil's eyes were like two pits of shadow, even deeper than the darkness gathering around them. "Mikey had. It was Mikey who killed Sean."

"How?"

"Why?"

Phil sighed profoundly. "It was an accident, right? From what I could work out from what Mikey told me, they got him to take part in one of their films. Stupid... If I'd been there I'd have told him no, but I wasn't, was I? And they asked, Sean asked, and like some big old stupid dog he goes along and does it, doesn't he? To please them. Only it goes wrong." There was another long sigh as Phil drew in the cooling night air to steady his nerves. "'Cause of course it couldn't be a straightforward film, could it? Oh, no. It had to be something a bit different. A bit more extreme." Claire thought back to Sean's flat. To the ropes, the cuffs. "Only thing is they don't reckon on Mikey's being... On the fact that... Hell he didn't know what he was doing. They'd got him all worked up and the kid behind the camera was egging him on and...and Sean wasn't in no position to be able to do anything and..."

"We know, Phil."

"It was an accident. By the time that Jonathan had realised something was seriously wrong it was too late. Pair of them were shit scared. Mikey comes straight to me. Took me the best part of an hour to find out what the hell had happened. And you know what Mikey wants to do? He wanted to go to the police."

"But you told him not to?" Claire pressed.

"Of course I did," Phil said flatly.

"So what did you do next, Phil?"

"When I finally calmed Mikey down enough to figure I could leave him on his own, I went back to Sean's flat."

"What for?"

"I wanted that camera. I wanted the film, or whatever it was, that showed Mikey...that showed Mikey killing Sean. But I didn't get there."

"You met Jonathan?"

Phil nodded. "Here. On the canal. I asked him for the camera, but he didn't have it. I think he'd been drinking. Could hardly put his words together. I think... I think that he actually laughed. And I... and I...." Phil covered his eyes with his broad hands. "I killed him." His hands flew away from his face. "I didn't mean to, I swear. But I... I saw red. The stupid little shit had just ruined Mikey's life and he was giggling and weaving about pissed out of his head, so I... I hit him."

"You punched him? With your fist?"

"Yes. In the stomach, in the face... I don't know. I was screaming, shouting, I don't know what I did or said but it was quick, and then he was up against the stone of the wall by the bridge over there and then...and then he was sliding down to the ground. And I knew. I knew he was dead. But I didn't mean to. I swear I didn't mean..." He buried his head in his hands. "Christ, Mikey, what am I going to do without you?"

Chapter Twenty-four

"First case cracked, Inspector Summerskill. Well done."

"Thank you, Chief Inspector Rudge."

And if the congratulations were twice as warm, Dave thought, this scene of jubilation could still be mistaken for a funeral. He sat at his desk in the Foregate Street office, idly running his finger up and down the crack that had developed down the side of the framed photo next to his computer screen. *That sort of thing will happen when you're forever being knocked into a bin, or onto the floor. Maybe a spot of that sticky stuff on the base to make accidents less likely. Yeah, like that's going to make a difference.*

Summerskill and Lyon had brought Phil in, and even now, the shambling big man was being processed elsewhere in the station. Dave thought he'd give it an hour, then he'd go along to see what was happening, make sure Phil was okay. As okay as he could be.

"Question now, of course, is can you keep up the pace?"

"We'll do our best, Jim."

"Right. Right." Rudge leaned back in his chair, hands clasped behind his head, and eyed the pair of them. For just a minute, Dave wondered whether the chief inspector was about to pass on to him the congratulations he had given Inspector Summerskill.

He should have known better. “C’mon, Terry. We’ve got a bit of catching up to do if we’re going to match this pair of Sherlocks.”

He rose and left without saying more, followed by Cortez. The sergeant stopped and turned in the doorway. “Nice one,” he said, to both or neither of them, then left.

Claire and Dave sat in the office, the sounds of the station dimly perceptible through the frosted glass of window and door. Eventually Dave spoke. “Permission to speak candidly, mum.”

“Knock it off, Dave,” Claire growled.

“He’s a pillock, isn’t he?”

Claire sighed. “He’s got more good years on the clock than you and me put together. But right now, yes, he is.”

Another minute passed. The inspector and the sergeant sat staring at the paperwork that was the immediate reward of a job well done. Neither made a move to start processing it. “So,” said Claire finally. “Want to tell me why you’ve got a face like a week of wet Fridays?”

“Probably for the same reasons as you,” Dave shot back immediately.

“Number ’em.”

“All right.” Dave held up two fingers. “As I see it, there’s two mainly. Firstly, we still don’t know who all these men running around terrorising people were. There were thugs scaring Mikey, Phil and others from the Old Navigator, thugs staking out Elijah, and thugs trailing Simon Wilson.”

“Never more than two at a time.”

"Then they were either a very busy pair or there were more than two of them altogether. Job-sharing."

"And it was Phil outside Elijah's house."

"At the end, yes."

"Presumably with some vague notion of recovering any discs or memory cards that might incriminate Mikey before doing away with himself. A last gift for... a friend."

"Like you said, he wasn't thinking straight, no pun intended."

"Although of course," Claire said, "that beggars the question of how Phil found out about Elijah's link with the case." Her attention momentarily focused on an obstinate spot of something or other that seemed to have become stuck to her desktop, she didn't have to see Dave's guilty twitch. "Not that it really matters any more. Phil didn't do any harm to Elijah, and Elijah's email sent us after him before he could do any harm to himself. So, one of these unknowns is accounted for. That still leaves whoever was threatening the Old Navigator crowd. And Simon Wilson's stalkers."

Dave didn't miss the significant tone.

Claire continued thoughtfully. "Our mistake was in thinking these men, whoever they were, and however many of them there were, were involved somehow in the actual murder of Jonathan and Sean. But now we know they weren't. So, what do you think they were doing?"

"Our job, I guess," Dave said bitterly. "Trying to find out who killed the boys."

"Most likely. And who apart from us most wanted to find that out? Or at least, who wanted to find out who killed Jonathan if not Sean?"

"Jonathan's dad."

"Exactly."

Dave nodded slowly. "A man with enough connections to the kind of guys who could go around shaking people up to see what fell out."

"That's one way of putting it."

"Yeah but, that doesn't quite work out, does it? Why would Wilson put a trail on his son, unless he thought he had something to do with the deaths, which seems unlikely. And even more unlikely, why would he have his hired muscle put the frighteners on his wife by messing about with her car?"

"The car I'll admit I don't understand yet, but as for the other matter..." She braced herself. "What if there weren't men following Simon at all?"

"That doesn't make sense," Dave said with a frown. Claire said nothing, letting him go on to actually think about her words. "You mean he was lying? Why would he lie about it?"

"Come on, Dave," she said softly. "You know why."

"No."

"He's...attracted to you. Possibly."

"What, so he cooks up phoney stalkers just to get my attention?"

"Think, Dave. He digs up evidence for you."

"For us. For the investigation."

"He bumps into you at the hospital. He bumps into you again outside some restaurant. He rings you at all hours of the day and night."

"A few phone calls. It's what we encourage people to do, isn't it?"

"And he throws a complete fit when he finds out you have a boyfriend."

"I haven't... That's not... You weren't there."

"No, but you told me about it. And I have to admit, sergeant, I've come to find your incident reports pretty accurate. In this case, it was just your conclusion that was a bit shit. You thought he was reacting to your coming out to him. But would that have been the reaction of a man who had an openly gay brother? He's not like some we could mention who only know gays from the telly. Has Simon ever expressed anything other than complete acceptance of Jonathan's sexuality? No. He was pissed off because he found out that you weren't available. Any more reports of stalkers since then? No, because after meeting Richard, he knew there wasn't any more point in trying to get your attention."

"Is that how straight people do it, then?" Dave asked acidly. "'Cause believe it or not, gay men have developed simpler ways of getting another guy's attention."

"I know," said Claire dryly. "I have done my share of duties on Gay Prides, and you're right. Some of the things I've seen to get attention have been very simple and very direct. Almost illegally so in public places." She tried to change her tone make it clear she wasn't accusing Dave of anything, not exactly. "He's a lawyer, what can you expect? They can't even walk straight."

"History. His degree was in history."

"Was it?" Claire's forehead wrinkled as she tried to remember. "I could have sworn someone told me it was in law."

"No, he told me it was in history."

"Oh. Right." She grew thoughtful for a minute.

Dave squared his shoulders. "What you appear to be telling me, ma'am," he said stonily, "is that you don't trust me."

Claire shook her head to clear it of a strangely nagging thought. "What? Of course I do. I'm just saying that, in this instance, your judgement was...compromised."

"Which is just assessment speak for saying you don't trust me."

"All right!" She jabbed a finger at him in anger. "You tell me, Dave. Do you fancy Simon Wilson? Yes or no?"

Dave stared at her. "You have no right..."

"Don't give me that bollocks! You're the one questioning my judgement, sergeant, so prove me wrong. Tell me you're not attracted to Simon Wilson."

For a long moment, inspector and sergeant glared at each other across the desk. A storm of conflicting thoughts whirled through Claire's head: the sheer bloody unethical nature of what she'd just done; the tribunals Lyon could drag her through for even suggesting it in this manner; the fact that he could leave the station now and it would be her fault he'd gone just as they'd earned their first success together. But if their working relationship was to continue and was to have any success at all, it had to be built on certainties, and you didn't get to them through pussyfooting around.

"Simon Wilson is...attractive," Dave said finally. "But I did not let that influence me in my work on this case. I think...I think I knew that his attitude towards me was more than just friendship, but I thought..." He trailed off.

"What?"

"I knew he was gay. And don't even mention gaydar. It was that first time when he was talking to me in Jonathan's bedroom about what it had been like for Jonathan being gay in that house. And I just knew he was also telling me about what it had been like for him, At least I think I did. It...it reminded me of what it had been like for me. There was common ground there, and that," he concluded with a heavy sigh, "was all it was." He lifted his eyes to look his boss in the face. "And I still do not believe that anyone, gay or straight, who isn't a complete basket case, would go to the extreme lengths of cooking up imaginary stalkers just to draw themselves to my attention."

"Okay. And thank you. For the moment, let's agree to differ, eh?"

The corner of Dave's mouth twitched. "About my not being besotted with Simon or about the likelihood of anyone turning bunny boiler over me?"

"Maybe both."

He shrugged. "All academic I suppose anyway now. No way we're going to be able to find out differently, is there?"

Claire nibbled her lower lip. "Maybe. Maybe not. We'll come back to that." She spoke more briskly again. "What was our other loose end?"

Mildly puzzled by his boss's thought processes, Dave went on. "Well, it's the timing, isn't it? Phil's story doesn't quite add up." Claire gestured for him to expound. "There's this godawful accident at Sean's place. Sean dies. Mikey runs over to Phil's, pours his heart out. Phil calms Mikey down, makes sure he's safe enough to leave and then heads out to the bedsit, probably to make sure there's nothing there to incriminate Mikey. And he meets Jonathan, apparently just leaving. Now Phil tells us that it took him ages to calm Mikey down enough to get the story out of him, and all this back and forth between Phil's place and Sean's has got to add more time on. So what has Jonathan been doing all that time?"

"Drinking?" Claire suggested, playing devil's advocate. "Mikey said he was weaving about as if drunk."

Dave shook his head. "We know Jonathan had his faults, God knows, but drink doesn't appear to have been one of them. He didn't even use the Navigator, remember?"

"And there was no evidence of drink in Sean's bedsit," Claire agreed.

"And then Phil starts beating on Jonathan and kills him. Just like that."

"Phil's a big man."

"He's a very big man. He could probably do you a lot of damage, if he was that kind of guy."

"He was upset, angry over what the lads had made Mikey do."

Dave swept his hand in the general direction of the cells. "You've seen him. You've got an idea what he's like. Upset, yes, of course, but angry enough to kill? I don't buy it. And where's the weapon Aldridge said he thought had been used?"

"Aldridge cocked up?" Claire suggested hopefully. "Or Jonathan caught his head on some projection in that bridge wall?"

"SOCO would have found the blood there and they didn't."

"No," said Claire, "they didn't." She sat back. "So, sergeant, having pithily summed up the mess of unanswered questions in which we still find ourselves, what answers do you have?"

Dave held his empty hands up.

"You're scared," Claire mused. "More scared than you've ever been in your life. You've just seen a murder. You've *filmed* it without realising and you're probably terrified you're going to go down for it. What do you do? Where do you go?"

Dave snorted. "Home?"

"Home."

Claire stood up. "Come on, sergeant. One last visit to the Wilsons."

Dave frowned. "What for? We've got the killers. Even if Robert Wilson did sic goons on people no real harm was done. The only person who was really hurt was poor Mikey, and he's..."

"A killer?"

"Not going to be pressing charges."

"True. But as we've just made clear, I still have a lot of questions I want answering. And everything takes us back to the Wilsons. Everything," she added pointedly.

Dave had to know she wasn't just talking about the deaths.

Chapter Twenty-five

As they pulled into the Wilsons' driveway another car was pulling out, gliding past them almost silently apart from the crunch of its wheels on the gravel. Dave craned his neck to get a view of its occupants: two men in suits and hard expressions, both resolutely determined not to catch the eye of either of the two police officers. "Would you buy a used car off either of them?"

"I think I'd want to see its log book and their charge sheets first."

Unlike their first visit, they weren't met at the door by Simon but by a mousy young woman who introduced herself as Liz and mumbled something about being a housekeeper. She offered to show them to the living room but Claire brushed past her. "No need. Trust me, we know the way."

Mr Wilson might almost not have moved since their last meeting. He was still standing with his back to the bar, still holding a glass of something in his hand. About the only thing Claire could guarantee was different was whatever was in the glass. "You've got the bastard, then," were his first growled words, even as Liz was offering faint apologies. It was not a question. He waved the housekeeper away peremptorily and she walked out practically backwards, pouting reproachfully at Summerskill and Lyon before closing the door behind her.

"You're very well informed, Mr Wilson," Claire said smoothly, and made a mental note to find out just how that came to be.

"Well? You have, haven't you?"

"We have made an arrest, yes."

"It was that... It was Evans, wasn't it?"

"It wouldn't be appropriate to say yet who we have in custody, Mr Wilson," Claire said smoothly, damned if she was going to show any reaction to the extent of the man's knowledge. "We would just like to ask you a few questions about..."

"More bloody questions?" Wilson slammed the glass down on the veneer finish of his bar. "What the hell do you want to ask questions of us now for? Enough of your bloody questions. Get out of my house now, Miss Inspector, and go and do your job. Bang the murdering sod up, and tell him from me that when he gets out, I'll be..."

Claire raised her hand and spoke softly but firmly over the man's ranting. "I would strongly suggest you do not say any more at this stage, Mr Wilson, as who knows what trouble that could lead to later on in events? And as for leaving, I would also strongly suggest you do help us this one last time with our enquiries." She gave a small smile that had almost no real humour in it. "Were I to leave now, I dare say, what with the reckless speed at which my sergeant here drives, I would very quickly find my car up the arse of the one that's just left, and, do you know, I have a crazy idea I might recognise the two gentlemen inside it. I can't quite place them now, but I'm sure a few questions would help jog my memory. May I sit down?" She did so without waiting for any formal invitation. Dave remained standing at her side.

"What do you want, inspector?"

"Were they the only two, Mr Wilson? The two you sent down to the Old Navigator, to lean on people—Mikey Henderson, Phil Evans among others—to try to find out who killed your son?"

"I don't know what you..."

"Don't waste my time, Mr Wilson. The sooner you answer my questions, the sooner we can leave."

Wilson deliberately turned his back on Summerskill as he recharged his glass from an open bottle. "You'd have done the same, if it had been either of your sons."

Either of your sons. Such a small piece of knowledge to suggest so much. Whatever sympathy she had harboured for this man died at that point, frozen out completely at the thought of his dabbling his fingers, however lightly, into the life of her family. "Yes. If either of my sons had been killed, I think I probably would have done anything, too. Leaned on people. Frightened them. Probably more."

"But why your own son?" Dave asked. "Surely you couldn't have thought...?"

"What do you mean?" Wilson growled.

"Simon told me, told us, that he'd been followed, too. He was quite worried about it. And what about the business with your wife's car?"

"The car's brake system was faulty. My wife hasn't got the sense she was born with when it comes to cars. Anyone else would have noticed something was wrong with the damn thing as soon as they set off, but not her."

"She was...on medication, Mr Wilson."

"She's been on medication for a very long time, sergeant. And as for the men supposedly following my son, I haven't got a clue what you are talking about."

"And where is your son, Mr Wilson?" Claire asked.

"I'm here, inspector." Simon Wilson was walking towards them from the far side of the room. He could have come through a door over there. Or he could have been sitting in one of the wing-backed chairs all the time. It was impossible to tell. Either way, always with his father. What was it his mother had said? That Simon took after his father. And always together. He nodded to her briefly, then did exactly the same to Dave. "Sergeant."

Dave nodded back but said nothing.

Claire glanced at Dave then back at Simon. The young man's attention was all on her, as if having greeted Lyon he was now refusing to acknowledge his presence at all.

"What's this about men following you, Simon?" his father demanded.

He's nervous, Claire realised. For all his apparent calm, Simon was very nervous. Maybe even scared. It was as if the young man was finally coming into focus for her and she could sense it clearly.

But not scared of them. *Of his father?*

"I think the inspector and her sergeant have got things a bit confused, dad."

"I wonder if we might have a word with Simon alone, Mr Wilson?" Claire said.

"Now what the bloody hell do you want to see him...?"

"It would just enable us to tie up one or two loose ends, sir, and then, as I said, we could get out of your hair all the sooner."

Simon was quick to support her. "It's all right, dad. Everything's sorted now. I'm happy to help the police tidy things up."

Cheeky bastard.

Wilson snatched his glass back up from the drinks counter, huffed his reluctant agreement and left the room with as much ill grace as he could manage. The door was slammed behind him.

Simon walked over to the bar and there was something, even in the way he walked, that was different. More relaxed, more confident now his father wasn't there? But it was more than that. He was different from how he had been when she and Dave had first come to the house. Then he'd been helpful, eager to please. That had gone, she could sense that, too. All because of what had happened between him and Dave? Or had even the infatuation she had so insisted on with Dave been pretence, too? "Simon," she began.

"I think Mr Wilson is more appropriate, don't you?"

Indeed. This was definitely not the Simon they thought they

had come to know. “Of course, Mr Wilson. Very well.” She paused, sorting her thoughts. They’d get maybe one shot at this and after that she doubted she and Lyon would be allowed back in the house without a warrant, and given the apparent solving of the case, the chances of getting that were extremely remote. Back in the station it had all seemed, momentarily at least, clearer—umpteen unresolved questions and this, the only possible point of solution. But where to begin? She thought again of that niggling point that had arisen during her conversation with Dave. “I wonder,” she began, “could you just set my mind at rest about something? Small thing, really, but, you know what it’s like, it’s been nagging away at me. What exactly was your degree in?” She was gratified to see a spark of surprise in Simon’s eyes. Nothing wrong with unbalancing him a little before moving on to the bigger questions. And such an apparently small question to discomfit him so much. Only then did she know for certain she’d been right not to simply let it go.

“It was in law, inspector. Though you didn’t have to ask. I’m sure any casual search of police computers could have thrown that one up.”

“I suppose it would,” she demurred. Such a prickly answer, and such a swift reference to checking police records. Connections were forming in her mind, shaping unexpected patterns. “Funny, I mean, I know this is such a small thing, but I could have sworn you told us it was in history when we first met.” She half turned to Dave who nodded, without having to check his notebook. “Silly mistake. Who would get confused over something like that?"

"Who indeed?"

"And it's not as if you'd have wanted to deliberately mislead us, is it?" she went on, thinking aloud as much as anything else at this point. "I mean, what would have been the point, eh?" She smiled, letting her words hang in the air between them. That was the great thing about rhetorical questions, something she'd always known as a Welshwoman but had most put to practical use after joining the Force—leave them around for long enough and people felt obliged to answer them as if they were real.

"It is a fact," Simon grudgingly said, "that, for some reason, telling people you've studied law unsettles them. Especially police."

Nice try at a barbed comment, and not quite an admission of a lie. Close enough, though. But why? "Yes," she agreed. "I can see how fudging the issue would make people a little more relaxed in your company. A little more off their guard, you might say."

And suddenly the patterns were beginning to make more sense, and she could feel, too, without looking, that something had clicked for Dave as well. *Go team!*

"You may say that, inspector," Simon said. "That's not actually what I said."

"No, but what you've actually said, at various times, seems to be a matter of some confusion, doesn't it, Mr Wilson?" Simon's eyes darted from her to Dave and back again. She pressed on. "I mean, you've also told us that you were followed by two men, on several occasions, and yet the only following done has been by men set on by your own father. And he doesn't appear to know anything about your stalkers."

"I think," Simon said quickly, gesturing at Dave's upheld notebook, "that you'll find my father has not actually, at any point, specifically admitted to having done what you've just accused him of."

"A very lawyer-like answer, Mr Wilson, if you don't mind my saying so. Yes, I can indeed see you studied law. Your family must be very proud of you. Especially your father. We know he didn't really approve of Jonathan."

"What do you mean?" Simon snapped.

"Of the direction Jonathan's studies had been taking him," Claire continued smoothly, "but he must have been very pleased with you. Yes," she said, her tone becoming more thoughtful, "nothing...awkward about you. And so helpful, too, to have a lawyer in the family 'business'."

"Are you accusing me of lying, inspector, because if you are I must insist that..."

"Lying, Mr Wilson? To me or to your father?"

"I...I don't know what you mean."

Now she'd got the little shit on his back foot. She pressed on. "So who do you think was following you, Simon?" She knew she had him rattled when he didn't challenge her use of his first name.

"The same men presumably who attacked that sad specimen Michael Henderson."

"Mikey," Dave said automatically.

"Mikey Henderson is dead," Claire said, "but he killed himself, deliberately or while the state of his mind was unbalanced."

"And his boyfriend killed my brother, inspector, or had you forgotten that?"

"I haven't. Though I am puzzled about how you know quite so much so soon, but that aside for the moment, I haven't forgotten your brother. In fact, I'm still very concerned about Jonathan's death. Aren't you? Isn't your father?"

"What do you mean, concerned? It's done. It's over. We know who killed him."

And there it was again in his eyes, much more noticeable now—fear. She watched as he reached for the bottle his father had been drinking from and poured himself a stiff measure. *So alike, father and son.* She felt the confusion and uncertainties that had bedevilled her and Lyon, even after the apparent solution of the case, begin to melt away. "You're very close to your father, aren't you?"

"Of course I am."

"Yes. Always together. Wouldn't you agree, sergeant? Every time we've come to see Mr Wilson—that is Mr Wilson *Senior*—Mr Wilson *Junior*—" and she enjoyed the spasm of irritation that caused to pass across Simon's features "—has always been there, hasn't he?"

"Yes, ma'am."

"Even, I suppose, when your father was in a meeting with

those two men we saw leaving as we were driving in. I assume it was some kind of business meeting?"

"That's..."

"None of my business? I know. Perhaps not. Although I have to ask myself what a law graduate might be doing in such company? I mean, we know your father has connections with, shall we say, operatives from the greyer areas of commercial enterprise." She held up a hand to ward off Simon's incipient and evident outburst. "Please, Mr Wilson. As you have already made clear, you know we have access to excellent records back at the station and your father's name is cross-referenced with some very interesting entries. Let's not waste time discussing those at this juncture. That's not what we're here about now. We're here to talk about you."

Simon placed his drink very carefully back down on the bar counter, but held onto it. Claire could clearly see the bone white of his knuckles as he clutched the glass tightly. "What about me?"

"It must be very handy for your father to have a trained lawyer on hand twenty-four seven. And not just someone he's hired, but someone who's linked. By blood. A cool, legal brain to rein in that hot temper of his. And he does have a hot temper, doesn't he, Simon? We've seen it. We've heard about it. You even mentioned it yourself." She paused for a moment, as if to give him time to answer though knowing full well he wouldn't. "Do you have a temper, Simon? Do you get angry? You are so very alike after all, your father and you. In most things."

"I don't know what the hell…"

"I think you do. I think Sergeant Lyon caught a glimpse of that temper recently outside an Indian restaurant. Yes, Simon, he told me about that," she said in answer to Simon's accusatory glare in Dave's direction. "Of course he did. I'm betting you're able to control your temper better, though. You've a trained mind. Lawyers don't win cases, make successes of themselves, by doing rash, hasty things." She paused for a moment, pointedly surveying the room they were in, the expensive furnishings, the extensive grounds clearly visible through the large windows. "It must be very worrying for a newly qualified legal mind like yours interested in joining the family business, taking it further perhaps, building it up maybe, having to keep an eye on his father's temper day in day out, making sure it doesn't ruin everything. I'll bet he didn't even consult you, did he, Simon, when he hired his muscle to find out who killed Jonathan? And that scared you, didn't it? I think that had you pissing yourself. For all sorts of reasons."

"That was what it was all about, wasn't it?" Dave said slowly as full realisation finally dawned. "The…helpfulness, the 'accidental' meetings, the… Everything. Keeping close. Keeping tabs. Trying to find out what was going on because your father, blind with anger and grief, had cut you out of the loop." His eyes momentarily widened in shock as a new implication hit him. "And the car. Your own mother's car!"

"You're mad! If you're suggesting I tried to kill my own mother…"

"Your mother wasn't killed, Simon," Claire said sharply, "and didn't even get close. Shaken up, yes, but nothing worse. And no, actually I don't think you put her life at risk. I don't think you're capable of that," she couldn't help adding. "I think quite probably her accident was just that—an accident brought about by being drugged up to the eyeballs and sick with misery. But what a marvellous opportunity for a bit of smoke and mirrors, eh? Just slip in to the garage *after* the accident and loosen the odd nut and bolt here and there. You'll have to forgive me. I don't know my way around a car, but I'll bet you do, the favourite son of car-mad Robert Wilson. A few twists of the wrench, a few hints to my sergeant here, and bingo, the strangers going round trying to scare confessions out of people couldn't possibly have been hired by your father because now they're turning on his own family. Clever."

"Why?" It was Dave speaking, regarding Simon with an expression Claire wasn't sure she would have wanted to try to put a name to. "Why couldn't you let us do it? Why couldn't you get your father to call off his thugs and let us get to the bottom of it legitimately?"

"You were getting nowhere." Simon stopped abruptly as if he'd already said too much.

But Dave wasn't listening. Claire knew that the truth was coming home to him, too, as it finally had to her. And for his sake, she let him give voice to it now. "You weren't just trying to cover for your father. You were deliberately muddying the waters, making it *harder* for us to find out what happened to Jonathan. But why would you do that unless...?" He turned to his notebook, rapidly rifled through the pages until he got to that series of events he had gone through with his boss just under an hour previously at the station: the murder; Jonathan's meeting with Phil; his own death. And that unexplained discrepancy in the timing. Where would a boy in the worst trouble of his life go? "You saw Jonathan that night, didn't you?"

Simon stood up straight at the bar, the hand holding the glass a white-knuckled fist. "I was with friends that night."

"Which friends?"

"Is this an official question?"

"No. Not yet," Claire admitted. "And I'll just bet by the time it became one you'd have conveniently remembered which friends and they'd be able to remember you. It doesn't matter. I think you were here that night, Simon. I think you were here when your brother turned up half out of his mind with fear about what had happened. And you got angry. Just like your father would have. There you were, faced with the brother who'd mocked you all your life, who was openly leading the kind of life you'd always wanted to but couldn't because you knew how your father would react..."

"What do you mean by that?"

"And who'd gone and got himself involved in some seedy, messy death that was going to drag in exactly the sort of police attention you didn't need focused on the family at this early stage of your expansion of your father's business. And you snapped.

That famous Wilson temper we keep hearing about, that Jonathan used to enjoy goading you into in all those films. Those films you hid from us or edited so we wouldn't see the real you. You snapped. So what happened then? What did you do? Hit him? Punch him?"

"Get out! Get out of here now!"

Dave stepped forward, ignoring Simon's enraged commands. Claire saw the pain in his eyes. "Was it here? In his bedroom? The hallway?" He must be trying to picture the scene, thinking back to Aldridge's report: that depression to the skull. The rounded impact crater. "The marble globes arranged the length of the staircase out in the hallway. You pushed him down the stairs. That was it, wasn't it? One shove in a moment of fury, and Jonathan goes all the way down the stairs. Except that's not all, is it? He smashes his head against the banisters. He's stunned, concussed, but you can't tell the difference between that and the sheer funk he was in when he arrived, so you throw him out of the house. Lock the door behind him. Was there any blood? Maybe if his hood was up you didn't even notice." Dave regarded Simon with clear astonishment. "Maybe you didn't even care."

"And Jonathan managed to drive back to the canal," Claire concluded. "Only just, I should imagine. Frightened. Concussed. Reeling like a drunk man. And he bumps into Phil."

"Who kills him. That bastard killed my brother!"

"Did he?" Dave shook his head slowly. "He attacked Jonathan, it's true, hit him, punched him, pushed him back, further and further, until his already fractured skull impacted with the brick wall of the bridge over the canal. And he died."

The two men stood, staring at each other, looking deep into each other's eyes. For what, Claire wondered. "Hard to say who killed who, wouldn't you say, Simon?"

"I... I didn't..." Simon closed his eyes, his mouth wide, gaping like some suffocating fish. When he finally opened his eyes again they glittered, with anger or unshed tears it wasn't possible to say. He set his jaw, unclenched his fists. He faced Claire, turning his back deliberately on Dave. "This is entirely conjecture. You can't prove any of it."

Claire nodded slightly as if agreeing. "You're right. We probably can't. We're just the police." She turned as if to go, then turned back to him again. "But maybe your father..."

This time there was no mistaking the fear in his eyes. For Summerskill and Lyon it was all the proof they needed.

"He does have his own ways of investigating these matters, doesn't he? C'mon, sergeant. Time we were going."

~~*

"So is that it?"

"What do you mean?"

"I mean, we don't arrest him, bring him in for questioning at least?"

Claire shook her head. "After we've had forensics check out a few things at the house, like those, what d'you call them, balustrades for instance, I guess so. But I have a feeling our tough nut will have cracked before then and will come in on his own. A last ditch attempt at damage limitation. And what have we got? Manslaughter at the worst. But if so by whom? Simon or Phil? Would whatever happened to Jonathan at home have killed him if not for Phil's shove into the wall? Would Phil's shove into the wall have killed him without that accident at home? I guess that's why I'm police, not a judge, because I haven't got a clue."

"But you had an idea about Simon's involvement. Is that why you took us back there?"

"Not...entirely," she said. "Not really." She moved on quickly. "You okay?"

"Course I am. Why shouldn't I be?"

"No reason," she said, and now she knew she meant it. She took a moment to gather herself. This was hard. "I was wrong," she admitted.

Dave pantomimed surprise but it was only a half-hearted effort. "About Simon's going to all those lengths just to cop off with me? Course you were. I told you so. I should find someone that eager to get into my trousers."

She laughed even as she tried to work out just what she was feeling at the thought of that image, suspecting Dave knew that wasn't exactly what she had meant,

"Back to the station, then?"

Claire sighed. "Yeah. You'll be wanting to see Phil, I guess, tell him the outlook might not be as bleak for him as he thinks. And I guess there's still enough time left today to rattle Jim's cage a bit before we go home. Consider it my treat for a job well done."

"Thanks, mum."

* ~ * ~ *

Claire drove them back to the station. For most of the journey Dave was silent. Finally, Claire had to ask him. "What are you thinking, sergeant?" It was an intrusion, an inappropriate question probably. But she'd made it official by adding his rank, so that was okay wasn't it?

Dave gave no indication he was offended. "I was thinking about when I was Jonathan's age and younger. Coming to terms with...things. What it was like for me and my family. My brother. It wasn't always...easy." He took a deep breath and let it out, as if letting go of the memories. "And what are you thinking about, ma'am?"

"The paperwork," she said grimly. "And then the evaluations. There'll have to be a formal meeting with Madden. And...." She shook her head to clear it of the mounting images of drudgery. "Reckon you're going to stay on?" she asked before she'd even realised she was going to say it.

"I didn't know I was being asked to think about leaving."

"You're not. But if you were going to this would be the point, wouldn't it? First case successfully wrapped up. Gold star and a tick in your record. If you then decided this wasn't the station for you, you could move on with no questions asked. Probably even be able to start a bidding war."

"You really do have this idea that everyone's after me, don't you?"

"Well," she said, eyes fixed firmly on the road outside the car, "if they aren't, they bloody well should be."

"Thank you." Dave, too, stayed focused on the road. They could have been taking a driving test together. "Do you want me to go?"

She took a second or two before she gave her answer, only because somehow it seemed the right thing to do. "No."

"You could get that WPC you wanted instead of me."

"You knew that?"

"I worked it out. Something to do with the way she arches her back and spits whenever I walk into the room. I'm sensitive like that."

"Hmm." Claire considered. "I think maybe it's time Jenny moved on. For her own good. New stations, new approaches. Good experience for her."

"Right."

"So? You staying?"

Dave nodded. "Yeah. I'm staying."

"Even though..." Hell, she couldn't pretend any longer she hadn't noticed. "Even though you find your desk photo...in a new place every time you get back to the office."

"You mean like in the bin or on the floor? It doesn't actually get much further than that. You've noticed, then?"

"It's a girl thing. Dust, moved photos and new hairstyles: things men don't notice."

"Straight men, though I'm not so good on dust and new hairstyles myself."

In for a penny, in for a pound. "That's not all I've noticed about the photo."

"Ah."

"Ah," she agreed. "So who is it? It's not Richard, not unless there was a time when he was a foot taller, carried about another stone in muscle and had different coloured hair. Past boyfriend?"

"I wish."

"Current second boyfriend, then, who you steal away to for dirty weekends whenever you can?"

Dave sighed. "Like I've got the time and energy. His name's Craig or Cliff or Conan, something like that, Bound to be fake anyway. He's a picture I found on the net somewhere."

"A site that specialises in pictures of handsome young men."

"You mean to say *you* don't browse them?"

"And it happened," she said quickly, "to come complete with a hand-written inscription saying, *To Dave, With All My Love*?"

"That's a little artistic touch of my own. I was quite proud of it, actually."

"Just one question, then. Why?"

He sighed. "Do you know when a gay man stops coming out? Never. You start a new job, you move to a new flat, you meet someone in a pub. Sooner or later someone says something like,

'So, do you have a wife? A girlfriend? Children?' And you have to decide, do you hedge, do you lie, or do you live an honest life. I decided years ago I wanted to live an honest life."

"By putting up photos of fake boyfriends on your desk?"

Dave scratched his head embarrassedly. "Yes, well, you've got me on a bit of technicality there. Think of it more as a short cut than an out and out lie. It just seemed a quicker way of getting things out in the open than going around telling people piecemeal as the occasions presented themselves." He grimaced. "In the end, I don't think I need have bothered. The world and his police dog seem to have known which side of the street's my beat right from the start."

"Okay. I'll let you have that one. Good idea, actually. Very neat."

"Thank you."

"Buuut..."

"Yes?"

"That doesn't exactly explain why it's not a picture of Richard."

"You're good, aren't you?"

"I am the inspector."

"Right." Dave sighed again. "I don't think it's working out between Richard and me."

"Oh. I'm sorry." And just for a second she was, selfishly sorry that she'd opened up another can of worms and was going to have to spend the rest of the journey counselling a grief-stricken colleague. She quickly cleared her mind of the unworthy thought, and was soon reassured in any case.

"Don't worry. It's not a biggie. It's not like we've known each other that long. And I'm only living with him at the moment because of the move to this area. Far too early in a relationship to try living together, but circumstances demanded, and sure enough we got to see each other's faults before we'd really had time to get to know our good bits. And, well, it's not the easiest thing in the world being a copper's partner, is it? You'll know better than me."

Claire leaned forward in her seat as if suddenly fascinated by the sight of a passing shop display. "No," she said off-handedly. "It isn't."

"So, fancy a drink before we get back to the station?"

Claire Summerskill sat back and considered. Yes, she did like the idea of a drink with her new sergeant. With just one proviso. "You're on. But let's make it somewhere where I'm the one who'll get eyed up."

About the Author

Steve Burford lives in one of the less well-to-do areas of Malvern mentioned in the novel. When not writing in a variety of genres under a variety of names, he tries to teach drama to teenagers. He has only occasionally been in trouble with the police.

NineStar Press, LLC

www.ninestarpress.com